SCORPIUS REX

WILLIAM BURKE

SEVERED PRESS
HOBART TASMANIA

SCORPIUS REX

Copyright © 2020 William Burke

WWW.SEVEREDPRESS.COM

ISBN: 978-1-922323-66-8

<u>DEDICATION</u>

Dedicated to my old Air Force buddy James Potts, who always

called me Beaker. A true friend.

This one's for you Jimbo! We miss you.

CHAPTER ONE

Matabeleland South Province, Zimbabwe
25 kilometers north of the South African border.

Zander Kotze leaned back against a water tanker and closed his eyes, savoring the cool air drifting off the drilling site's three-story liquid nitrogen tanks. After fifteen hours of work, the exhausted drilling engineer's head was throbbing. Now all he wanted in life was a few minutes of silence, but the chirping alarm on his watch chopped that vacation down to fifteen seconds. The incessant beeping meant it was ten pm—time to make the long walk back to the monitoring van and check his readings before the night's final detonation.

Getting to the van meant navigating through the city-block-sized network of cryogenic fracking equipment. The massive liquid nitrogen tanks fed into a maze of fracking tanks, blenders, hydration units, and proppant tanks full of toxic chemicals, all supported by a fleet of two-thousand-gallon pumping trucks. The miles of hose and pipe all converged at the Christmas Tree, the drilling term for the collection of valves and fittings resting atop the wellhead—the final connection point before everything went subterranean.

Looming over it all was a one-hundred-and-twenty-foot steel derrick that on any sane job would already have been torn down. With drilling completed, the ten-story derrick was just one more safety hazard in an already dangerous environment. But taking it down meant lost time— something the company man, Aaron Momberg, wouldn't stand for. Momberg was Graaff Energy's on-site representative. Most company men were smart enough to keep their traps shut and let the engineers do their job. But Momberg was the exception; a safety last corporate monkey, intent on getting somebody killed.

Zander walked along listening to the cacophony of pumps, engines, and turbines. To anyone else it was just noise, but to him it was a symphony. He paused near one of the hydration units and listened, thinking it sounded a hair off balance, but after a few seconds he nodded and moved on. The fracking process was as complex as the human body, but Zander knew every gear, connection and sound by heart.

He heard raucous laughter and noticed two roughnecks near the blowout preventer, tightening drill strings with pneumatic wrenches.

Without stopping, Zander shouted, "Hey, you clowns know the rules. No screwing around while you're tightening drill strings! That's how guys get killed."

One gave him a thumbs up. "Won't happen again, boss."

"Good, 'cause I'm not breaking the news to your wife, unless she's pretty, rich or both."

The men laughed and Zander kept moving, passing the mud engineer, who was too wrapped up in his work to notice him. He knew every man on the drilling crew, mostly South Africans with a few Brits tossed into the mix. The only strangers were the new security specialists—a polite term for mercenaries.

He nodded to one of them. The khaki-uniformed Shona tribesman gave him a broad smile, looking just about as friendly as someone toting an assault rifle could. These security specialists were the only Zimbabweans on the site.

The mercenaries were just one of the insane security precautions Graaff Energy had put in place since discovering the mystery gas. That was three months ago, and since that fateful day, Zander had been a virtual prisoner, unable to leave the compound or even call his wife without security listening in. The company had gone so far as to surround the entire two-square-kilometer site with a steel fence that would be the pride of any maximum-security prison. In his fourteen years as a drilling engineer he'd never experienced anything like it. Strangest of all was that he still didn't know what the mystery gas was or why it was so precious. All he knew was that it wasn't flammable, but just one whiff could put a man into a coma.

Zander climbed into the monitoring van and massaged his temples, muttering, "Relax, the brain work's all done. Pretty soon you'll be out of here."

Under Zander's expert supervision the crew had drilled vertically through twenty thousand feet of shale. From that kickoff point they'd bored another five thousand feet horizontally—practically a record. That's when the cryogenic fracturing, or 'fracking', began. It entailed lowering down a perforating gun lined with explosive charges to blast fissures into the rock. The next step was stimulating that now fractured rock with high pressure liquid nitrogen, water, and a toxic soup of hydrochloric acid, cobalt and lanthanum. Then they'd suck out that contaminated flowback water, put in a temporary plug and repeat the entire process every hundred feet. They'd done it eight times already with no major problems … except for the earthquakes. Three of them in the past forty-eight hours, each bigger than the last.

Zander's blessed silence was interrupted by a harsh voice.

Jaco Botha, the site's gun loader engineer, leaned into the van shouting, "Boss, we need to talk about fucking Momberg!"

Zander took a deep breath. "What's he doing now? And Jaco, do me a favor, and use your indoor voice, my head's splitting."

"Sorry boss, I just got riled up. After the last runs you and I agreed to go back to the standard-shaped charges."

"Uh huh."

As the gun loader engineer, Jaco was responsible for the safe handling and detonation of all explosives. Nobody on a drilling site argued with or even questioned the gun loader.

Jaco continued, "So after I lowered the perforating gun, Momberg came at me, bitching about why we weren't using those oversized charges again."

Zander saw a golf cart rolling up to the van and said, "Speak of the devil."

Momberg climbed out of the cart. The gangly company man looked like a Halloween skeleton draped in a fat man's suit.

Momberg made a beeline for the van, barking, "Why's this guy using small charges?"

Zander said, "And a good evening to you too, sir. We're using the standard charges because that's what Jaco and I agreed on."

"It's slowing things down."

"No it isn't. We ran a nodal analysis and there's no advantage to using those monster charges. I mean we're fracturing shale here, not bombing Afghanistan. All you're doing is damaging the formation, plus maybe you noticed those earthquakes."

"Probably a natural phenomenon."

"Natural my ass, they happened because you forced us to use mega charges and oversaturate the well with liquid nitrogen. I don't have time to explain the concept of negative skin factor right now, but, trust me, oversaturating isn't helping the well and it sure as hell ain't making things safer. Plus, I suspect there's a fault line we don't know about."

Momberg was fuming. "The geologist didn't find anything."

"Because you ordered him not to find anything! He's too scared of losing his job."

"That's a valid fear, if you catch my drift."

Fighting the urge to deck the scarecrow, Zander calmly said, "If you

3

want to fire me, go ahead. We can all sit around waiting for my replacement, who's just going to tell you the same damn thing."

Jaco added, "Yeah, and I'm not doing fuck all till Zander says go."

Knowing he'd lost the argument, Momberg said, "I'll be reporting this to the board."

Zander said, "That's your prerogative. Jaco, go run your final checks for detonation and blow the klaxon at the two-minute mark."

"Got it, boss. I just need a few minutes." And he ran off.

Zander shouted, "Take your time." But that was just to yank Momberg's chain.

A trio of five-thousand-gallon water tankers pulled into the adjacent lot.

Zander asked, "Are those the flowback water trucks coming back?"

Momberg nodded.

"Aren't they supposed to be dumping at a disposal site across the border?"

Momberg said, "That's what they did," already sounding defensive.

"Except they only left an hour ago and now they're back already. You've been dumping the flowback locally, haven't you?"

"That's not your department."

"For Christ's sake, there's a village about seven kilometers from here and that water's toxic."

Momberg turned and headed back to his golf cart, shouting, "Just do your job!"

Zander watched him drive off, feeling depressed. He gazed out at the sprawling complex he'd helped design. Directly adjacent to the fracking area was the gas separation plant—a technical marvel of machinery, piping and steel spanning six city blocks. Beyond that stood the hundred-foot derrick known as Rig Tower-1. Nestled around it were blocks of Quonset huts housing the welding shops, sleeping quarters and mess halls. Zander had erected a miniature city in the desert that operated at peak efficiency. But now, instead of pride, he felt ashamed. He'd spent much of his life defending his work, while taking every precaution to protect his men and the surrounding communities. Now he'd discovered that Momberg was callously contaminating the local water table. All because of that god damn mystery gas.

He looked wistfully at Rig Tower-1, its flare stack billowing flame into the night sky—a good old-fashioned tower pumping clean-burning natural gas. He muttered, "Ah, the good old days."

The first klaxon blew, indicating they were two minutes from the blast. After this final round it was just a matter of pumping out the mystery gas—something any other competent engineer could do. Soon he'd be on his way home to Johannesburg, forgetting this place ever existed.

Hansie Bekker shuffled the cards and said, "My deal." He heard the first klaxon blow in the distance. "Here we go again."

He was sitting in the security team's barracks at the opposite end of the drilling compound. Anton, his oldest friend and second in command, sat across the table, studying his cards. The two had been playing the same running game of *Klawerjas* for three decades. They chatted in Afrikaans to maintain some privacy from their men.

Anton said, "I tell you, something bad's going to happen."

Hansie chuckled. "You've been saying that since Angola."

The pair had fought side by side for the past thirty years, first as young recces with the South African Special Forces, until circumstance pushed them into the world of private soldiering. Bush wars, civil wars, coup d'états—they'd been hired guns in them all. Both men were going on sixty, but decades of combat experience kept them in demand.

Anton continued, "And I'm usually right. I hear the drilling crew grumbling. They're not happy."

"That's just because I won all their money, just like I'm about to win yours." Hansie pointed to the flipped-up card. "You good with clubs as trump?"

Anton nodded.

Hansie glanced over at the far wall where five of his men lounged on army cots, listening to Zim-dancehall music and gossiping in Shona. All were former Zimbabwean Defense Force troops turned mercenaries that he'd commanded in the recent fight against Boko Haram. His other five men were on duty, patrolling the drilling complex.

Hansie said, "Makanaka."

Makanaka jumped up from his cot, eager to please. "Sir!"

In near-perfect Shona, Hansie said, "Run over to Rig Tower-2. If any of our men are over there, tell them to fall back by Rig Tower-1. I don't want you boys anywhere near those idiots while they're playing with bombs."

Anton grinned and said, "See you have that bad feeling too."

Hansie tapped the last Princeton out of his pack and lit it, "I don't feel anything, I just know they'll need all of us to pick up the pieces after those morons blow themselves up."

Makanaka grabbed his gear and ran for the door.

Hansie shouted, "Stop!"

Makanaka froze in place.

"Where's your rifle? I know we're not shooting our way across Nigeria anymore, but that's no excuse to let your guard down."

Makanaka grabbed his Vektor R-4 rifle, looked to Hansie for approval and hustled out the door.

Hansie made it a point to be tough on the Zimbabweans, who saw it as a sign of affection. He laughed and said, "They're all young and full of piss."

Anton dropped down a card and said, "You're just old and full of shrapnel."

Hansie went back to his cards, taking four tricks in rapid succession. "Aren't you going to accuse me of cheating? Something must have really crawled up your ass tonight."

Anton said, "I'm just getting tired of all this."

"What's the problem? We're not shooting it out with Boko Haram anymore. This is a cushy security job, the closest thing to retirement we'll ever see."

"Screw this. It's another damn desert."

"Technically it's a savanna."

"Screw that too. We should be on the water."

Hansie took another trick and asked, "Is this about buying a boat again?"

"We can take fishermen out around Cape Vidal during the day then eat lobster and drink ourselves stupid at night. I've got some money put away."

"Not when I'm done with you." And he started dealing another hand, adding, "Plus you know less about boats than cards. Face it, my friend, we're old recces, all we do is tell boring war stories until somebody shoots us or we break our neck falling off a barstool."

The klaxon blew again, followed by a second, longer signal.

Hansie said, "Fire in the hole."

Zander sat in the monitoring van, switching his gaze between a stopwatch and his screens. When the stopwatch hit zero, he muttered, "Fire in the hole."

The signals on his monitors jumped, verifying the blast had gone off on schedule.

The klaxon blew three times in rapid sequence, indicating all clear. Nobody had heard the explosion, or felt anything above ground, but his sensors had measured and recorded the blast.

He muttered, "Good, everything's normal."

Almost instinctively he reached for a walkie talkie before remembering that the company's new cell and satellite phone blocker had rendered them virtually useless. He climbed out of the van humming under his breath, until his feet touched the ground. The shale was vibrating.

"Another tremor?"

But it didn't feel like a tremor, which usually came in short bursts. This was continuous—like a giant never-ending subway train rumbling beneath his feet.

"Shit!" Zander sprinted through the site, leaping over obstacles, shouting, "Blow out! Drop everything and fall back, fall back!"

It took him a solid minute to reach the blowout preventer, the mechanism that stood between them and disaster. The two roughnecks he'd seen earlier were already running in the opposite direction.

Momberg grabbed his shoulder. "What's happening?"

Zander shouted, "It's a blowout!" He pulled himself free and ran to a cabinet marked "Emergency." Inside was a Scott Air-Pack emergency breather. As he pulled on the mask, he saw Momberg trotting over to the blowout preventer to investigate. "Get away from there, you id—"

It was too late. Momberg stiffened for a second then keeled over. The toxic mystery gas was leaking out.

Zander turned on the air pack and scrambled over. The pack only held ten minutes of air, and he might need all of it to prevent a full-on blowout. But now he was wasting precious time saving Momberg, of all people. A low hiss emanated from one of the pipes. Zander twisted a nearby shut-off valve. The hissing ceased. He hauled Momberg up over his shoulder and cleared the area.

One of the security team watched him, resisting the impulse to run.

Zander raced over, gesturing for him to take the seemingly dead man, shouting, "Infirmary, understand? Infirmary," his voice muffled by the air mask.

The guard nodded and took off, carrying Momberg.

The vibrations grew more violent until Zander could barely stand. He saw the rig tower swaying.

"Oh Jesus!"

With a scream of tortured steel, the legs buckled, sending the ten-story derrick tumbling down onto the fracking setup. The girders slammed down onto a pair of tanker trucks, rupturing them like water balloons. Wirelines snapped, whipping across the ground, mowing down everything in their path. The work lights around him exploded in showers of sparks, plunging the area into darkness.

The vibrations jumped to a full-on earthquake. Splinters of shale flew up, ricocheting off his air mask. He dropped to the ground for stability and watched in awe as a crevice opened two hundred feet away, spreading in a jagged line towards him. The fracking equipment was swallowed into its maw, and the crevice just kept growing.

Hansie Beeker threw down his cards, shouting in Shona, "On your feet! Form up!"

Anton stood, feeling the steady vibration beneath his feet. "You think it's a blowout?"

"Could be, or an earthquake, or a bomb."

The four Zimbabwean mercenaries grabbed their gear and assembled at the door.

The vibration increased and Hansie watched the playing cards flipping into the air. "It's a full-on quake."

Anton nodded. "Hell of a lot bigger than the other ones."

Hansie tossed the lead man a medical backpack. "We'll probably have casualties. You men go out in two-man teams. Pull any wounded to the central split, then go back and look for more."

The central split marked the end of the site's welding shops and housing unit before entering the gas separation plant.

Hansie turned to Anton. "We'll head for the fracking area and find out what those idiots have done. Now move out!"

The Zimbabweans raced out the door.

Anton smiled and said, "Maybe next time I say something bad's going to happen you'll listen."

"Yeah, that boat's looking better and better."

And they stepped out into the chaos.

Zander pressed his belly to the ground, fingernails clawing at the shale, feeling like he was adrift on a rippling sea. The crevice widened, swallowing everything in its path. He watched a thousand-gallon water tanker being sucked into the growing void.

A massive jolt tossed him upward. He slammed down hard, knocking the wind out of him. An instant later the trembling ceased. The crevice stopped advancing and the night became eerily quiet.

Zander lay there in numb amazement until he heard someone shouting his name.

"Zander, you okay?"

Jaco ran over, a cluster of technicians trailing behind. Zander saw that the gun engineer was now wearing an air pack.

Jaco helped Zander back onto his feet, clapping him on the back. "That was fucking insane! If you hadn't spread the word, we'd all be down in that hole."

Zander nodded and reeled off the names of every man on the fracking crew.

All twelve responded with, "Here."

"Okay, good news is we didn't lose anybody." Looking east he was relieved to see Rig Tower-1 still standing, a healthy column of flame issuing from its flare stack. The fracking area was dark, but there were still lights on across the rest of the complex, meaning it had power. Most importantly, he didn't see signs of fire or smoke.

Jaco said, "I checked the nitrogen tanks and they're intact."

Zander laughed. "Good, 'cause otherwise we'd be ice sculptures."

Rupturing the three-story liquid nitrogen tanks would have unleashed a tsunami of minus 320-degree liquid.

A group of engineers and technicians ran out from the gas separation plant, eager to help, or at least find out what was going on.

Zander shouted, "Stop!"

The group halted.

"We may get aftershocks, so I want every flare valve opened, now! If it's flammable I want it routed to a flare stack and burning off. Get moving; in five minutes I want that sky lit up like it's New Year's!"

The men raced back into the gas plant, where raw natural gas was separated into its valuable elements. The steel labyrinth was jammed with miles of pipe, all connected to a network of two-story separating tanks. Those towers and pipes contained enough compressed butane, propane and methane to level the entire complex. Routing it all to flare stacks would burn off a quarter of a million dollars' worth of gas, but that beat losing a fifty-million-dollar plant and all the men in it.

Zander turned and addressed his group. "Boys, I think we made it through."

The hardened drillers whooped with joy.

Zander felt raindrops on his head, smiled and said, "Jaco, if you say it could be worse—"

Jaco finished his sentence, "It could be raining?" earning a round of laughter. Then something caught his eye and he pointed to the crevice. "What's that?"

Zander said, "It's the biggest earthquake crevice I ever saw."

"No, I'm talking about that thing coming out of it."

Zander strained to see what he was pointing at. "Yeah, you're right."

A black shape was rising from the crevice, clearly moving under its own power.

Jaco asked, "Should we take a look?"

Zander put on his air mask and said, "Put on your mask. The rest of you wait here in case there's any mystery gas."

Flashlights in hand, Zander and Jaco picked their way through the debris field of twisted metal and broken shale. The increasingly heavy rain didn't make things any easier.

Jaco said, "It looks like a war zone."

They were twenty feet from the crevice when they saw the dark shape slip back inside. It suddenly occurred to Zander that there weren't any trucks or equipment sticking out of the crevice. It was as if everything had been sucked straight down into hell.

Zander wondered aloud, "How deep is this thing?" and shined his flashlight down. All he saw was a black void.

Jaco crouched down, straining to see into the darkness.

Zander heard a dull thud in the distance and looked up. "They've got the stacks going."

A series of flare stacks kicked in, shooting columns of blue and red flame high into the night sky. The flames reflected back off the rain clouds, casting a flickering light into the crevice.

Zander turned to Jaco. "At least now we'll be able to—"

But the gun engineer was gone.

"Jaco!" Zander knelt down, shining his flashlight into the crevice, shouting, "Talk to me!" Then Zander realized that he wasn't looking into a dark void—it was a writhing black mass. Dozens of intertwined shapes crawled over one another, hundreds of legs thrashing in an obscene dance. Another flare stack lit up, illuminating the crevice, giving Zander a clear look at one of the things. It stared back at him, the aerial flames illuminating its black eyes and glistening off its exoskeleton. It was a perversion of nature—a living nightmare.

The undulating mass burst upward. A huge pincer clamped around his chest, hoisting him into the air. Suspended there he watched dozens of the creatures stampeding from the crevice. Zander tried to scream, but the pincer only tightened, crushing his ribs, slicing into his flesh. In his final moment he saw the lower half of his body fall away, tumbling into a sea of black monsters.

Hansie and Anton scrambled past the rows of Quonset huts until they reached the central split leading into the gas separation plant. The burning flare stacks bathed the steel maze in flickering shadows. The steady rain had dragged the smoke down to ground level, shrouding everything in a noxious haze.

Anton said, "I can't see fuck all."

Hansie muttered, "A two-year drought and it has to rain tonight."

Despite the dense smoke the pair effortlessly weaved through the warren of pipes, machinery and separation towers. As seasoned reconnaissance soldiers they'd run dozens of drills, committing every turn to memory.

Makanaka emerged from the smoke up ahead, an unconscious man slung over his shoulder.

Hansie waved, shouting, "Over here!"

Anton looked at the unconscious man and said, "It's that idiot, Momberg."

Makanaka said, "He sniffed the gas and went down."

They heard a scream in the distance, followed by another until it grew into a chorus. The shrieks echoed off the steel pipes, making it impossible to pinpoint their origin.

Anton said, "That don't sound good."

Hansie pointed to a steel compartment labeled, "Emergency shutdown wrenches." "Makanaka, shove that guy in there and follow us. We'll come back for him."

Makanaka put Momberg into the compartment, secured the door and fell in behind Hansie.

The screams grew closer until a pack of technicians charged out of the haze, tripping over pipes and colliding with each other in their panic.

Hansie grabbed one, demanding, "Tell me what's going on!"

"It's a swarm! They're killing everyone!"

"A swarm of people?"

"No!" The crazed man tore himself away and ran.

Hansie turned to Anton and Makanaka, shouting, "Come on!"

Off in the distance, Hansie heard four rifles firing in unison, releasing short, controlled bursts.

He said, "Good boys! Just like I taught you, concentrated, disciplined fire."

After three more bursts the guns fell silent, and the screams began.

The trio raced another twenty feet. Through the haze Hansie could make out one of his mercenaries crouched behind a network of pipes, firing wildly into the distance. Then his body shot straight up, vanishing into the haze above. There was a long, agonized shriek then silence.

Looking up, Hansie saw indistinct black shapes crawling among the pipes and rigging. All he could make out was that they were big and fast.

Hansie shouted, "We're holding here. Makanaka, you cover up top; Anton, left flank."

Makanaka aimed high, firing at the nearest shape.

To their left, Hansie saw an animal the size of a cape buffalo dart out from behind a gas storage tank. It charged at them, vaulting over the network of pipes with feline grace.

Anton shouted, "It's mine!" and fired a series of three-round bursts into the oncoming creature. Every bullet hit the target, but the beast barely slowed.

Hansie saw another to their right. He pivoted, unleashing a series of bursts. Every shot was dead on target, but the barrage only served to draw the creature's attention.

Anton's target was charging straight at him. He switched to full auto, emptying his rifle at point-blank range. The beast slammed into him head-on, sending both to the ground in a tangled mass.

Another creature leapt off a two-story tower, landing on Makanaka. It slashed his chest, ripping him in half.

Hansie kept firing at his target. The darkness, the smoke, and the creature's speed made identifying it impossible. It bore down on him then broke right without losing any speed, tearing into a cluster of fleeing technicians. Hansie watched helplessly, unable to fire without hitting the men. Seconds later, it didn't matter—they were all dead.

The creature paused, savoring its kill. Hansie went on the offensive, charging forward, firing extended bursts. In the muzzle flashes he could make out that his target was at least nine feet long with some kind of claws. It grabbed the nearest corpse, clamped its legs around a vertical pipe and scuttled straight up, vanishing into the steel rigging above.

Anton groaned, pinned beneath the dead creature. Hansie ran over and dragged it off, giving him his first clear look at the enemy. For an instant he froze, unable to process what he was seeing, then quickly pulled himself back together. He'd survived a lifetime of combat through a combination of situational awareness and pragmatic thinking—abstract, irrational thoughts only got you killed. What he was seeing couldn't exist, yet there it was—an inarguable fact. He couldn't waste precious seconds denying or rationalizing its existence. All that mattered now was basic math. It had taken Anton thirty rounds to kill one beast, and they only had three hundred bullets between them. Judging by what he'd seen and the distant screaming there must be at least two dozen more. He slung the rifle over his shoulder, knowing attack was pointless. The battle was lost.

He knelt down over his wounded friend. Anton's Kevlar vest had been slashed clean through. It was soaked in viscous yellow fluid that was melting the nylon outer shell. Hansie pulled it off, revealing a deep gash on Anton's chest. There were splotches of the yellow fluid, and the skin it touched was already putrefying. Hansie recognized it as necrotic venom.

In a weak voice, Anton asked, "How bad is it?"

"Remember when you got bitten by that ring-necked cobra?"

Anton grunted.

"This'll be worse."

Anton winced in pain and whispered, "Leave me, save your own ass."

Hansie hoisted Anton over his shoulder and said, "I can't, you owe me too much money."

He grabbed the spare ammunition off Makanaka's dismembered body then worked his way back towards the workshops, keeping to the shadows. Just ahead he saw one of the beasts leap down from the overhead pipes, tearing into a pair of fleeing technicians. More creatures were slinking through the haze, running men down and dragging them off. He resisted the impulse to fire, knowing the sound would only bring the creatures down on them.

He managed to clear the gas plant, entering the network of tightly packed Quonset huts. Most of the rounded steel buildings were workshops or sleeping quarters. Unfortunately, the workers usually kept the steel rollup doors open to escape the African heat—a fatal error.

From the shadows, Hansie watched a screaming man being dragged from the nearest hut. Another of the creatures stood outside, awaiting its turn to hunt.

But he saw one Quonset hut further down the row. The rollup door and windows all looked secure and the creatures showed little interest in it.

The second creature charged into the open hut.

Trying to ignore the screams coming from within, Hansie whispered, "Hang in there, Anton, I think I found us a safe house."

Seizing the opportunity, Hansie scrambled down the access road till he reached the hut. He set Anton down and yanked open the rollup door. The interior was pitch black, but anything was safer than being out here.

After dragging Anton inside, he paused for one last look at the carnage unfolding around him. Over the course of his life, Hansie had witnessed famine, butchery and even genocide, but nothing had prepared him for this. Tonight, hell had opened its gates, releasing an army of giant scorpions to feast on humanity.

A ten-foot scorpion emerged from the nearby hut, a dismembered corpse clutched in its pincers. Two slightly smaller ones charged into the open building, eager for whatever scraps the larger left behind.

Hansie slipped inside, bolting the door behind him. The room was dark and silent, save for the steady patter of rain on the tin roof. He groped along the wall until he found a light switch. A bank of flickering fluorescents came on. The room was sixty feet long with rows of workbenches. The walls were lined with tools, welding torches ... and blood. There was blood everywhere.

"Shit!"

Hansie raised his rifle just as the ten-foot scorpion leapt from the shadows, barreling at him like a charging rhino. He let loose on full automatic, emptying his magazine directly into the creature's face.

And then it was on him.

CHAPTER TWO

Matabeleland South Province, Zimbabwe
18 hours later

Dave Brank hated flying on the best of days, and today didn't qualify as one of those. He made a second attempt to fall asleep, but closing his eyes just sent him straight back to Syria, reliving the Battle of Khasham. That was the night four hundred Russian mercenaries backed by MIG-29 fighters pounded his platoon with artillery and air-to-ground missiles. American warplanes eventually crushed the assault. But on the last wave of attacks, a hunk of Siberian shrapnel had sheared off half his index finger.

Brank snapped awake, hoping nobody noticed the sweat on his forehead. He wasn't prone to combat flashbacks, but today was an exception—and he didn't need a psychiatrist to tell him why. Although the Russians had dropped the ball at Khasham, it looked like they were getting another crack at killing him today… at least in spirit. This time the terror wasn't from high-tech MIGs swooping down at him; today's angel of death was the decrepit Soviet-era Antonov AN-24 cargo plane he was sitting inside. It was a twin-engine casket held together with duct tape older than he was. The aircraft shuddered, violently listing to its left. Brank anxiously twisted at the prosthetic cap on his index finger, convinced the portside engine had stalled again. Or maybe the wing had just fallen off completely.

The plane's PA system crackled and the pilot cheerfully announced, "This is your captain speaking. We have a little bit of turbulence, but, you know, nothing to get freaked out over. We are making our final approach and *The Mayor Urimbo* will be landing in … I don't know, like ten minutes. Thanks, and remember, *The Mayor Urimbo* will always bring you home."

This was Brank's fourth flight on the Soviet-era relic named *The Mayor Urimbo* and each trip had been a protracted near-death experience. The pilot was a Zimbabwean maniac named Nhamo who'd somehow endeared himself to the American embassy—probably by showing them pictures of a different plane.

The kidney-bruising three-hour flight from Harare to the Matabeleland South District might have been almost bearable if he wasn't sharing it with three goats. The nervous animals prowled the aisle, bleating piteously and gnawing at loose cargo straps. The aircraft's interior consisted of a few canvas bench seats along the fuselage broken up by crates of live chickens, piles of grain sacks and other relief supplies, all strapped down with cargo netting.

A goat stopped in front of Brank, hungrily eyeing the shoulder strap of his M82 .50 caliber rifle. He gave the animal a hard look, so it settled for urinating on his boot before moving on.

Brank leaned back into the canvas seat, allowing himself a thirty-second pity party over how his life had changed. He'd spent six years with Special Forces, being shuttled around the Middle East in Blackhawk helicopters and Humvees. Now, as a private military contractor for Talos Corporation, he'd been reduced to cavorting with livestock aboard a Russian suicide machine.

Brank shook his wet boot, muttering, "Welcome to the private sector."

The guy next to him said, "Sorry, I didn't catch that, Stumpy."

Brank turned to Arnaud Cloutier, known to everyone as Goon. The Canadian giant grinned maniacally at him, exposing the void where his front teeth should have been. Goon had given Brank the nickname Stumpy, though he was the only person brave enough to use it.

Brank said, "You think that's funny, Goon?"

Goon shook his head. "Absolutely not."

Brank cracked up. "Come on, a goat urinating on your boss' foot. It's everything you love all rolled into one."

Goon laughed uproariously—a terrifying sight for the uninitiated. The towering brute stood six-six, sported two missing front teeth, a flattened nose, and a Frankenstein worthy scar across his forehead, all framed by scraggly red hair and a Viking beard. Goon was Brank's closest friend, despite being the most frightening looking human being he'd ever seen. Ironically, Goon hadn't received his roadmap of scars serving with the Canadian Forces in Afghanistan. They were all souvenirs of his earlier years as college hockey's most vicious enforcer. He'd earned the nickname Goon long before he'd signed on with Talos and wouldn't answer to anything else.

A sleepy voice grunted, "*Vete a la Mierda*!" from across the aisle.

The goat had awakened Rodrigo Flores who'd been contentedly curled up atop a pile of grain sacks. Brank envied the pint-sized Honduran's ability to sleep virtually anywhere, even on this kamikaze flight. Flores gently tapped the goat's butt with his fifteen-inch bolo machete, shooing it away. The machete had been his trademark during his time with Honduras' elite anti-gang unit, *Policia Tigres*, and he never traveled without it.

Brank said, "Aw, be nice, Tigger, it's just being friendly."

Back in Honduras, terrified M-13 gangsters called Flores *El Cuchillo* or The Blade. But the day he joined the team, Goon had christened him Tigger, and, despite his protests, the nickname had stuck.

Tigger lay back down and said, "Never trust goats, man, I saw one bite off a guy's *cajones* once."

With a toothless grin, Goon proclaimed, "So that's why your voice is so high."

Tigger rolled over, muttering, "*Soplame*," roughly translating to "Blow me."

Goon roared, slapping his knee. The big Canadian's laugh made Santa Claus sound morose by comparison. Brank ignored the pair's mutual insults, knowing that Goon and Tigger were inseparable—like a homicidal Laurel and Hardy.

A few seats down, Ezekiel Jones was gently patting the goat's head, cooing, "The lamb will provide the clothing and the goats the price of the field."

Brank asked, "What's that from, Easy?"

"Proverbs 27:26. But the proverb is really a business lesson, meaning the lamb's wool may clothe you, but you must have the goat's milk to sustain you."

"Well, don't try milking that one; it's a billy goat."

Goon added, "You can tell by its big hairy balls."

Easy shrugged. "We didn't have many goats back in Compton."

Brank found that every unit, military or mercenary, always had one evangelical on board. Everyone liked Ezekiel, or Easy as they called him, mostly because he was a solid soldier who loved talking about Jesus but knew when to shut up. The burly, sweet-faced African American had escaped gang violence at home by enlisting in the Marines, where he saw nothing but violence for four years. Through it all he'd clung firmly to his beliefs, which was more than most could say.

Brank asked him, "You getting any closer to your goal?"

"Getting there," Easy replied. "The GI Bill will cover Divinity School, and I figure one more year of this and I'll have enough saved to start my own parish. God willing. But—"

Goon muttered, "Here we go."

Brank elbowed him.

Easy continued, "Maybe I'll stay here in Zimbabwe and open a mission. Bring people to Jesus, work with my hands, feed the starving—"

Brank added, "And marry one of those pretty African girls?"

Easy looked embarrassed. "You know, they're mostly Christians and from good families."

A voice chimed in, "You better be careful, half of 'em have AIDs."

Brank took a deep breath, thinking, *Fucking Flynn.*

Craig Flynn took off his earbuds and said, "That's what I heard anyway. Tons of AIDs and other shit like incurable clap. Get 'em tested, and wear double rubbers till you're sure. That's my advice."

Easy just nodded politely, while silently praying for Flynn's soul.

Flynn was the newest addition to the team. The former Army infantryman sported a buzz cut, goatee and neck tattoos—all the affectations beta males used to pass themselves off as alphas. He'd started off on the wrong foot by bragging about his exploits in Iraq and showing pictures of himself posing with dead bodies. The kind of creepy, amateur night stuff that turned seasoned men off. Brank didn't know why Flynn left the army, but he bet some NCO was glad to see him go. It spoke volumes that all the other team members had earned nicknames while Flynn was still just called … Flynn.

Brank was about to say something when Goon elbowed him, whispering, "Pipe down, it's the boss."

Ruby Jenkins strode out of the cockpit. As their assigned US Aid officer, she was indeed the boss, with all the bravado and swagger that came with the title.

Ruby announced, "Alright gentlemen, and Goon too, listen up. We're getting ready to land. Just in case we survive that landing we'll meet our village contacts who'll start unloading the aid materials." A curious goat nuzzled at her leg. "Shouldn't these critters be tied up in the back?"

Brank said, "They kept trying to eat the grain bags, so we let 'em go free range."

She shooed the goat away. "Whole Foods would be proud of you. Brank, when we land, have your team do a quick sweep for any threats and try not to frighten the locals."

Goon said, "Hey, I resent that remark."

Ruby continued, "And since there's no doctor, I need you to give the sick ones the once-over. At least twenty are showing symptoms."

Brank nodded. As a Special Forces operator, he'd had more medical training than most paramedics. His team's primary responsibility was protecting Ruby, or occasionally protecting other people from her. Zimbabwe was peaceful overall, but the village they were entering was only thirty miles from the South African border. Roving SA gangs would jump at the chance to slip across and kidnap an American Foreign Service officer—especially one who was obviously a CIA agent in disguise.

The statuesque African American woman sat down on the bench across from Brank, legs stretched out. Brank tried to ignore them; after all, Ruby was his boss. He wondered where she found Eddie Bauer outdoor pants that clung like silk stockings.

The PA crackled again, and Nhamo announced, "Please prepare for landing."

Goon said, "About time," and slapped a magazine into the Mossberg 590 pump action shotgun he called "the stick." With its twenty-round double stack magazine full of double-aught buckshot, the Mossberg was the close-range equivalent of Brank's .50 rifle—pure, devastating brute force.

Brank glanced over at Easy, who was in silent prayer, and said, "Put in a good word for us, buddy."

Goon laughed uproariously.

The runway was nothing but a drought-ravaged field the villagers had picked clean of rocks and obstructions, now reduced to a swamp by the heavy rain. The twin-engine plane slapped down onto the wet ground, spraying jets of water and slewing from side to side until Nhamo gained control.

Brank felt like a middleweight was pummeling his kidneys as the plane bounced down the airstrip. The moment it stopped, he started barking out orders that really didn't need to be stated.

"Alright, work in twos, secure the area around the plane and check the horizon, make sure nobody's coming at us."

The men moved to the exit. Brank shouted, "Full battle rattle, gents, including buckets. That means you, Flynn!"

Flynn begrudgingly took off his ball cap and slipped on a tan ballistic helmet. Helmets weren't standard for Talos military contractors, but Brank had seen too many head injuries in his day. When Talos deemed the 3M Foxtrot helmets an unwarranted expenditure, he'd gone out of pocket himself.

The props were still spinning as the men hit the ground and broke off in twos, ignoring the waving villagers huddled beneath umbrellas.

Brank worked alone, using the scope of his M82 .50 caliber semi-automatic rifle to scan the horizon. The thirty-five-pound weapon was a beast, but Brank knew their greatest threat came from vehicle assaults, be they armed gunmen or suicide bombers. The M82 could tear through an engine block at long range, stopping any vehicle in its tracks. Following that up with a few armor-piercing or high explosive rounds would reduce any bad guys to hamburgers. True to form, Talos had declared his request for the M82 as extravagant, so he'd maxed out his credit card to the tune of seven thousand dollars. It was becoming a bad habit.

The rain was still coming down, but visibility was decent. The village sat to his east, a collection of round hut style homesteads clustered around an open-sided building serving as a church and school. In every other direction Brank saw nothing but flat sand broken up by rocks and a few baobab trees.

Goon stood at the rear of the aircraft, giving a thumbs up, shouting, "Clear!"

Easy stood at the front, shouting, "Clear!"

The closest thing to enemy combatants was a horde of chickens racing over to peck at the grubs their landing had stirred up.

Brank shouted, "We're clear." And the men relaxed.

Ruby Jenkins strode down the gangway, her tight khaki pants stretched over what Brank assumed were an amazing pair of legs. A pair of nuns greeted her, their skin jet black against pristine white habits. A pair of village elders trailed behind them. Ruby greeted them in passable Venda, even getting the male and female greetings correct—something Brank always screwed up.

Nhamo swaggered down the gangway, carefully adjusting his yachting style captain's cap while flashing a toothy grin at the cheering locals. It was the kind of smile only the truly happy or insane can manage. He looked over at Brank and asked, "Do you remember what I always tell you?"

Not wanting to disappoint him, Brank said, "Why don't you remind me?"

"*The Mayor Urimbo* will always bring you home!" He slapped the engine, and a plume of black smoke poured out. Looking embarrassed, Nhamo then went running for his tools.

The deranged pilot had christened his plane *The Mayor Urimbo* as a tribute to one of Zimbabwe's national heroes. The name was stenciled across its pitted fuselage, barely covering the faded Angolan Air Force insignia beneath. Rumor had it that Nhamo had found the plane after it was shot down and rebuilt it himself, using god knows what.

A group of villagers filed aboard, emerging with sacks of grain and caged chickens. There was a huge cheer when the three goats were led down the gangway like celebrities at a red-carpet event.

Brank muttered, "I guess Easy was right about the goats."

Tigger stood on the gangway holding a pair of soccer balls he'd purchased in Harare. He kicked them to a throng of children who went wild. Brank wished he'd thought of something personal like that, then remembered that he was already two lifetimes in hock on military equipment.

The grain and chickens were loaded into a pair of decrepit pickup trucks and driven to the village. Ruby and Brank's team walked, flanked by smiling locals and the newly arrived goats.

The village consisted of about thirty thatch-roofed, round homesteads. The buildings were crafted out of sun-dried brick, decorated with artwork depicting African symbols and flowers. Each was surrounded by red-leafed pig's ear plants, renowned as nature's snake repellent. Barrels and clay pots were set out everywhere, catching the rare and precious rainfall.

To Brank it was like something from another century, an illusion only marred by the children's T-shirts emblazoned with faded soccer logos.

Goon commented, "It's sad, eh? These folks, they've got nothing."

"Oh I think they've got something," Brank said, marveling at the dignity, community and kindness they all showed in the face of hardship. Zimbabwe was considered impoverished even by African standards. But over the past months he'd grown to admire the people of this drought-ravaged country.

Ruby walked over accompanied by one of the nuns, her habit indicating she was a nurse.

Ruby said, "Sister Estelle here will show you where the sick folks are. Give me a quick assessment."

"What's the current diagnosis?"

"I already know what they think. Now I want your take on it."

"Got it. Goon, you, Tigger and Flynn keep an eye on things here. Easy, you come with me."

Brank and Easy visited seven homesteads. The symptoms were the same at each stop, with varying degrees of severity—weakness, severe coughing and chest pains. The more acute cases were coughing up blood.

Brank whispered, "It's not cholera."

Easy nodded. Cholera being the most common waterborne illness.

Brank dug through his medic satchel and doled out some iodine pills. "Looks more like radon or lead poisoning. Something must have contaminated the well."

With a smile, Easy said, "The Lord has provided rain during a drought, to protect his children from the contaminated well."

"True enough," Brank said, "now I hope he protects me from Ruby when I break the news. Let's go."

Goon and Flynn stood near the community borehole, flanking Ruby as she chatted with the elders.

Flynn cocked his head towards Tigger, who stood about a hundred feet away by the open-sided community building, and asked, "So, the little guy was like a cop or something in Mexico?"

Goon said, "It was Honduras, and he ran an elite paramilitary unit. Trust me, Tigger's dropped more bodies than all of us combined."

"Then why's he out here in ooga booga land?"

Goon took a breath, ignoring Flynn's latest racist comment. "The gangs that *Policia Tigres* took down were more like armies. The job was so dangerous they had to wear masks so the bad guys couldn't hunt them down and kill their families. But somebody ratted Tigger out, and ten of the bastards hit his house. He got away, even took some of them out in the process. But then he and his wife had to haul ass out of Honduras with just the clothes on their backs. She's lying low in Mexico and he sends her money."

Flynn watched Tigger with a newfound respect, or at least fear. Two of the nuns approached the community center, and he watched Tigger move away from them, looking visibly uncomfortable.

Flynn said, "He don't like those nuns very much, does he?"

"It's a personal thing."

"Like what?"

Goon grew annoyed. "Like if he wants you to know, he'll tell you."

One look into Goon's eyes inspired Flynn to change the subject. "Uh, Brank's coming."

Seeing Brank's grim expression, Goon said, "Let's give them some space."

Ruby saw Brank approaching and asked, "What's the scoop?"

Brank didn't bother mincing his words. "It's definitely the water."

Ruby's face tightened. "USAID spent a lot of time and money ensuring these people had clean water." She pumped the well handle a few times until water started flowing. "Anybody got a lighter?"

Brank dug out the zippo he carried for emergencies. She flicked the lighter and held the flame near the running water. There was a burst of blue flame that continued burning for a good ten seconds.

Brank took a step back. "I'm no expert, but that ain't supposed to happen."

Ruby handed the lighter back and said, "Bastards."

A village elder rattled off an excited stream of Venda.

"He's telling me they had an earthquake last night. Not a tremor, the real McCoy."

"That happens."

Ruby shook her head. "In the north or central part of the country maybe. Out here, I don't buy it. Brank, give me your binoculars."

He handed them over and she focused her attention to the south. "There it is, about seven clicks out."

Using his rifle scope, Brank made out a blurry cluster of towers in the distance. "It looks like a small city."

"It's a South African natural gas mining operation."

"Aren't they on the wrong side of the border?"

"They paid for the rights to drill here. But the burning water and the earthquake tells me they're breaking all the rules."

"How so?"

"That's a fracking operation, and its backwash is contaminating a well that was bought and paid for by Uncle Sam."

"Are you going to file a report?"

She handed the binoculars back to Brank. "Screw reports, we're going to pay those bastards a visit ourselves. Oh, somebody's already been poking around here."

"Who?"

"A Zimbabwean reported that some white ladies were here a few hours ago. They're probably already over there and I don't like being in second place, so have your team mount up."

"Uh, mount up in what?"

"The nuns are loaning us their pickup trucks. Get on it."

Ruby walked off, leaving Brank and Goon to sort out the details.

"Well," Brank said, "you heard the lady, get 'em loaded."

Goon pointed out, "It's going to be dark in an hour."

"Relax, we're not going there for a fight, just to lend support and look mean."

Goon trotted off yelling, "I'll dust off my war face!"

Brank studied the distant mining operation through his scope, amazed that something so large had been built in less than a year.

A high-pitched voice said, "Hey, you big boss soldier?"

Brank turned around to find a boy no more than nine standing behind him, his hands hidden behind his back.

"Yeah, you could say that."

"You boss soldier, with the big gun, so you want to look badass. Yes?"

Brank nodded, curious what rapper the kid learned his English from.

The sales pitch continued, "You need animal, like pit bull, so other soldiers know you're bad motherfucker." He pulled his hands out from behind his back. The kid was holding two long twigs, like chopsticks. Clamped between them was a seven-inch emperor scorpion. "You buy this, cheap!"

Brank stared at the writhing scorpion, its pincers snapping at the air, black exoskeleton gleaming in the rain.

The sight took him back in time to his childhood in New Mexico. He couldn't have been any older than this kid, but it was already the third or fourth time he'd run away in a futile attempt to escape his father's drunken beatings. He'd been hiding behind some rocks, only a few miles from a drilling complex like the one they were about to visit. That's when he'd been stung by a bark scorpion. It was a tiny thing, one tenth the size of the wriggling thing dangling in front of him, but its venom was infinitely more deadly. Its sting was pure, undiluted agony. Brank lay there for an hour, wracked with pain, until he was forced to crawl home crying. Going home only earned him another beating before being taken to the emergency room. To this day he had a dime-sized divot in his shoulder where the necrotic flesh had to be cut away. The rest of his childhood scars were on the inside.

"You buy?" the kid shouted, holding it closer.

Brank calmed himself and said, "You keep him, kid," and walked away. Between the Russian plane and the scorpion he'd had enough nostalgia for one day.

The disappointed boy threw the scorpion onto the ground, where it was assaulted by a pair of hungry chickens.

The scorpion didn't stand a chance.

CHAPTER THREE

The road between the village and the drilling complex really amounted to a seven kilometer unpaved goat path. The congealed mud combined with the pickup truck's busted shocks and rotted suspension only added to the punishment. Brank drove the lead pickup, with Goon riding shotgun. Tigger sat in the truck bed, while Easy, Ruby and Jenkins trailed them in the second truck.

Between moon craters, Goon asked, "So, you think Ruby Doomsday's looking to start a fight like back in Iraq?"

Brank said, "I hope not, 'cause I'm pretty happy with this backwater assignment."

"Yeah, out here nobody's trying to kill my arse, except maybe this truck."

They'd first been assigned to protect Ruby during her previous posting in Iraq, where her reckless bravado earned her the handle "Ruby Doomsday"—though nobody dared call her that to her face. While claiming to be a USAID worker, she had coordinated a spy network of Iraqi women. For six months the operation yielded a goldmine of actionable intelligence, until one of those operatives was compromised. Many CIA case officers would have left the asset to fend for themselves, but that wasn't Ruby's style. Without authorization, she led Brank's team on an extraction mission that was hairier than any of his Special Forces operations. The rescue was a success, but Ruby had ruffled enough feathers to earn herself a backwater posting in Zimbabwe. Impressed by Brank's team, she insisted they accompany her there for more suicidal frolics.

They were about one kilometer out when the rain lightened up enough to give them their first clear view of the facility.

Goon said, "Christ, look at that goddamn place!"

Brank was thinking the same thing.

The derrick stood at least a hundred feet high, its flare stack emitting a ten-foot jet of fire. Sprawled around it was what appeared to be a full-on gas separation plant; looking at it brought back memories of his drunken father who'd worked oil rigs until he became too unreliable and therefore even more violent. Brank quickly shoved those memories back into the dark recesses where he kept them locked up.

"It's big alright," Brank said, "must be a kilometer on each side. Like a small city."

"It looks more like a prison."

Goon was right. The entire complex was surrounded by a twenty-foot steel fence capped with razor-edged concertina wire.

Brank said, "Well, we're only about twenty clicks from the border, so maybe they're trying to keep roving SA gangs out."

"That fence could keep the damn Marine Corps out."

The fence was odd, but Brank was more concerned about the flare stack. "See that flame coming off the derrick? It should be constant and steady, but it's sputtering."

"Is that bad?"

"It ain't good."

Brank pulled to a stop just outside the open main gate. He'd expected to see trucks rolling in or out, but there was nothing. "This isn't right. An operation this size needs around thirty workers per shift. The place should be a hive of activity."

The only other vehicle in sight was a vintage Range Rover parked alongside the fence.

Goon asked, "You think that's the reporters Ruby mentioned?"

"We'll find out soon enough."

Easy swung his pickup around, pulling up driver's side to driver's side. "What's the plan, sir?"

"With Ruby's approval I say we sit right here and wait for someone to invite us in. That way, we keep it all friendly."

Ruby said, "I agree. We'll sit tight. But let's be ready for trouble."

Goon leaned over to Brank, whispering, "I told ya, brother, she's Ruby Doomsday."

And wait they did—for a solid twenty minutes. By that point the sun had set and the rain had died down.

Climbing out of the truck, Brank said, "Okay, change of plan."

The team formed up behind him.

Goon asked, "So, nobody's home, eh?"

A series of lights inside the compound flickered to life. Goon glanced over at Brank and pointed.

Brank said, "Don't get excited. Usually the night lighting at these sites comes on automatically."

"You really know these places, eh?"

"I worked at one for six months after I got out of high school. One day, I saw a guy fall off a crane and I was at the army recruiting office an hour later."

Goon chortled. "Yeah, 'cause that's safer."

"I never claimed to be smart." Brank turned to the group. "Ruby, may I offer my recommendation?"

"I'm listening."

"I'm no expert on these places, but I'm the closest thing you've got. If this facility's running with nobody at the wheel, it presents a legitimate danger to the village, maybe the whole district. I say we run a brief recon. If we don't find anyone, you call in a team of engineers from Harare to double time it out here and secure the place."

"I concur."

Brank looked at the team. "Okay, we're going in. Weapons slung, don't look threatening and don't take any aggressive action. Flynn, you stay out here on lookout with a walkie. Yell if you see anything. Goon, dig out the radios."

"All three of them?"

"Don't be a smart ass."

Like the helmets, Talos Corporation considered walkie talkies a luxury, allotting only three units to Brank's team.

Ruby strode through the open gate.

Brank shouted, "Ruby, do you mind if we go first, since we're supposed to be guarding you and all?"

She smiled and said, "Lead on, Macduff."

Brank took the lead, Goon following directly behind, with Tigger, Easy and Flynn covering the rear.

Flynn whispered to Easy, "Hey, who's Macduff?"

Easy said, "It's Shakespeare."

Flynn nodded once then asked, "Who's Shakespeare?"

Just inside the main gate was an open area the size of a baseball field surrounded by loading ramps, tool sheds and a cluster of gas pumps. Rows of steel and wood track mat formed crude laneways, while the rest of the area had been reduced to mud by the rain. The lot was empty except for a few trucks clearly undergoing maintenance.

Brank said, "This is the vehicle dispatch area."

Goon asked, "Then where're the vehicles, eh? Did everybody just up and leave?"

"This would be reserved for outgoing trucks and maintenance, so I'm guessing they're making a delivery to South Africa. There wouldn't be any personal vehicles since the workers all live on site."

"They must be deep sleepers."

They pressed on. The vehicle dispatch area transitioned into a hive of steel Quonset huts standing beneath platforms and towers connected by overhead pipes.

Brank sensed his team's apprehension. The drilling site resembled a series of narrow alleyways, except in place of buildings there were multistory machines connected by acres of steel pipe. The endless din of that machinery echoed through the man-made jungle. Residual rainwater dripped down onto the hot machinery, hissing angrily as it turned to steam. The stark work lights shined brightly in some sections, leaving others shrouded in deep shadow.

Tigger summed up their concerns, muttering, "You could hide an army in this place."

Brank pointed to the steam jetting from the separation units on the second level and said, "The main gas separation plant's deeper inside, but that kind of machinery extends out all over the place. There are hundreds of miles of pipe and girders in these places."

A massive fan roared to life behind Goon. He spun around, shouting, "Son of a—"

Brank said, "Relax, that's just a heat exchanger. This place is jam-packed with that kind of crap. Wait till we get into the gas separation plant."

"Can't wait."

Brank saw water dripping down from the second level and caught a few drops in his palm. He sniffed it."

Goon asked, "Thirsty?"

"Just checking to see if it's contaminated, but I think it's just rain runoff."

The narrow walkway emptied onto a wider access road running between the pumping stations and the hundred-foot drilling tower. Brank watched its flare stack sputter again—a bad sign.

"Alright, Goon and Tigger break right, Easy and I go left. Go to the end of this roadway or two hundred meters, whichever comes first. If you don't see anybody, come straight back here. I want this to be a Domino's recon."

Flynn looked puzzled.

Easy said, "That means thirty minutes or less."

Brank said, "Ruby, you're with me."

Brank, Easy and Ruby continued down the laneway. Easy pointed to the steel and wooden traction mats covering the ground.

"Sir, there're no muddy tire marks on these mats."

"Good eye. That means no vehicles have been through here since the rain started, which is funky 'cause at a drilling site this is pretty much Main Street."

Brank signaled to stop in front of a Quonset hut. The rollup door was open but the interior was dark, save for the dim glow of a vending machine. Brank could make out sets of coveralls hung up to dry over rows of rubber boots. From the corner of his eye he caught a flicker of movement. A second later, something crossed in front of the vending machine. Whoever it was, they were trying to stay hidden but doing a lousy job of it.

Brank said, "Nothing here, let's move on." But after five paces he tapped Ruby's arm while giving a hand signal to Easy.

Brank spun around, raising his .50 caliber, shouting, "Don't move!"

Easy dropped into a crouch, his sights locked on the same target.

Ruby shined a blinding tactical flashlight inside, while shouting, "Stop!" in Venda.

A petite woman stood in the doorway, looking like a deer caught in headlights. She raised her hands shouting, "Whoa, whoa, don't shoot!"

Brank kept his weapon trained. "Easy, check her out!"

Easy slung his rifle and patted down the woman. Based on the "whoa, whoa," Brank suspected she was an American.

She announced, "Hey, watch it, pal, I'm a journalist."

Brank thought, *Yeah, definitely an American.*

Easy stepped back, holding a laminate. "She's clean. I found this, looks like ID."

Ruby snatched it out of Easy's hand. Giving the young woman an icy look, she demanded, "Name?"

Here we go, Brank thought, *it's Langley time.*

The young woman wasn't easily intimidated. "It's right there on my press pass. Emily Lennox, *Vice Magazine.*"

Ruby nodded. "Yup, it's right here on your *temporary* press pass, and, hey, what do you know, it expired nine months ago." She tossed it back to Emily. "I'm Ruby Jenkins, US State Department. How long have you been in here?"

"As a journalist, I don't have to answer your questions."

Keeping the flashlight in her eyes, Ruby declared, "And as an attaché of the United States Embassy I don't have to seize your passport and accidentally shred it, but I might. You ever been adrift in Africa with no passport?" She leaned closer, adding a dash of menace to her voice. "You'll probably wind up in some Burkina Faso harem."

Damn, Brank thought, *Ruby's really cranking up the heat.* But Emily impressed him by not backing down right away. Despite her grease-stained jeans and rain-soaked jacket she was clearly attractive. Her dirty blonde hair was pulled back, and, thanks to the blinding flashlight, her honey-brown eyes glowed. He was looking at a prime example of what an army buddy called a BCS, being an acronym for buddy's cute sister. Brank had a fatal weakness for BCS's.

Finally relenting, Emily confessed, "Fine, we got here a couple of hours ago, expecting to be harassed and run off. But the place was a ghost town."

Ruby said, "So you decided to trespass onto a South African drilling site? That's jumping the fence from reckless to plain stupid."

Brank added, "And from the size of that fence outside I'm guessing they don't like visitors."

Ruby asked, "Why were you here? Bear in mind, I might be willing to share some of our own findings with you. Scratch my back, I'll scratch yours. Big hint, I already know about the waste water."

"Okay," Emily said, "I'm an environmentalist and a journalist."

"Oh girl, please! You're an unemployed blogger who eats Ramen noodles four times a week to survive, but do go on."

Easy looked over at Brank with an "ouch" expression.

Emily asked, "Did any of you wonder how this place got built so fast?"

Lowering the flashlight, Ruby said, "You've piqued my curiosity, do continue."

"They did it in nine months because this whole facility was originally on the South African side. But there were huge environmental issues, so they made a deal with Zimbabwe and moved it across the border piece by piece. But instead of trucking the waste water off for safe disposal—"

"They're dumping it back into the ground. I figured that part out."

Brank interjected, "Who's we?"

Emily turned to him. "What?"

"When you started talking you said, 'we got here a couple of hours ago.'"

"His name is Tatenda, and he's with the ZBC."

Ruby explained, "That's the Zimbabwean Broadcasting Corporation."

Brank's walkie crackled, between bursts of static he barely made out Goon's voice.

"Stumpy, I found something."

Goon knelt, picking through the pile of bullet shells. Keying the walkie talkie he said, "I've got expended shells, 5.56 brass. Looks like a full magazine's worth."

Brank came back. "You're breaking up, I copy you found shells."

"Affirmative." Goon played his flashlight across the steel pipes and girders. "But I don't see any impact marks. It looks like whoever fired these hit their target one hundred percent."

Tigger moved ahead of him, checking for bodies or anyone in hiding. He saw a bolted compartment labeled, "Emergency shutdown wrenches." Curious, he opened the bolt, swung the door open and jumped back. The body of a gaunt man tumbled out of the compartment.

"Got one!" Tigger shouted. "A body!"

Goon gave the body a once over, but nothing about it seemed right. It was cool but not cold and there was no rigor mortis. He checked the pulse—nothing. Just to be complete, he pulled up the man's eyelid and shined the flashlight into it. The pupil responded.

He keyed the radio. "Boss, we found one of them."

Brank came back, radio barely audible. "Dead or alive?"

Goon replied, "Um, I'm not sure."

"Grab the body and both of you head straight back to the entrance gate."

"Copy."

Brank turned to Ruby and said, "I want us out of here, ASAP." He looked over at Emily. "Where's your partner?"

"I don't know. Tatenda's in here someplace, but we split up."

"Well, you're going to wait for him at the car with us. Let's get moving."

The radio crackled again. This time it was Jenkins, his voice barely audible through the static. "We got company. I repeat; we got company." And then there was only static.

Emily fell in behind the group, hoping that Tatenda was okay and could find his way out.

Tatenda was okay; in fact, he was having one of the best days of his life.

The ZBC reporter pointed the video camera at himself and pressed record, keeping his voice barely above a whisper. "This is Tatenda Dutiro, reporting from inside this natural gas drilling installation. I must be quiet as I'd certainly be arrested, or worse, if caught. I've already discovered barrels of toxic chemicals on the site, but here, in this trailer, I've found concrete evidence of callous environmental abuse." He panned the camera around, capturing the inside of a construction trailer jammed with open file boxes. "These documents prove that the operators have been dumping contaminated waste water locally, poisoning at least one village." Satisfied with the take, he switched off the camera and rooted through the files.

Tatenda had been prowling the drilling site for three hours, shooting incriminating video at every stop. In his fifteen years as a journalist he'd never stumbled onto such a gold mine of evidence. Once his report aired, the government wouldn't be able to ignore the truth or hide its complicity. If they tried to cover it up, Emily's American media connections would still get the message out. Tatenda would prove that big business couldn't callously exploit his country and poison its people just to turn a profit. And if he became Zimbabwe's own Bob Woodward in the process, well, that was just a bonus.

After photographing the documents he pressed on, coming to a pair of three-story white tanks labeled, "Liquid Nitrogen."

He turned the camera on them while narrating, "What you're seeing is clear evidence of cryogenic fracking, a process that produces highly toxic waste water." Turning the camera back on himself, he continued, "But I've also uncovered a mystery. A site this size requires at least seventy people to operate it, yet I haven't seen a soul. So where has everyone gone?"

Tatenda liked this added mystery angle. Finding the installation empty but still functioning was akin to discovering the ghost ship *Mary Celeste* abandoned at sea. It was exactly the kind of story the BBC or even CNN might pick up. Yet, despite the site being seemingly abandoned, Tatenda couldn't shake the sensation he was being watched.

Chalking that sensation up to trespasser's paranoia he moved past the tanks, stepping into what appeared to be a war zone.

"My God, what happened here?"

A huge rig tower had collapsed, crushing several trucks. Nearby, another water tanker lay on its side, surrounded by twisted metal and broken shale.

He rolled his camera. Though he could make out the demolished trucks, anything beyond that was shrouded in darkness. He tried shining his flashlight, but it was as useless as a birthday candle.

Tatenda fumbled with the camera's switches, trying to remember which turned on the night vision feature. After a few seconds, the dark viewfinder switched to green.

"There we go."

The once black void sprang into a murky, green-tinted image of more wreckage and broken rock. But much of the area remained veiled in shadow. He zoomed in all the way, straining to make out any details, but the viewfinder's image kept shifting and blurring.

"Damned auto focus."

He reached down to disable the auto focus function but discovered it was already switched off. The problem wasn't shifting focus—it was the shadows that were moving. Through the video noise he glimpsed dark shapes, like huge animals prowling in the blackness. Then he saw distant eyes reflecting back, livid green against the darkness.

"Oh shit!"

His first thought was Cape buffalo—an animal so dangerous it was nicknamed "The Black Death." But how could buffalo get inside this fenced installation? Tatenda switched off his flashlight, deciding it was safer to let the camera's night vision guide him back to safety. A hot breeze blew across his back and he caught a whiff of something—a noxious blend of rotting meat and sulfuric acid. He turned back the way he came, eyes glued to the viewfinder.

A gigantic, nightmarish face stared back at him, its fetid breath burning his eyes. Its mouth was a gaping vertical slit, oozing yellow fluid, with wriggling pincers on either side. He tried to scream, but the mouth pincers shot out, latching onto his head, yanking him forward. The slit mouth opened wide then clamped down onto his forehead, tightening like a vice. The yellow mucus seared Tatenda's skin as razor-sharp teeth whittled into his skull.

The camera tumbled to the ground, capturing his final agonizing moments until the lens became too soaked with blood.

CHAPTER FOUR

Brank and his team double timed it towards the vehicle area, Flynn's walkie talkie signal growing clearer with each step.

Flynn blurted, "We've got a shit ton of vehicles coming. I make two, maybe three and a bus and... Oh shit!" The transmission ended.

Brank and Easy cleared the jungle of pipe and steel just as a truck sporting blinding running lights barreled through the gate. Brank stopped, shielding his eyes, its diesel engines growing closer. It screeched to a stop twenty feet in front of him. The running lights shut down, leaving Brank momentarily blind.

Once his vision cleared, he muttered, "What the hell!"

The vehicle wasn't a truck—it was a South African Ratel-90 tank. The six-wheeled, eighteen-ton armored vehicle was similar to the Ferrets used by American anti-terrorism units. Its open turret sported a .50 caliber Browning machine gun.

The gunner shouted, "Stop where you are. Drop your weapons and raise your hands!" His machine gun was aimed squarely at Brank.

Brank yelled, "I'm raising my hands, but we're keeping our weapons until you identify yourselves!"

Easy stepped up next to Brank, further shielding Ruby and Emily. Following Brank's lead, he held up his hands.

A second vehicle roared through the gate, screeching to a halt next to the tank. Brank recognized it as a Mamba—the South African equivalent of a Humvee. The vehicle looked like an old-school Range Rover and a rhinoceros had a baby, equipped with full armor, bullet-proof windows and massive puncture resistant tires. It was a cruel-looking vehicle custom made for African warfare. Three men in tailored tiger stripe fatigues and maroon berets piled out, weapons at the ready.

Easy whispered, "They're toting South African R4s."

Brank nodded. "Good eye, but they ain't South African or Zimbabwean troops."

Two things had tipped Brank off. Firstly, none of them wore name tags, rank or unit insignia. Secondly, their Vietnam-era tiger stripe camouflage was useless for concealment in this arid terrain. The pattern was chosen solely to intimidate people, and it was almost working.

Brank whispered, "They're mercenaries, and not friendly ones like us."

A burly white man climbed out of the Mamba's gun hatch. He stood on the roof, staring down at them, tugging at his thick walrus mustache, his shaven head gleaming in the moonlight.

In a hushed voice, Brank said, "He looks like an old-time circus strongman."

The bald man turned left and right, barking out orders to his men in Afrikaans. That's when Brank noticed his missing ear. It looked as if it had been chewed off years earlier but never properly stitched up or healed.

The man turned back to Brank and, in a thick Afrikaans accent, bellowed, "My name is Kruger. We represent the rightful owners of this facility, and you are trespassers. Therefore you will drop your weapons, or..."

On cue, a pair of mercenaries emerged from the Mamba, leading a man with his hands secured behind his back.

Brank instantly recognized the prisoner. *Fucking Flynn*, he thought.

Flynn said, "Sorry sir, they snuck up on me!"

In a hushed tone, Brank told Ruby, "We're outnumbered and outgunned, so this might be a good time to flex some diplomatic muscle."

A second Mamba drove through the gate, parking beside the first. Two civilians climbed out of the back. The taller was a man in his fifties wearing pressed khakis topped with an Aussie slouch hat. Around his waist hung a big game hunter's culling belt, looped with high caliber .404 bullets—the very model of the great white hunter.

Ruby muttered, "Hooray for Captain Spaulding."

Brank whispered, "Be nice."

The new man spoke in a more refined accent. "I am Gerhard Hertzog, vice president of Graaff Energy, and I demand an explanation for this trespassing and attempted sabotage."

Ruby stepped forward. "Ruby Flynn, US State Department. We entered your facility on the suspicion it presented a danger to the adjacent village."

Unimpressed, Hertzog replied, "This facility is not American, nor is it on American soil, nor are the villagers United States citizens, therefore you have no justification for bringing armed troops onto our property."

"Well, considering that your own people have abandoned the place, I'd say it falls under international jurisdiction."

Hertzog was silent for a moment.

Brank got the impression that the news wasn't a surprise. It was more like it confirmed his suspicions. Sensing an opportunity, he chimed in, "She's right. There's nobody here"—he pointed to the derrick and its sputtering flame—"and that flare stack ain't looking too healthy."

Hertzog turned to his men, shouting orders in Afrikaans. Seconds later, what appeared to be an armored bus pulled into the yard.

Brank was impressed. "That's a Rhino-Runner."

Easy replied, "Yeah, they used to run those between Baghdad and the Green Zone. I saw one take an RPG round and keep right on rolling."

"These guys definitely got some cash behind 'em."

A stream of men dressed in coveralls, all carrying toolboxes, piled out. The technicians formed up in a line, awaiting instructions.

Goon emerged from the maze of pipes with a body slung over his shoulder, Tigger right behind. When they saw the South Africans, they stopped and looked to Brank for direction.

Brank waved them over, saying, "It's okay, Goon, bring him out."

Goon stepped forward, laying the inert man on the ground. "He's in some kind of coma, no pulse, but his pupils respond to light."

Brank knelt over the man, checking his vitals.

Looking down, Hertzog said, "It's Momberg, our company man."

Brank said, "He looks dead."

"He always looks that way." Hertzog shouted for the other civilian, who raced over carrying a medical bag. "Dr. Vorster will examine him." Then he shouted orders to the line of technicians. They scrambled into the facility, accompanied by five of the mercenaries.

Tigger glanced over at Brank, who nodded. Goon slipped Tigger the walkie talkie and the Honduran slipped in behind the parade of technicians.

Dr. Vorster briefly examined the unconscious man then asked Goon, "Where was he found?"

Goon glanced at Brank, who gave him a silent nod of approval. "He was just inside the gas plant."

Vorster put a stethoscope to the man's chest.

Goon whispered to Brank, "What kind of shit show have we got here?"

Brank whispered, "I estimate at least thirty armed men, likely outlaw military contractors, along with those twenty gas technicians."

"Plus armor. They came loaded for bear."

"I think they lost contact with this place. So they came in with private troops expecting a coup or terrorists."

Brank had a decent view out past the main gate, where he saw two more Mambas idling alongside a flatbed truck with a heavy generator mounted on it.

He whispered to Goon and Ruby, "That generator's at least six hundred kilowatts, enough to power the whole place."

Ruby asked, "Emergency backup?"

"Yeah." Brank watched men run heavy cable out from the generator. "But what're they doing out there?"

Dr. Vorster turned to Hertzog. "His symptoms are the same as the previous three. No pulse, zero respiration, yet his reflexes respond as if he's alive."

Hertzog said, "Do the test."

Forster pulled a scalpel from his bag and cut a short incision into the man's chest.

Brank asked, "What the hell are you doing?"

Ignoring him, Vorster said, "No bleeding. It's incredible."

The twenty technicians scrambled into the maze of pipes then split off for their individual work stations. A pair of them stopped at Drilling Tower-1. The hundred-foot derrick's controls were located on a second-level platform known as the drill floor. The technicians ran up the steel steps and went straight to work. A mercenary followed behind them.

Tigger climbed up the stairs but hung back in the shadows, trying to hear them over the din of equipment. Thankfully the men spoke English, and the mercenary seemed too distracted to notice him.

One shouted, "Should we engage Blowout Prevention?"

His partner replied, "No, Hertzog will kill us if we shut down. Let's try balancing the load first."

Working in unison, they spun heavy steel wheels while monitoring a series of gages.

Tigger looked up, watching the sputtering flare stack stabilize until it was burning smoothly.

The lead technician leaned back. "That was too close."

His partner agreed. "Another hour and we would have had a blowout. Where the hell's the regular crew?"

The South African mercenary stepped up to Tigger, blocking his view, demanding, "Get back!"

Tigger smiled and took ten steps back, satisfying the mercenary. Tigger had just learned that the technicians were as in the dark as they were. He looked up at the flare stack again, but this time he saw something else—a dark shape moving among the pipes overhead. At first he thought it was some of the drill crew, but it looked like one solid, undulating mass.

Tigger approached the mercenary and pointed up. "Did you see that?"

Without bothering to look, he ordered, "Just get back down there, now!"

Tigger walked down the steps, muttering, *Pendejo.*"

Then he heard the first scream.

Hertzog stared down at Momberg's seemingly dead body and said, "Bring him back."

Dr. Vorster protested, "But instant revival hasn't been tested on humans."

"Then test it now!"

Vorster dug through his medical kit, producing a cardiac needle and a compact oxygen bottle. He filled the syringe with what Brank assumed was epinephrine and jammed it into the man's chest. Curious mercenaries hovered over them for a closer look.

Vorster checked his vitals and said, "Nothing yet."

Brank shoved the mercenaries aside, shouting, "If you're not helping, make a hole." He knelt down and started pumping Momberg's chest. Without protest, Vorster placed a bag valve mask over his face and started squeezing. Brank and Vorster hummed the Bee Gees song "Staying Alive" in harmony as they alternated CPR actions.

The doctor said, "He may need another shot."

Momberg's chest heaved and he let out a gasp. Brank held down his flailing arms while Vorster placed the oxygen mask over his mouth. After a few seconds of panic, Momberg began breathing normally.

Vorster asked, "How do you feel?"

Momberg replied, "Okay. Tired."

Then Vorster asked him a series of questions, ranging from personal information to current events. Momberg answered some of them, with difficulty.

Brank bent down for a closer look at the scalpel incision and muttered, "Holy shit." The freshly cut wound was already at proliferation—the second stage of healing.

Vorster turned to Hertzog. "It's incredible; he's alive and responsive despite being technically dead for at least fourteen hours. New tissue is already growing over the wound. His memory's cloudy, but that could just be post-operative delirium. That's normal after anesthesia. Hopefully it wears off with time."

Hertzog just nodded. The he turned to Kruger and gestured for him to follow. The two talked back and forth while sneaking looks at Brank's team.

Brank sensed they'd seen too much.

Tigger heard screams echoing from deeper within the gas plant, followed by the distant pop of rifle fire.

The South African mercenary raised his rifle at Tigger, shouting, "Touch that weapon and I'll blow your ass away!" convinced that Tigger's team was responsible.

That's when the creature dropped down ten feet behind the mercenary.

In the darkness, Tigger could only make out that it was huge, the size of a racehorse, but slung close to the ground. When its tail curled above its head, Tigger realized he was looking at an impossibly large scorpion.

Tigger yelled, "Behind you!"

The mercenary's final words were, "Nice try, asshole!"

Huge black pincers grabbed him by the neck. The scorpion hoisted him up high then slammed him to the ground. In the same move, its tail plunged downward in one lightning-fast strike. The beast stood there, toying with its still squirming prey.

Two more of the creatures skittered down the drill tower. These ones were pony sized but even faster, their eight legs flowing like water across the steel landscape. The drill technicians tried to escape, but the first scorpion pounced on the slower one. It grasped him in its claws, whipping its stinger down into his chest.

The other technician raced towards Tigger, a second scorpion in pursuit.

Tigger opened fire, sending a three-round burst of 5.56 bullets into the oncoming creature. It reared back from the impact, more shocked than hurt. Tigger fired again, placing eight rounds dead center into its abdomen. The bullets jarred the creature but failed to penetrate its exoskeleton. The technician ran past Tigger without looking back.

Another mercenary raced out of the darkness, followed by a pack of screaming technicians. In their rush to escape, the men stumbled over the network of pipes. A wave of monstrous scorpions was in pursuit, effortlessly clearing those same obstacles.

The mercenary turned, firing a low, full auto burst into the escaping technicians. Two went down screaming, clutching at their bleeding legs. A heartbeat later, the scorpions were on them, razor-sharp pincers tearing at their flesh.

This cowardly act bought the mercenary a few seconds. Mistaking Tigger for one of his own people, he raced to him, shouting, "Go! Go!"

Tigger used one hand to fire at an approaching scorpion. With the other he drew his machete and swung, slashing across the mercenary's stomach.

Tigger shouted, *"Cobardemente joder!"* while scooping up the bleeding coward's Vektor rifle. As a seasoned jungle fighter, Tigger instinctively shifted his attention upward. It saved his life. Another scorpion was poised on the steel pipes above, ready to pounce. Tigger emptied the Vektor's magazine into its underbelly, tearing it open. He leapt to one side as the thrashing beast crashed to the ground. Its pincer lashed out, slashing through his Kevlar vest. Miraculously it didn't draw blood. Tigger threw down the now empty Vektor rifle and retreated. Another huge scorpion dropped down behind him but opted to dine on the wounded mercenary.

Brank heard shots echoing over the cacophony of machines, followed by distant screams. He keyed his walkie, shouting for Tigger. All he got was static. Turning to his team he ordered, "Easy, you're with me. Goon and Flynn stay with Ruby and Emily. And don't trust these bastards!"

Brank ran into the maze of pipes, Easy right behind.

A panicked technician bolted past them screaming, "Scorpions!"

They ran another twenty yards and saw Tigger. He was cornered, with a huge scorpion coming at him from the front and another poised to attack on his left.

Upon seeing the scorpions, Brank had a reaction he'd never experienced in his years of combat—he froze. There it stood, his every childhood nightmare made flesh, only a hundred times worse. An icy tremor shot through his body, and his hands trembled.

Tigger fired a burst into the front creature, momentarily pushing it back. Unharmed, it charged forward.

The gunshot yanked Brank out of his paralysis, allowing his instincts to take over. He fired the .50 caliber, striking the creature in its side. The armor-piercing round tore through its exoskeleton in an explosion of indigo-blue gore. Tigger sprinted forward, leapfrogging over the dying creature as the second launched its attack.

Easy fired a three-round burst, which only seemed to annoy the creature; Brank fired again, nearly blowing the second scorpion in half.

Tigger ran up to him shouting, "We gotta go, *pronto!*"

Brank saw massive shapes moving among the pipes and girders and yelled, "Fall back, in order!"

Brank walked backwards, .50 caliber at the ready, Easy guiding him past any obstacles. Tigger took point, scanning for oncoming scorpions.

A huge one dropped down twenty feet behind them. Brank loosed another round, tearing it open. The next wave of scorpions descended on the wounded one in a cannibalistic frenzy.

Tigger's direction was no more promising. A technician raced past him only to be pounced on. This time the scorpion didn't use its stinger, instead clamping its pincers onto the screaming man and dragging him off. Then Tigger spotted a wave of scorpions to his right, advancing toward the vehicle yard.

They saw him too. A group broke from the herd to pursue them.

Tigger shouted, "The way back's cut off!"

Brank saw more coming in his direction and shouted, "We're surrounded!"

To his left was a conduit pipe with a maintenance ladder running alongside it. He shoved Easy towards it, shouting, "Up!"

Easy scrambled up the ladder, Tigger right behind. Brank let off five rounds, certain three of them had struck targets. While some of the attacking scorpions turned on their fallen brothers, others kept coming.

Easy climbed the twenty-foot ladder to an overhead platform and peered down. Brank was clearly in trouble, but he knew his M4 lacked the stopping power to kill these things. Then he saw wisps of steam escaping from a ground-level horizontal pipe. Easy fired a three-round burst, rupturing the pipe. A cloud of high pressure steam shot out, scalding the oncoming scorpions. Seizing the moment, Brank scrambled up the ladder, a scorpion in pursuit. Tigger extended an arm, hoisting him up to the platform. The moment he landed, Brank spun, loosing a .50 caliber round into the creature's face. The dead scorpion tumbled down the ladder, landing on a cluster of others below. That group quickly took off, following the main herd.

Watching them, Brank said, "They just made a tactical decision."

Easy asked, "What?"

"A tactical decision. Coming up after us would be too costly, so they opted for the easier meat."

"You mean Goon and Ruby?"

CHAPTER FIVE

Goon kept one eye peeled for Brank while also watching the South Africans, who'd made no attempt to rescue their own people. Turning to his group he whispered, "What say we mosey over to that gate and out of here? Just act casual, eh?"

Goon, Ruby, Flynn and Emily slowly walked towards the gate.

Kruger shouted, "Stop!" and stood blocking their path, flanked by three mercenaries.

In a polite tone Ruby asked, "What's wrong? You wanted us to leave, so we're going."

"I'm afraid that's no longer an option." Kruger's mercenaries brought their weapons to bear on the group.

A piercing scream came from the gas plant. The mercenaries swung around, weapons at the ready.

A technician staggered out of the alleyway, clothes soaked in blood, screaming, "Scorpions! Huge scorpions!"

Kruger strode toward the man, shouting, "What the hell are you ranting about?"

Before the technician could speak, a scorpion galloped out of the alleyway, grabbing him in its pincers. A split second later, he was impaled on its stinger.

The mercenaries just stood there, too stunned to react.

Goon wasn't. He raised the Mossberg 12-gauge shotgun, unleashing a fusillade of buckshot into the creature. Three shells struck home at near point-blank range. The sheer force threw the scorpion backwards into a mass of oncoming beasts. Goon fired four more shells into the swarm, wisely aiming for their legs, slowing them down.

Ruby grabbed his shoulder, yelling, "Down!"

Now recovered from their initial shock, the South Africans opened fire. Goon, Ruby, Emily and Flynn hit the dirt, bullets zipping overhead.

Goon pointed ahead. "Crawl towards the trucks."

The rain of bullets hit the alleyway swarm, but a split second later, the rigging on either side was alive with scorpions. Three attacked from the right, descending on Dr. Vorster and the barely conscious Momberg. The first snapped up Momberg, tearing him to pieces. Vorster tried to run but was overtaken by the other two. The pair fought a brief tug of war with the screaming doctor until each got half.

The six-wheeled Ratel tank rumbled forward, its gunner unleashing a hail of .50 caliber machine gun fire. Four charging scorpions were shredded in the first burst.

That's when Goon saw the scorpions do something incredible. A pair of them launched a flanking attack, leaping onto the back of the Ratel. One scrambled across the roof, decapitating the machine gunner with its pincers. It tossed the cadaver aside and began ramming its stinger through the top gun port, down into the vehicle. The Ratel swerved wildly, running down one of the mercenaries. The scorpion pulled its tail out of the gun port, the driver impaled on its tip.

Mercenaries scrambled in every direction, firing into the creatures while losing ground every second.

Goon knew the Ratel and its .50 caliber were their only hope of survival. He charged at the slowly rolling tank, firing three loads of buckshot at the scorpion atop. The first severed its tail, while the other two blasted its left side legs apart. Unable to balance, it tumbled forward, under the wheels. The driverless Ratel lurched to a halt.

Goon kept moving, firing at the second scorpion. The sheer volume of fire knocked the creature from its perch atop the vehicle. Goon climbed aboard, nearly slipping in the scorpion's inky blood. Within seconds he was firing the .50 caliber machine gun.

A mercenary toting an SS-77 medium machine gun scrambled over. He kept firing the belt-fed weapon at distant targets, to little or no effect.

Goon threw a fistful of expended brass at the man, getting his attention. "You protect me! I'll take care of them!"

The mercenary got it, shifting his focus to any scorpions attacking the Ratel. Knowing he was covered allowed Goon to choose viable targets.

Emily climbed aboard the Ratel, crouching behind Goon. "I'm sticking with you."

"Then be a doll and feed the ammo," Goon yelled, "like this."

He gave her a one-second demonstration, which was all she needed.

Goon shouted, "My kind of girl!" and resumed firing.

Knowing their rifles were underpowered, Kruger rallied his men into an old-fashioned firing line.

"Concentrate all fire on one target." He waited until one of the creatures charged. "Fire!"

Fourteen rifles fired in unison, loosing three-round bursts. The sheer intensity of lead jackhammered through the beast's exoskeleton, dropping it.

"Good work!" Kruger shouted. But he knew they couldn't afford to waste a hundred rounds killing a single opponent.

Hertzog slipped inside one of the Mambas and emerged carrying his personal Heym Express .404 big game rifle. He'd brought it along hoping to sneak in some big game hunting on company time. The fifty-thousand-dollar rifle was chambered to take down elephants, and his first bullet tore open a distant scorpion.

He slapped the bolt, chambering another round, shouting, "Beautiful!"

Goon slapped a fresh belt into the Browning and resumed firing, shredding two more scorpions. He noticed something had changed. "Hey," he shouted to Emily, "am I nuts or are they retreating?"

Peering over his shoulder, Emily said, "You're right. They're running, or crawling, away."

He fired a short burst into a retreating scorpion. "Here's a going away present ya eight-legged fuck!" Goon ceased firing.

Emily leaned close to him and whispered, "We've got a problem," and pointed down.

Kruger calmly stood below, hands folded in front of him. One of his men had Ruby in an arm lock, his pistol pressed against her temple. Flynn knelt on the ground beside her, hands behind his head. Twenty mercenaries clustered around them, weapons trained on Goon and Emily.

Goon said, "You one-eared bastard! We just saved your asses!"

"And we thank you for that. Now drop your weapons!"

Knowing they were licked, Goon threw down his Mossberg shotgun. A mercenary caught it and took a moment to admire the weapon.

Kruger said, "Now come down slowly or I'll have to shoot the ambassador."

Hearing gunfire coming from the yard, Brank and his team climbed through the maze of pipes and girders, following the sound. Progress stopped when they reached a twenty-foot gap spanned by a horizontal length of pipe. Beneath were two massive fans blowing hot air straight up.

Brank shouted, "Those are heat exchangers." The distant gunfire abruptly ceased. He said, "I'm not sure if that's good or bad."

Tigger heel-toed across the narrow span of pipe like an aerialist.

Muttering, "Show off", Brank wrapped his arms and legs around the pipe, shimmying over boot camp style. The fan's benzene-laced wind burnt his nostrils. He told himself that this was just like an army obstacle course, except they were twenty feet in the air, dangling over whirling steel, surrounded by man-eating scorpions.

Easy fell in behind. They'd only made it halfway across when Tigger stuck his head down and signaled to stop. He pointed left. Shifting his gaze, Brank saw a scorpion inching up a nearby vertical pipe. This one was colossal, at least nine feet long, not counting its stinger. Rippling shadows in the distance indicated at least five more creeping through the darkness. Brank and Easy froze, not daring to breathe. Tigger lay down on his back, his M4 trained at the nearest scorpion, waiting.

The scorpion inched up, its eight legs gripping the steel pipe until it was barely ten feet away. Brank's stomach tightened and chills rippled through his body. Up to now he'd been too busy fighting his enemy to think about them. But now, standing this close, all those childhood nightmares came rushing back.

Stay focused, he told himself, *don't let fear take over. Your enemy's right up close, so learn something!*

Brank saw the wirelike hairs on its legs bristling from the exhaust fan below and remembered something useful from his New Mexico childhood. The scorpion's hairs were actually sensory organs, and it looked like the exhaust fan and benzene fumes were raising hell with them. That's why they weren't attacking—they couldn't find them.

Brank felt his grip slipping on the damp pipe and squeezed tighter against it, his core and leg muscles burning. The bulky .50 caliber rifle hung from his back like an anvil.

The scorpion latched onto a horizontal beam, offering Brank a nightmarish view. The thing's back was covered in some kind of pale growths, like a rippling mass of white boils. After a breathless minute the beast slipped past, followed by the rest of its herd.

Hand over hand, Brank shimmied forward until Tigger grabbed his arm and pulled him over. Easy was across a few seconds later.

Tigger and Brank crawled to the edge of a platform, getting an overview of the vehicle yard below. Easy kept an eye peeled for any attackers coming from behind.

Tigger said, "They're alive."

Brank said, "But something ain't right."

Using his rifle scope, Brank took a closer look. Kruger had a gun pressed to Ruby's head and Goon was climbing down from the tank, unarmed.

Kruger leaned close to Hertzog, speaking in Afrikaans. "They've seen too much. I say we execute them now and then deal with those monsters."

Hertzog nodded and said, "Agreed."

The two had arrogantly assumed Ruby couldn't understand them. But she'd learned enough Afrikaans to catch their drift. Their only hope was that Brank was out there, somewhere. She shouted to Goon, "Well, sorry about how this all turned out, guys, but you know these missions are always a crap shoot!"

Brank could barely hear her shouting over the machinery, but he clearly made out one word—shoot.

He whispered, "Get ready," and fired.

The .50 caliber round whooshed past Ruby's ear, straight into the mercenary's forehead. The massive round detonated his skull in a shower of blood and brain matter.

In the same instant, Tigger opened fire, killing the mercenary holding Goon's shotgun.

The headless mercenary crumpled to the ground, pinning Ruby under him. Grabbing his sidearm, she snapped off three fast shots. One struck Kruger squarely in the chest. His Kevlar vest stopped the bullet, but the ballistic impact threw him to the ground.

Brank opened fire on the nearest Mamba armored car. The round tore through the bullet resistant windshield, killing the driver. His next shots sent mercenaries diving for cover behind the vehicle.

Goon charged forward, sending the nearest mercenary to the ground with an NHL worthy body check. With three more strides he scooped up the fallen shotgun.

Flynn grabbed his M4 off of a dead man and opened fire on a pair of fleeing mercenaries, killing one.

And then the scorpions attacked.

Three bolted out from the machinery, charging towards the troops. The mercenaries opened fire, but their erratic gunfire did little to slow the onslaught. But some had learned from their first experience. Two fast-thinking men scrambled aboard the Ratel tank and threw it in gear. It rumbled forward, unleashing a barrage of heavy machine gun fire.

Emily rushed over to Ruby, pushing the headless corpse off her.

Ruby yelled, "Look out!"

A scorpion barreled towards them. She got off four shots, but the 9mm handgun was useless. The beast was only inches away when its abdomen burst open in a shower of indigo blood.

Ruby looked up, shouting, "That's our guardian angel!"

Brank slapped another magazine into the .50 caliber, relieved that Ruby and Emily were momentarily safe. Tigger grabbed his shoulder and pointed to their left. Forty feet away, a massive scorpion hung motionless from a pipe ... as if it were waiting. It was the same boil-encrusted creature he'd seen up close.

Brank looked down and saw the Ratel tank rolling directly underneath the suspended monster. That's when he realized what the quivering mass on the creature's skin was.

"Goddamn paratroopers!"

The Ratel's gunner reached for a fresh ammo belt then heard something land behind him. He turned, trying to aim, but it was too late. A white, dachshund-sized scorpion latched its pincers onto the gun barrel then skittered down, embedding its stinger in the man's forehead. The screaming man's hand clamped down on the trigger, sending a long burst into the nearby gas pumps. A jet of flame roared into the air. Man and scorpion tumbled off the roof and were crushed beneath the vehicle's six massive tires.

Still hanging from the pipe, the mother scorpion shook its body, releasing more of the pale, almost translucent, infants clinging to its back. Two dropped directly into the Ratel's open gun port, attacking the driver. The six-wheeled Ratel slewed wildly, sending terrified men diving out of its path. It slammed into the flaming gas pump, and the spraying gas detonated it in a ball of fire. Within seconds the Ratel was engulfed in flames.

Up above, Brank fired a .50 round into the mother scorpion, blowing its abdomen wide open. Its death throes released a dozen more infants.

Kruger was back on his feet and bellowing orders. On his command both Mamba armored vehicles shifted into reverse, backing towards the main gate, terrified men clamoring up onto the chassis.

Hertzog stood just inside the gate, gleefully firing his big game rifle into the wave of scorpions. A Mamba screeched to a halt next to him.

Kruger leaned down, extending a hand, shouting, "Get on, this ain't some goddamn safari!"

Hertzog was hoisted aboard and the vehicle backed out. A waiting mercenary hit the gate switch, and, with a rumble, it began sliding shut.

Goon, Emily, Ruby and Flynn were already making a beeline for the closing gate when Kruger's men fired on them. The barrage forced them to retreat back into the drilling area—directly into scorpion territory. A pair of nine-footers closed in on them, only to be shot from above by Brank. The .50 caliber was perfect for huge scorpions, but the infants proved too small and nimble. Now ten of them were racing towards Goon and his team.

Goon let loose with the 12-gauge, taking out two of the lead scorplings. Flynn opened fire on full auto, loosing fifteen rounds but only hitting one target.

Emily held up a five-gallon can of gasoline, asking Ruby, "Can this help?"

Ruby grabbed the jerry can out of her hand, yelling, "Goon, it's skeet shooting time!" And she hurled it with all her might at the approaching scorplings.

Goon fired, hitting it mid-air like a clay pigeon. The jerry can exploded in a shower of flames, immolating the horde. Goon gave Ruby a toothless grin. "They teach you that trick in the CIA?"

"That's only a rumor."

The group scrambled into the maze of machinery and pipes.

The second his vehicles cleared the fence, Kruger jumped down, shouting, "Now, now!" to the generator truck.

The generator operator nodded, throwing a bull switch just as the gate slammed shut.

A seven-foot scorpion was already scaling the fence, with two more right behind. There was a loud hum, followed by a wave of static electricity and ozone stench. The scorpion trembled, smoke pouring off its body, then tumbled to the ground, motionless. The second scorpion grabbed the fence with its pincers, only to be catapulted back by the high voltage. Another tried, meeting the same fate.

Kruger watched with satisfaction then turned to Hertzog. "See? You cheap bastards whined when I requested an emergency generator."

Hertzog eyed the fence. "Do you think it's enough to stop them?"

Kruger nodded. "It's eight hundred amps. Hell, the old electric chair was only twelve."

"What if they learn to dig?"

"We're sitting on a shale rock bed, so digging's not an issue."

"Can the fence handle it?"

"My contract demands that every fence is capable of being electrified. Usually it's to keep the enemy out, but it works both ways." Kruger saw his adjunct, Major Van Shoor, running over and asked, "What's the butcher's bill?"

Van Shoor reported, "We lost twelve men, leaving us twenty-seven in total, but we also lost the Ratel and the fifty caliber."

Kruger waved Van Shoor away and turned to Hertzog. "I requested three heavy machine guns, but you were only willing to pay for one. When old soldiers talk, you should listen."

Hertzog scowled then asked, "We need to regain control of the drilling complex. So, how does an old soldier propose we do that?"

Kruger dug a can of *Jakobson* from his pocket and jammed a wad of the tobacco into his cheek. "Those things might be huge, but they're still scorpions. I say we wait."

Hertzog was puzzled. "Wait? For what?"

"Scorpions are cannibals, so once they run out of food they'll turn on each other. We let that happen, then go in and kill off the survivors."

Hertzog said, "Are you forgetting that we just murdered a member of the American State Department? The US embassy will come looking for her, and this time they won't just bring a couple of mercenaries for backup. It'll be a company of ZDF troops." ZDF is the acronym for the Zimbabwean Defense Force. "The mystery gas we've uncovered is beyond priceless, and the pocket under Rig Tower-2 appears to be pure. We must be in full control of the site when they arrive, or they'll come up with some bullshit kaffir law and take possession."

Kruger sucked at the tobacco for a moment then suggested, "What if we lure the scorpions out by offering them something to eat?"

"Are you suggesting feeding your own men to those bastards?"

"Of course not, those are my boys. I'm saying we arrange a banquet they can't pass up. I can rig a timer on the fence to kill the power once we get to a safe distance. Once the bastards are clear, we move inside and electrify the gates again."

"What do we feed them?"

Kruger turned, spitting a stream of tobacco north, and asked, "How far away is that village?"

CHAPTER SIX

As soon as he saw his people scrambling into the complex, Brank shouted, "Let's move!"

The team trekked through the upper level of machinery with Brank on point, Tigger and Easy covering the rear. Brank spotted a ladder leading down and gestured for them to halt.

Brank said, "We need to get back down to ground level."

Looking down, Tigger said, "Looks clear."

"Don't bet on it. Scorpions are ambush predators." He handed the .50 caliber rifle to Tigger, grabbed the outside of the ladder and slid down.

The second his feet touched ground he dropped and rolled left onto his back. Staring down at him was a six-foot scorpion clinging to the bottom of the steel platform. It dropped to the ground, nearly landing on him, lashing out with its stinger. But the strike missed, its tail becoming caught in the ladder. Tigger dropped the .50 caliber into Brank's waiting arms. In one move he caught it, sat up and fired. The round split the scorpion's head wide open.

Easy hit the ground, rolling up onto his knees, ready to fire.

A heartbeat later, Tigger landed, covering the opposite direction.

But the second attack never came.

Brushing off some scorpion blood, Brank said, "We just learned two things. First off, some hunt alone."

Easy asked, "What's the other?"

"They've already figured out what ladders are for."

Tigger and Easy stepped around the dead beast and looked to Brank for direction.

Brank waved them forward, saying, "Goon's smart. He'll head for the rally point where we split up."

They'd run thirty feet when Brank raised his fist to stop then pointed to the ground. It was covered in steel and wood track mat. In a hushed voice he said, "Those access mats keep trucks from sinking in the muck, but they'll vibrate if you run on them, and that's how scorpions hunt. So, step lightly, like little ballerinas."

They moved on, stepping gingerly. Those six months Brank had spent working on a drilling site were finally paying off.

Within minutes they reached the rally point. Brank peered around the corner but didn't see people or scorpions. He pulled his red-lensed tactical flashlight and flicked it three times. A few seconds later, the signal was returned.

He muttered, "I hope my Morse code isn't too rusty," and flashed what he hoped was "You okay?"

Goon flashed the reply, "Okay, coming to you."

Brank raised his .50 caliber. Tigger crouched beside him, his weapon trained on the rigging above, while Easy covered the rear. In Morse, Brank flashed, "Go."

Goon's group scrambled forward.

As soon as they made it around the corner, Goon gave Brank a helmet-to-helmet headbutt, saying, "Nice to see ya, Stumpy."

"Good to see you in one big ugly piece."

He grabbed Goon's arm, steering him in front of a nearby exhaust fan. The group followed, huddling in the wind.

Brank caught a whiff of benzene and smiled. "This is a sweet spot. The fan screws with their sensory hairs and the benzene vapor means they can't smell us." He asked Ruby, "Were you able to get an SOS call out?"

Ruby held up her embassy satellite phone. "I've got zero signal."

"Well, we've still got to warn the village."

Ruby nodded. "Agreed. If those things get loose they'll be slaughtered."

"It's a good thing I'm packing these." Brank dug out a pair of seven-inch aerial flares from his vest pocket, one red, the other white. He tossed one to Goon. "I'm gambling that Nhamo's still patching up his plane and sees 'em."

He held one up high, tugging the release cable, firing the red flare up through a gap in the overhead rigging. Goon waited two seconds then fired his.

Both flares soared to five hundred feet before bursting in brilliant red and white light. They slowly drifted down on parachutes, lighting up the sky.

Brank looked up and said, "Let's hope he's paying attention."

Flynn asked, "Is anybody gonna talk about this? I mean we're fighting giant fucking monsters! This is crazy."

Ruby glared at him. "What's the point? They're real, they're here and that's the situation we've been handed. You're a soldier; accept it and deal with it."

Easy asked, "Speaking of them, where'd they all go?"

Tigger shrugged. "Off doing bug stuff."

Brank shook his head. "Stop thinking of them as bugs, they're smart."

Goon chimed in, "He's right. Taking out that tank wasn't an accident. They'd seen what it could do, so they launched a goddamn baby bombing raid on it. They're learning fast."

Brank asked, "How'd you guys slip past them?"

Ruby said, "It was luck. First, they all went for the fence but then turned around and started marching right past us, deeper into that pile of weird machinery."

Brank said, "That weird machinery is the gas separation plant." He turned to Emily, asking, "How you holding up?"

Forcing a smile, she said, "Okay, just trying to stay out of the way."

Ruby pressed her shoulder, saying, "Lois Lane here saved our asses with that gas can."

Emily said, "Oh, I almost forgot," and dug under her coat, producing a belt of .50 ammo. "I remembered you had a fifty-caliber rifle, so I grabbed this one off that tank looking thing."

Brank held up the precious ammo. "Shucks, and I didn't get you anything. So, where'd a liberal snowflake like you learn about fifty-caliber ammo?"

"I wrote an online piece called 'The Ten Best Weapons to Defeat the New World Order.' That cannon of yours was number three. Goon's Mossberg made number two."

Goon said, "Get a load of little Miss Militia."

"I know squat about guns, so I just cribbed it all from the internet. When you're broke, you write anything you can for a buck; survivalist paranoia, top ten lists, Bigfoot porn... I'm not proud of that last one. I also jabber when I'm scared beyond recognition."

Brank grinned and said, "You're doin' great," genuinely impressed at how resilient she'd proven to be. He took a moment to survey the group. Serving with Special Forces had taught him the healing power of talk. Even two minutes of it allowed troops to decompress, transforming fear into focus. With the exception of Flynn, everyone looked borderline sane, which was the best he could expect in this situation. He turned to Goon. "If this place uses the standard engineering layout there should be earth-moving gear parked on the other side of the complex. Backhoes, bulldozers, that kind of stuff."

Goon nodded, and said, "Armored vehicles. I like it."

"Exactly. Plus, if there's a bucket truck we can use it to put people over the fence without touching it. I'm betting those mercenaries electrified it, that's why those things are trapped in here."

"Just like us. We're pretty much surrounded."

Easy, being an ex-Marine added, "They're in front of us, they're behind us … so they can't escape this time."

Brank smiled and tapped Easy's helmet. "Gotta love that twisted jarhead logic. Let's move out in twos, civilians in the middle."

They headed out, Brank and Easy taking point, Tigger watching above, while Goon and Flynn covered the rear.

Brank had only gone fifty feet when he felt the ground tremble. He signaled to stop, worried that it was an earthquake. He touched the nearest run of pipe. The ground trembled again—the pipe didn't.

He yelled, "They're under us!"

A section of track mat burst upward, slamming Emily back against the machinery. A seven-foot scorpion clawed its way out from the mud beneath, coming at her. Brank peeled off a shot, striking it in the back. Its abdomen burst, drenching Emily in inky viscera.

The mat beneath Ruby erupted, but she clung to the edge then latched on to a section of overhead pipe. The second scorpion reared up, trying to grab her.

Goon fired the Mossberg, launching three buckshot loads into its underbelly. The creature went down.

Brank shouted, "Fall back!" He felt the mat beneath him shimmy and fired three .50 caliber rounds straight down, stitching the board. The shimmying stopped.

Ruby lost her grip, dropping down on top of the dead scorpion. Emily got to her feet just in time to see another burrowing out from under the mat. It advanced on Ruby, its stinger raised. Emily grabbed the dead scorpion's pincer, heaving it upward. The attacker's stinger struck it, embedding in the hard exoskeleton. The scorpion struggled to free itself, offering both women a glimpse into its vertical mouth. Ruby pulled her 9mm, pumping six rounds straight down into its open maw. It vomited a gusher of blackish gore and went limp.

Tigger shouted, "They're up top!" firing bursts into a descending cluster of scorpions.

The group fell back to the exhaust fans as the rigging above came alive with crawling monstrosities. The things leapt off, slamming to the ground ahead of them, ready to fight.

Flynn shouted, "Behind us!" and fired at a pair of ten-footers lurching towards them.

Brank ran a split-second tactical assessment—they were trapped.

That's when a column of flame shot past his head, nearly roasting him. He jumped back, trying to locate the source. Another burst of flame jetted out from overhead. Through the smoke, Brank made out a man standing on the second level rigging wielding a flamethrower. His face was covered by a welder's mask.

Another blast of flame seared the scorpions above them, knocking them to the ground. The next jet of flame engulfed the creatures in front.

Brank instantly knew their fiery savior's strategy— he was clearing the upper levels and cutting off the scorpions' frontal assault. His group was being herded back, but defending the rear was up to Brank.

Brank pivoted, shouting, "Fall back!"

Flynn was pinned behind a pumping relay by a pair of scorpions tearing at the machinery. Brank fired two .50 caliber rounds, knocking one onto its side. Goon charged at the second, pumping five tightly grouped buckshot shells into its face. The first three merely softened up the target, allowing the last to tear through its exoskeleton, killing it.

The man with the flamethrower loosed another column of fire, turning the alley in front of them into an inferno. He turned, trotting along the overhead beams. At an intersection he slid down a pipe, fire fighter style, and gestured for the group to follow. Thirty seconds later, he yanked open a Quonset hut's rollup door. The group scrambled inside, Brank covering the rear.

Flynn took three steps inside, yelled, "Oh shit!" and opened fire on a scorpion at the far end of the hut.

His M4 was in full auto mode. Half the rounds ricocheted off the Quonset hut's steel walls.

Ruby grabbed Emily's shoulder, shoving her to the floor as bullets pinged over them. Emily landed squarely on top of a dead body and rolled off, fighting back the impulse to scream.

Goon grabbed Flynn's rifle. "Stop firing! It's already dead!"

Finally realizing the beast was dead, Flynn stopped.

The man in the welding mask slammed the rollup door closed then jumped onto a nearby forklift. He lowered the blades onto the door's inner lip to secure it.

Satisfied, he hopped down, turned to the hyperventilating group and asked, "*Gee da n gwai?*" When he got no reply, he yanked off the welder's mask, revealing a tanned, weathered face capped with a silver brush cut. In a thick South African accent he said, "Ah, you're *Amerikaans*. I asked does anybody have a cigarette?"

Nhamo had spent hours pulling apart one of the *Major Urimbo's* engines. After isolating the problem he picked through his collection of spare parts. Some had been salvaged from junked aircraft, while others were machined by his cousin in Harare. He shouted to the small boy hovering nearby, "So, Prince, which village girls are of marrying age and do not have suitors?"

The boy, who insisted on being called Prince, said, "There are a few. My sister is the prettiest, but she won't marry you."

"Why not? I'm a successful businessman."

"Because you laugh too much and she likes serious men."

Tossing a rag at him, Nhamo said, "You don't know anything about women," and went back to his repairs.

The boy pointed into the sky, shouting, "Hey, pilot man! You need to look at the sky!"

Nhamo climbed out from under the wing, wiping grease off his hands. Two parachute flares, one red, the other white, were drifting to Earth.

Nhamo muttered, "What the hell?"

The colors gave a mixed signal, indicating danger at the flare's origin point but also warning.

Nhamo said, "Prince, fetch my binoculars from the cockpit." The boy stared in bewilderment until Nhamo gestured holding binoculars to his eyes.

A minute later, the boy emerged with the binoculars. Using them, Nhamo could make out three sets of headlights approaching from the drilling complex. One military style vehicle turned off the road, making a circuitous route toward the village from the rear—a flanking maneuver.

Nhamo leaned down, grabbing Prince's shoulders. "Get the elders and the nuns, bring them to me. Run, boy, run!"

The boy took off. Nhamo grabbed a pair of wrenches and beat them against the engine cowling, making an unholy racket. As a child soldier he'd survived brush wars and coup d'états by knowing how to recognize an impending attack. The cardinal rule was that troops only came to villages for two reasons: to attack or to loot. In either case, innocent people died.

Within five minutes he was begging the villagers to flee into the desert. They refused. At least twenty people were too sick from poisoned water to move and they wouldn't abandon them.

Nhamo cursed his luck. If *The Mayor Urimbo* had been in flying shape he could have airlifted the sick out, but his plane was still an hour from airworthy. By his reckoning, they only had fifteen minutes. After much back and forth they formed a plan. It was a terrible one, but there was no better solution.

The mysterious flame bearer eyed Brank's group silently. His silver hair and blue eyes accentuated a lean, tanned face, deeply creased by decades in the African sun. He wore a Kevlar vest over a khaki fatigue shirt along with those strange short-shorts that only hardened South African troops could pull off.

Brank said, "Hey Flynn, you smoke, so give the man a cigarette."

Flynn handed a crumpled pack of Marlboros to the man, who tapped one out then shoved the pack into his own pocket.

"Hey!" Flynn protested.

In a gruff Afrikaans accent, the mystery man said, "What? I saved your asses, isn't that worth a pack of smokes?"

Brank already liked the guy. He watched their mysterious savior stripping off the improvised flamethrower—an amalgamation of welding torches and fuel tanks, all ratchet strapped onto a backpack.

Glancing around the hut's interior, Brank figured out how the mystery man had cobbled together his weapon. The Quonset hut had belonged to the site's oil rig welders; tough customers even the meanest roughnecks didn't mess with. Blood spatters across the metal walls told the grim tale of their fate. But their tools proved all the parts to construct a DIY flamethrower.

From a tactical standpoint, the Quonset hut was a good choice. The rounded building was about sixty-foot-long and forty wide with sheet metal walls supported by exposed steel ribs. Best of all, the floor was made of anchored, corrugated steel, offering protection from burrowing scorpions. All things considered, the hut made for a decent bunker. Half a dozen workbenches lined the walls, all laden with tools. A pair of thirty-foot steel sewer pipes lay lengthwise across the floor, ending over by the dead scorpion. Large oxygen-acetylene welding rigs straddled the long pipe. It must have been the welder's final project.

Brank extended a hand to the mystery man. "Thanks for saving our asses. I'm Dave Brank, US Embassy security detail."

The man extended a calloused hand. "It's pure luck that I was out looking for survivors. I'm Hansie Bekker, security officer for this site, or what's left of it."

Brank pointed to the dead scorpion at the far end of the hut. "Did you take that one out?"

After a long drag on his cigarette, Hansie said, "Barely. My friend was wounded so I dragged him in here. That *fokker* was waiting. But I got lucky and emptied a full magazine straight into its gullet. That's about the only spot where a bullet's worth a damn." Hansie noticed Brank's .50 caliber rifle and added, "Except maybe one from that *oilfant geweer*."

Ruby translated, "That's elephant gun for you non-Afrikaners."

Hansie grinned and said, "Ah, the lady speaks the language, now I'll have to watch my filthy mouth."

She extended her hand. "Ruby Jenkins, US State Department."

Shaking her hand, Hansie politely replied, "*Aangename kennis.*"

"Pleasure to meet you too."

Goon plopped down on a stool and set to work reloading his Mossberg's double-stacked magazine. Brank was always amazed at how many shotgun shells the Canadian managed to jam into his pockets—his pants were like an ammunition clown car.

Tigger dug three magazines from his pockets and said, "I grabbed a few South African mags on the run, we're lucky Vektors take the same loads as our M4s." He started transplanting rounds into his own magazines.

Emily knelt down over the dead man. The eye sockets were black empty holes, and what skin remained looked more like melted candle wax. His mouth was frozen open in an agonizing scream. Even more disturbingly, there was a bullet hole in his forehead.

Hansie walked over and solemnly said, "That's Anton. He was my oldest *chommie*, going all the way back to the bush wars in Angola. He got soaked with venom during the attack. Scorpion venom breaks down its prey for easy digestion, literally melts them alive like acid. He was in such agony he begged me to put that bullet in his head."

Emily said, "I'm sorry about your friend."

Hansie picked up the Vektor rifle and a magazine pouch lying next to Anton and handed them to Emily. "You hang on to these, since you're the only one who isn't armed."

Slinging the pouch over her shoulder, she said, "Uh, thanks, I guess."

After a respectful moment of silence, Ruby said, "Your other friends outside just tried to put bullets in all of us."

"Friends?" Hansie draped a tarp over Anton's body. "My friends all died last night."

"It was a guy named Hertzog from the gas company and some security guy. Bald bastard, looks like somebody bit his ear off."

Hansie spat on the floor. "That's Kruger, and he's no friend of mine, or anyone. I may be a mercenary, but Kruger and his team are just killers for hire. Kruger used to be with BOSS, running C1 unit back in the apartheid days."

Ruby explained, "BOSS was the Bureau of State Security. Unit C1 was their private death squad." She turned back to Hansie. "Kruger's got at least thirty armed men outside."

"Murderous bastards, one and all." He hauled his improvised flamethrower over to a workbench and began bleeding off the air pressure. "If Kruger's out there, you're safer in here. At least you'll die faster and the women won't get raped. Kruger loves making women suffer, maybe because one bit his ear off."

Hansie poured a mix of diesel fuel and gas into the flamethrower's tank, the lit cigarette still dangling from his lips. Everyone except Goon took a nervous step back.

Leaning closer, Goon asked, "You made that sweet little flamethrower, eh?"

"I've been a soldier for thirty-five years, so you learn to improvise." He replaced the small red oxy acetylene tank with a fresh one. "Adding a dash of acetylene is like the olive in a martini." Hansie kicked the now empty gasoline can. "But even I can't make one without gas, and that was the last of it."

Emily asked, "But aren't we safe in here? I mean you survived all night."

"I was safe in here because scorpions are lazy bastards, and there was too much easy meat outside. Then the rain came, and those things took cover. All scorpions hate rain, even the giant ones."

Brank nodded. "That's why they didn't attack us when we arrived. They were still hiding."

Ruby said, "Maybe that's why they burrowed under those traction mats."

Hansie nodded. "*Ja*, scorpions can flatten out and crawl under anything. Once the rain stopped you and Kruger's *holnaairs* arrived there was plenty of easy meat again."

Ruby said, "*Holnaairs* means ass—"

Brank held up a hand. "I think we get it."

Hansie continued, "But now all that easy meat's in here, so next time they're hungry they'll rip through these metal walls like opening a can of Spam."

Everyone quietly contemplated their future as lunchmeat.

A thunderous crash echoed from across the room. Brank, Goon and Tigger spun, weapons ready.

Brank lowered his rifle, shouting, "Easy, for Christ's sake!"

Easy put down the toolbox he'd just overturned and said, "Sorry sir, I just had an idea." He rooted through the tools strewn across the floor until he found a hacksaw.

"What're you thinking?"

Easy hauled some tools over to the dead scorpion. "Well, back in the sandbox we used scrap metal to up-armor the Humvees." He began sawing into the dead scorpion's thorax.

Brank got the drift. "So you want to make hillbilly body armor out of that thing?"

"It's like in James 1:22, 'But be doers of the word, and not hearers only deceiving yourselves.'"

Brank said, "You lost me."

"It means doing something always works better than doing nothing."

"Amen to that."

Ruby held up her satellite phone and took pictures of Easy and the dead scorpion.

Brank asked, "Something to remember this by?"

"Do you think anyone's going to believe my 911 call without pictures?"

"Fair enough."

"Easy's right," Emily said. "When that one outside attacked me, its stinger couldn't get through the dead one's armor."

Goon said, "She's a fast thinker this girl," and gave Emily a pat on the back that nearly knocked her over.

After recovering, she said, "Not that it's worth anything, but I think these things are Plumono-Scorpius-Rex. They were giant scorpions that lived in the Viséan Age, about four hundred million years ago."

Brank asked, "And you know that ... why?"

"I wrote an online list called 'Top Ten Most Nightmarish Prehistoric Monsters.'"

"Where'd they land on the list?"

"Number two."

"So, there you go... Things could be one worse."

Hansie seemed lost in thought for a moment then smacked the workbench, shouting, "Viséan Shale!"

Brank said, "What?"

"She said Viséan Age and I remembered something. I played cards a lot with the geologists here, smart guys, but they couldn't play *Klawerjas* for shit. Anyway, a couple of them were excited because we were drilling into a layer they called Viséan Shale. The first rig tower found natural gas, but aside from the usual benzene and other shit they have to separate, there was another gas nobody'd seen before. Three of the drillers caught a whiff of it and went to sleep right there. Like dead men."

Brank asked, "You mean into a coma?"

"Worse. We damn near buried one of them."

Brank turned to Ruby. "Just like that guy we found."

"Yeah, that must be why that doctor was so excited."

Hansie lit another cigarette and continued. "After that happened, the bosses were jumping up and down, like they'd found diamonds in a pile of shit. From then on, nobody was allowed to leave the site or make calls."

Ruby said, "I can't get a signal on my satellite phone."

"You won't. Once they found the mystery gas, the company installed a cell and satellite phone jammer. Top of the line rig too, probably Chinese military. No phones or even walkie talkies, unless they're line of sight."

Brank asked, "Any chance of shutting it down?"

"Nope, it's in the generator blockhouse at the far end of the complex, right where all those scorpions are. And don't even think about shooting at the building with that cannon of yours 'cause you'll damage the generator. We're blind in the dark, but those bastards are right at home. The only place you can get a clear signal out is from the top of Rig Tower-1. But it's about a hundred feet straight up."

Brank said, "Well, I guess we'll be doing some climbing."

CHAPTER SEVEN

The first of the Mamba armored vehicles roared into the village, switching on its blinding spotlights and nearly running down two women. The second swung around the rear to block any escape attempts.

A dozen mercenaries piled out, firing rifles into the air while shouting threats in Zulu and Venda. They grabbed any villagers within reach, throwing them to the ground and zip-tying their hands. Three of the mercenaries prowled the outskirts with flashlights to catch any runaways.

Major Van Shoor climbed out of the lead vehicle and watched the proceedings with amusement. The hawk-faced white man took a long drink of Klipdrift brandy from his canteen then offered some to his adjunct, Lt. Steyn, who declined.

Van Shoor said, "This takes me back to the good old days at Vlakplass."

Vlakplass Farm had been the headquarters of BOSS's infamous Section C1 where he'd been Kruger's interrogator.

The younger lieutenant said, "A little before my time, sir."

"Good times, my friend. Good times." Van Shoor saw one of the mercenaries kicking a villager and shouted, "Stop that! We need these *munts* in one piece!" With a sigh he said, "I wish we had dogs. It's always more fun with dogs."

The Rhino-Runner armored bus pulled in next to the Mamba and sat idling.

A pair of mercenaries charged into a round homestead, shouting threats, then backed out slowly. A pair of nuns pushed past them and strode towards Van Shoor, ignoring the obscenities hurled at them.

Seeing them, Van Shoor muttered, *"O. Fok,* here we go. *"*

Without a trace of fear, Sister Estelle shouted, "I demand to know what you're doing here. You have no right! These are innocent people trying to live their lives!"

Van Shoor said, "And they'll keep living, as long as they come peaceably." He yelled to the mercenaries. "Search every homestead. If we find one person trying to hide, we'll burn this whole village!" He leaned closer to the nun, asking, "Is that clear, Sister?"

Sister Estelle smelled the liquor on his breath. She turned, directly addressing the mercenaries, many of whom were clearly Zulu. "Why are you doing this? These people are Ndebele, brothers and sisters to the Zulu." She pointed at Van Shoor. "This man's no brother to you. I bet he misses the days when he could have you all flogged!"

Van Shoor muttered, "She's got a point there."

The assembled mercenaries listened to her impassioned pleas, then started laughing.

Van Shoor said, "Sister, you're barking up the wrong ancestral tree. I've seen these boys kill women and children from every tribe. They're stone-cold murderers; that's why we have to pay them so much."

Leaning directly in his face, Sister Estelle said, "There are laws to protect people."

Tapping the barrel of his rifle, Van Shoor said, "I'm holding the law right here," and without warning he slammed the rifle butt into her stomach. She sank to the ground, moaning. He turned to Steyn, announcing, "I want every villager zip-tied. One third of them go into the bus, the rest wait here."

Sister Estelle started to rise until a sharp kick sent her back to the ground. Sister Mary raced over, trying to shove Van Shoor away, earning a punch in the jaw.

Van Shoor said, "And make sure these nuns are in the load that goes to the drilling site." He leered down at Sister Estelle. "Kruger's got a thing for nuns."

Steyn ran off to supervise the loading. Van Shoor leaned back against the Mamba, enjoying the show.

After a few minutes, Steyn returned. "We've got about seventy in all. The first thirty are being loaded into the bus. Once we dump that load, we'll come back to grab the second."

With a smile, Van Shoor said, "When you come back, leave twenty here and disperse the rest along the road. That'll be a nice trail of kaffir breadcrumbs to lead the scorpions away."

Steyn watched the villagers being loaded into the bus and said, "They're going along pretty damn quietly."

His observation was accurate. Despite the verbal and physical abuse, the villagers weren't screaming or crying.

Van Shoor shrugged. "As dumb cattle should."

Steyn said, "I'll leave three men on guard here until we come back for the second load."

Van Shoor eyed the villagers squatting in the dirt. Noting some attractive young women among them, he said, "I'll stay here, just leave me two men."

Two Zulu mercenaries approached, dragging a man wearing a captain's hat.

One announced, "We found this one sneaking around by that plane."

Van Shoor slapped the captain's hat off the man's head and ground it into the dirt. "Are you the pilot of that shit heap?"

The man nodded, averting his eyes.

"Does it fly?"

The man shook his head.

Van Shoor drove the butt of his rifle into the pilot's crotch, shouting, "Lying piece of *kak*! As soon as we were gone, you'd be trying to fly out of here!"

The moaning pilot lay in the dirt, clutching his groin.

The mercenary asked, "How about we break his arms, boss? That'll sure keep him from flying."

Van Shoor turned his rifle around and casually put a bullet through the back of the pilot's head. Shouldering the weapon, he calmly said, "Why trouble yourselves?" He looked over at the villagers. Despite seeing a man executed they were still peacefully climbing into the bus. Taking another swallow of *Klippies,* he muttered, "Fucking cattle."

Hansie finished filling his flamethrower and announced, "This should give us a few minutes of fire. Better than nothing."

Flynn asked, "Hey, how flammable is this place? I mean, it's a gas well and we're using flamethrowers and bullets like crazy."

Lighting another cigarette, Hansie said, "They burned off the flare stacks last night, so most of the tanks are empty. So, probably a twenty percent chance we hit something and blow ourselves to hell. But there's a hundred percent chance those things will send us there if we don't. Did I answer your question?"

Flynn muttered, "Christ, this sucks ass."

Brank asked, "Hansie, where'd these scorpions come from?"

"Oh, right, I was getting to that. After finding the first gas, the drilling geniuses built Well Tower-2 so they could go even deeper. It hit some kind of open pocket that was pure mystery gas and plenty of it. But the fracking got too intense. The idiots started using depleted uranium-shaped charges for extra bang."

Brank said, "Is that what caused last night's earthquake?"

"No question. A real shaker too. I was in the Mbabane quake, and this was bigger. I heard someone yelling about a sinkhole opening up out by the nitrogen tanks. A minute later, those *vokken gediertes* were killing everyone in sight."

"That's got to be it," Emily said, sounding excited. "We saw that gas put somebody to sleep, but it also healed that cut on his chest."

Hansie said, "I remember something about that with the first drillers. One guy's broken arm just mended itself in an hour. They were all airlifted back to *Joburg* right after that, all secret like."

Emily paced in a circle. "Okay, so what if those things were entombed in that pocket of gas, perfectly preserved, sleeping like babies?"

Catching her drift, Brank said, "Until the drilling sucked the gas out of their bedroom and woke them up."

"Then the earthquake opened up the ground and they came crawling out."

Ruby took a deep breath and added, "And they haven't eaten in, what, four hundred million years?"

Goon said, "Hell, I get cranky after five hours."

They heard something huge bouncing around on the roof of the hut. There was another thud as something slammed against the outside wall.

Hansie muttered, "They're getting hungry."

Brank said, "Hey Easy, whatever you're doing, wrap it up. We're moving out."

Easy tore a section of exoskeleton away from the scorpion's body and said, "Just a few more seconds."

Goon asked, "Where are we going?"

Brank said, "Well, we can't stay in here."

"True that. But if we go outside the fence those mercenaries'll nail us."

"Then we need an alternative." Brank grabbed a site diagram someone had taped over their workbench and laid it out in front of Hansie. The group huddled behind them. Brank asked, "Is this the current layout of the place?"

Hansie nodded.

"Ruby, if you get to high ground you can call in the cavalry on your satellite phone." He turned to Hansie. "So where's that tower you mentioned?"

Hansie ran his finger across the diagram. "This is Rig Tower-1. It's a good hundred feet high with a ladder straight to the top."

"Can those things climb up the tower?"

"If there's a meal on top they can climb anything."

Brank pointed to another mark on the diagram. "What's this?"

"The construction crane. It's only sixty feet high, but the arm extends a good two hundred feet."

"So could it reach over to Rig Tower-1?"

Hansie nodded. "Yeah, but do you know how to run a crane?"

"I won a SpongeBob doll with a claw machine once."

"Then I guess I'm tagging along."

Ruby asked, "So why don't we all make a dash for the crane, run me up a hundred feet and I'll make the call?"

Brank shook his head. "Good in theory, except Hansie's the only one who can run the crane. So, not to sound negative, but what if he gets eaten?"

Hansie shrugged. "It could happen."

Goon said, "Then we'd all be stuck pulling our dicks on a crane that's too low to make the call from."

Brank said, "Exactly," and pointed to the diagram. "Plus, Rig Tower-1 is here, a straight run, so you won't get ambushed. The crane's only about two hundred feet further away as the crow flies, but it's all twists and turns through this funhouse of machinery. So, here's what I'm thinking. Me, Easy and Hansie make a dash for the crane, creating a load of noise as a diversion. Then Ruby, Goon, Tigger and Flynn run for Rig Tower-1. By the time you get there I'll be up on top of the crane giving you supporting fire with the fifty-caliber. That should keep those things off your back while you're climbing."

Hansie kicked the flamethrower. "The big guy should take that; it'll give you an edge while you're running for the tower."

Brank said, "Sounds good. Ruby, you make the call to your CIA friends and get the army, or the navy or the *X-Men* over here. If those things start getting too close to you, we'll swing the crane arm over, grab you, and then swing you over here." He pointed to an area just beyond the fence. "You'll be outside the fence line and far away from the main mercenary force. But don't touch the fence because I'm sure it's electrified."

Hansie said, "If Kruger's outside you can bet it's electrified, with enough juice to fry a side of beef on."

Brank said, "Good to know. If those mercenaries come after you, I can offer suppressing fire from on high. As soon as you're clear, Easy, Hansie and me will haul ass down the crane arm and bug out."

Ruby asked, "Not to be gloomy, but what if you don't make it to the crane?"

"Then you're still on the highest ground, with a fighting chance of survival, which we don't have in here. Simple, right?"

Goon said, "Dumbest fucking plan I've ever heard. Count me in."

Ruby said, "The Canadian moose's right. It's batshit crazy, but it's the only game in town."

Tigger said, "Where you go, I go *el jefe*."

Flynn just shook his head, muttering, "This is so fucked... Yeah, I'll go."

Goon handed Flynn the flamethrower. "Good, you're on fire detail. I can't handle that thing and the 12-gauge."

Brank shouted, "How about you, Easy? You in?"

Easy shouted, "Your word is a lamp for my feet and a light for my path," and went back to wrestling with the dead scorpion.

"I'll take that as a yes."

Emily asked, "Um, where am I in this scenario?"

Brank said, "I suggest you go with them, but, being a civilian, it's sort of 'choose your own adventure'." He folded up the diagram and shoved it in his pocket. "Easy, leave your friend and let's move out."

Easy said, "Just one second," and tugged at a large section of exoskeleton. The plate was still attached to the animal carcass by a strand of tissue. He drew the K-Bar knife from his belt and sliced into the stringy tissue.

And something grabbed him from inside.

Nhamo peered out the side window of *The Mayor Urimbo*, watching helplessly as an innocent man was murdered in his place. His grip tightened around the AK-47 cradled in his arms, and it took every ounce of will he possessed to resist using it. But he couldn't give in to his anger because the villagers had made him swear an oath to defend the village's hidden treasure.

That murdered villager had allowed himself to be captured while claiming to be the pilot. The villagers felt that, with the pilot in custody, the attackers would be less likely to search the plane. That's where they'd hidden their only treasure—the children.

Nhamo saw their small faces peeking out from behind the cargo crates. There were twenty in all. The older ones were tucked behind the empty cases, while the youngest were hidden in secret compartments he'd installed during his smuggling days. A pair of *ambuyas* were down there with them, and the elderly women had done an amazing job of keeping the children quiet.

Nhamo rubbed the AK-47's grips, worn smooth as glass with age. He'd only been ten years old when the warlord had handed him the weapon, claiming he was bestowing a great honor upon the boy. It was just one of many lies the bastard had used to transform an innocent child into a murderous beast. Eventually Nhamo had found his peace in the sky, only keeping the weapon as a reminder of how far he'd come. But if anyone threatened the children, they'd meet the beast he kept chained within.

Prince squatted behind him, whispering, "What's happening?"

"Quiet, go back behind the crates and make sure the little ones don't cry."

"They won't."

Nhamo nodded, thankful that African babies so rarely cried.

He watched the villagers being herded into the bus without voicing any protest. But their silence wasn't out of fear or submission—it was to prevent the children from hearing their mothers' voices and crying out in return. In all Nhamo's years of fighting as a child soldier, he'd never seen such courage.

Prince whispered, "Can I have a gun too?"

Nhamo snapped, "No, children shouldn't touch guns!"

He watched the armored bus pull out, followed by one of the Mambas. The second Mamba remained parked in the center of the village, a pair of mercenaries idly leaning against it. An older white man patrolled around the homesteads, silently appraising the bound villagers squatting in the sand.

One of the mercenaries ground out a cigarette under his boot and leaned back against the Mamba. His gaze drifted to the plane.

Nhamo's heart skipped a beat and he whispered to himself, "No, no, nothing to see here."

The curious mercenary was carrying a belt fed SS-77 medium machine gun, and Nhamo had seen the devastation that weapon could create. The mercenary tapped his partner on the shoulder then pointed to the plane. After a few seconds of chatter, he started walking over.

And the beast inside Nhamo began pulling at its chain.

Easy yanked his arm away from the carcass, screaming in pain. A newborn scorpion dangled from his hand, its pincers locked around his index finger. Ten more scorplings erupted from the freshly cut opening, swarming up his legs. Each was nearly a foot long, with pale white skin and black eyes. Easy frantically tore at the creatures as a second wave of newborns erupted from their dead mother.

Brank raced toward him.

Something hit the side of the hut like a wrecking ball. The wall buckled and a workbench rocketed out in a shower of tools. A flying sledgehammer struck Brank in the side of the head, knocking him to the floor. The Kevlar helmet saved his life, but the impact reduced the room to swirling white lights.

A black pincer ripped through the metal wall where the workbench had been.

Emily pulled Brank back onto his feet, yelling, "It's a mass attack!"

Another pincer tore through the rounded ceiling above Easy, peeling back the metal like tin foil.

A five-foot scorpion burst through the damaged wall to Brank's left, targeting him and Emily.

Goon charged forward, unleashing four blasts into the creature's midsection. The impact sent it rolling onto its back. Goon fired twice more, the buckshot tearing through its soft underbelly.

A ten-footer dropped through the ceiling, landing mere feet from Easy.

Emily physically spun Brank in Easy's direction, pushing his rifle barrel up, yelling, "Shoot it!"

Still punch drunk and dizzy, Brank tried to aim. His blurred vision showed three identical scorpions advancing on Easy—he aimed for the one in the middle.

The armor-piercing round tore the beast wide open.

Goon ran to Brank, asking, "You okay?"

Regaining his balance, Brank pushed the Canadian away, shouting, "Your team has to go now! Same plan, different order. Move!"

Upon hearing that, Hansie slapped the flamethrower onto Flynn's back, lit the pilot light and said, "You're good to go!" He jumped onto the forklift, opening the rollup door just enough for someone to slide through. A set of pincers groped under the door, trying to pry it wider. Hansie leapt off the forklift, shouting, "Now, now!"

Flynn let loose with the flamethrower, showering the doorway's gap in fire. The attacking scorpion shrank back from the inferno.

Goon dropped low, loosing a barrage of buckshot under the gap, yelling, "Flynn, go now!"

Flynn slid under the door, Goon right behind. Tigger was next, firing short, controlled bursts, with Ruby glued to his back. Within seconds the trio was out, and Hansie slammed the door down behind them.

Brank shouted, "Emily, you're supposed to be with them!"

But she wasn't there. Then Brank saw her feet disappear into the sewer pipe.

Emily squirmed through the narrow length of sewer pipe, the Vektor rifle cradled in her arms. Up ahead she saw Easy writhing on the floor, covered in a blanket of infant scorpions.

One of the ten-inch monsters crawled into the sewer pipe, scuttling towards her. Emily couldn't risk firing, for fear of hitting Easy. She spun the rifle around and slammed the butt down onto the creature. Its soft, newborn exoskeleton cracked, and a second hit crushed it. She kept moving forward, heartbeat pounding in her ears.

She crawled out of the pipe, only ten feet from Easy, who was covered in scorpions. Six of them saw Emily and attacked. They were moving too fast to shoot, forcing Emily to back-pedal till she slammed against one of the workbenches. In desperation she swept her hand across the top, showering her attackers in loose tools and bolts. The onslaught stopped them for a moment. Groping blindly for a weapon, her hand landed on a fire extinguisher. She yanked the pin, unleashing a cloud of CO_2 at the scorpions. The freezing cold fog forced the scorpions into retreat.

"Yeah, back off, you little shits!"

Emily crawled to Easy, blasting the extinguisher at the creatures as she went.

Brank shouted her name from across the hut.

She yelled back, "I'm getting Easy!"

Brank saw Emily from across the room and tried to run to her.

With a scream of tortured steel, the wall to his right tore open. A ten-foot scorpion pushed its way through the jagged opening, headed straight for Brank.

He raised the .50 caliber rifle, nearly putting it against his cheek—until he saw a newborn scorpion clinging to the stock. He tried to shake it off, but the little monster leapt onto his forearm and raced up, its stinger zeroing in on his face. Brank lowered his head just in time. The stinger missed, embedding in his helmet. The creature writhed, desperately trying to dislodge it. In a single move, Brank yanked off the helmet and threw it while firing his .50 caliber rifle—He didn't need to aim.

The round hit the ten-foot scorpion point-blank, entering its gaping mouth and exploding through its tail in a shower of indigo-blue gore.

Emily reached Easy, emptying the extinguisher at the scorplings covering him. It worked. The monsters scuttled away to safety. She rolled Easy over and gasped. His face and hands were a swollen mass of stinger wounds. His left eyeball was so swollen it had popped out of the socket, dangling by its roots. Seizures from the acidic venom wracked his body.

Easy looked up at her, slurring, "I'm dying. Go, get out!" And he went limp.

A five-foot scorpion dropped down from the jagged ceiling opening, landing ten feet away. Emily raised the Vektor, firing five times. The beast retreated a few paces, more confused than hurt.

Brank shouted, "I'm coming!"

Emily yelled, "No, stay there!" She looked down at Easy and said,

"I'm sorry."

She could have sworn the dead man was smiling.

The five-foot scorpion lunged forward. Emily dove for the sewer pipe, crawling inside. The creature slammed against the lip of the pipe, its pincer groping for her. She crawled deeper as the scorpion furiously tried to squeeze inside. After a few futile attempts it moved away—making room for the newborns.

Brank peered into the other end of the pipe and watched her coming.

A pair of adult scorpions tumbled through the gap in the ceiling, landing close to Easy. Thankfully, they became intertwined, lashing at each other.

Emily glanced over her shoulder and saw a pair of baby scorpions in hot pursuit. She yelled, "I'm coming, but I've got company!"

Brank saw a ten-footer struggling to squeeze through the tear in the ceiling above Easy. He fired one round, blasting its head clean off while leaving its twitching body jammed in the gap. Scorpions behind it pushed, frantically trying to remove the obstruction.

Emily's head emerged from the pipe. Brank grabbed her shoulder and yanked her out. She landed on her back, kicking furiously at a newborn scorpion clinging to her boot. Brank whacked it away with the butt of his rifle.

Two more infants emerged from the pipe.

Brandishing a sledgehammer, Hansie yelled, "Out of the way!" With two thunderous blows, he crushed both.

Easy opened his eyes. Pretending to be dead had been his way of keeping Emily from needlessly sacrificing her life. He watched as the two scorpions ceased fighting. The larger one came at him. He fired his M4 twice. The lead creature slunk back, but the second grabbed his leg with its pincer. It pulled furiously, trying to drag him away. Easy clung to the lip of the sewer pipe, screaming as the beast's grip tightened. Unable to drag off its prey, the scorpion clamped down, severing his leg below the knee.

Emily heard his scream and shouted, "Easy's alive!"

Easy screamed, aimed his rifle and shouted, "Everybody clear out, now!"

Brank grabbed Emily's arm and turned to Hansie, asking, "How's the door?"

But Hansie was already on the forklift, yelling, "This way's clear, they're too busy chasing the others."

Without another word, the three raced out through the rollup door.

The headless scorpion wedged in the ceiling tumbled free, followed by three live ones. They landed on the other two in a tangled mass. Once again, the beasts fought each other.

Easy smiled, knowing he'd just seen God's intervention, offering him precious seconds to contemplate his final action. He stared at the advancing scorpions but felt no fear. Instead he experienced a moment of serenity, whispering, "Greater love has no one than this; that someone lay down his life for his friends." Then he fired his last bullet—directly into a five-foot acetylene tank.

Brank had barely cleared the rollup door when the explosion tore through the building. The blast wave threw him to the ground. He rolled onto his back and saw a ball of fire burst through the Quonset hut's ceiling. There was a dull thud, followed by a second blast as another acetylene tank detonated. Hansie yanked him away just as the rollup door disintegrated in a shower of shrapnel and flame.

Brank muttered, "Thanks Easy," and got back on his feet.

Hansie ran off in the wrong direction, following the first team. Then he let loose with a volley of three-round bursts. He jogged back, shouting, "Just getting their attention."

Looking past him, Brank saw a cluster of scorpions turning in their direction and said, "It worked."

CHAPTER EIGHT

The other group ran full tilt for Rig Tower-1; Goon and Tigger in point position, Ruby and Flynn right behind. Tigger constantly shifted his focus left and right, while Goon kept his eyes trained above. Their logic paid off. Goon spotted one of the beasts poised in the pipes above and sent a shower of buckshot into its soft underbelly.

Flynn unleashed an inferno at the pursuing scorpions, keeping them at bay.

When they heard the Quonset hut explosion, Tigger turned and watched the ball of fire rising behind them.

Goon grabbed his shoulder, yelling, "Stay on mission, brother! Stumpy's got it under control!"

Tigger nodded and kept moving.

Flynn heard bursts of gunfire from behind and was relieved to see three pursuing scorpions turn away, attracted to the noise.

Ruby shouted, "Flynn, keep up!"

Goon looked up at the hundred-foot rig tower looming in the distance, the flare stack at its peak belching fire into the night sky. It was a hellish sight, but it sure beat being on the ground.

Goon doubled his speed, shouting, "Not much farther!" With any luck his group would make it to the rig tower alive. Off to his right he could see the massive yellow crane. It was only about two hundred feet away, but getting there meant navigating through a maze of drilling equipment with scorpions lurking around every corner.

Goon told himself, *If anybody can get through a suicide mission and come out laughing, it's Stumpy.*

Kruger stood, contemplating the bizarre sight resting just inside the fence line.

Minutes earlier, a massive scorpion had emerged from the drilling area and advanced within ten feet of the fence line. It abruptly stopped then backed up to its current position. Since then it had sat there, motionless as a statue.

Hertzog asked, "What's it doing?"

Kruger spat tobacco juice in the sand and said, "It's a scout."

"A scout?" Hertzog asked incredulously. "I think you're giving them too much credit. They're only insects after all. They barely even have a brain."

"Really? During the first engagement, the only weapon that stopped them was the heavy machine gun mounted on the tank. Their second attack went straight for that tank and destroyed it. Does that sound like stupid insects to you?" He studied the massive scorpion. "That one walked close to the fence, right to the edge of what we call the 'zap zone,' where the electricity can jump off like lightning. When it felt a twinge, it backed up, just a bit. See those thick hairs along its body? Those are sensors that can feel the electricity pulsing through the fence."

"So?"

"The moment the power shuts off, it'll send a signal to the rest, and a dozen of those bastards will be climbing over."

Hertzog threw the bolt on his Heym Express big game rifle. "I ought to stroll up to the fence and put a bullet in it. Did you see what this baby did to them?"

"I should let you. But if you fire that cannon within fifteen feet of the fence, a lightning bolt will shoot out, go straight down the barrel and fry you."

"Thanks for the warning."

Kruger shrugged. "I just don't want to damage the fence."

A thunderous blast echoed through the night air, and the earth trembled. A second, shorter blast followed.

"What the hell was that?" Hertzog shouted.

Kruger raised his binoculars and saw a ball of fire rising into the air, followed by a plume of black smoke. "Looks like something blew up."

"Christ, it's not the well, is it?"

"No. It was over by the welding shops. Either the Americans or those monsters must have set something off. The whole place is jammed with acetylene and propane, so it was almost inevitable a few things would get torched." He turned and shouted to a nearby pair of mercenaries, "Boys, I need that drone in the air now!"

The men were busily prepping a black Mavic-2 Quadcopter. One of them gave Kruger a thumbs up, yelling, "Three minutes, sir."

"Make it two!" He turned to Hertzog. "That'll give us a better idea of what's going on."

Hertzog asked, "Do you think those Americans are still alive?"

"If they are it won't be for long. Those bastards must be getting hungry. I just hope they don't stuff themselves on American food before we serve dinner."

He focused his binoculars on the scorpion near the fence. Despite the explosion, it hadn't moved a muscle. Kruger swore the goddamn thing was staring straight back at him. He heard the rumble of engines and saw headlights approaching from the north.

He said, "Looks like the chuck wagon's arriving now. Not much meat on those *munts*, but they should do the trick."

Two minutes later, the Rhino-Runner bus pulled to a stop, followed by the Mamba. Kruger's men descended on the bus, yanking the bound villagers out and shoving them to the ground. Two of the mercenaries spotted a pretty young girl and dragged her aside. One held her down while the other shoved his hands beneath her blouse.

Seeing this, Hertzog ran over to Kruger, shouting, "Do you see what they're doing?"

Kruger shrugged. "So? It's just part of soldiering."

"It's disgraceful, and I won't have it!"

"But you're fine with us feeding them to the scorpions?"

"That's different. It's simply … business."

With a long exhale, Kruger strode over and pulled the men away from the girl.

"No time for that today. I want them lined up neatly with no fuss."

Both men started to protest until a hard look from Kruger silenced them.

Then Kruger grinned and said, "Don't worry, Mister Hertzog just offered us a big bonus, so as soon as we're back home, the whores are on him."

The mercenaries did as he ordered, taking out their disappointment on the villagers.

Lieutenant Steyn climbed out of the armored car and reported to Kruger, "Sir, we've brought thirty over here, and we'll leave another twenty at the halfway mark. That'll still leave enough in the village to keep the beasts occupied."

"Good work."

"There was an airplane parked just outside the village."

Kruger nodded. "The one that brought those Americans no doubt."

"Van Shoor shot the pilot to make sure it can't go anywhere."

"That's what I like about Van Shoor, he's not afraid to get his hands bloody."

"Oh, and he wanted me to personally present these two." Steyn shouted in Zulu to the men standing by the armored car then turned back to Kruger. "I think you'll find them … entertaining."

Steyn's men yanked the two nuns out of the armored car and led them to Kruger.

Kruger looked them up and down and said, "Entertaining indeed." He cupped Sister Estelle's chin, forcing her to look him in the eye. "You know, Sister, I spent my childhood in an orphanage, surrounded by witches like you."

The frightened woman tried to look away, but Kruger held her in place.

"And you know what I remember from those years? I remember this!"

Kruger slapped her with all his might, knocking her to the ground.

One of his men shouted, "The drone's ready, sir!"

"Damn it." He crouched down, putting himself at eye level with the sobbing woman, and said, "Sorry *liefling*, we'll have to pick this discussion up later."

Kruger turned and walked off. Hertzog looked down at the sobbing woman, wondering what kind of animals he'd hired.

Brank, Emily and Hansie raced through the maze of machinery.

"Go left!" Hansie shouted, steering them toward an open dirt lot. "It's the truck turnaround area."

Brank was glad the old Afrikaner was with them, knowing he'd already be lost.

As soon as they entered the space, a ten-foot scorpion emerged from the shadows on the opposite side. It galloped toward them, stopped and pivoted right. A second, slightly smaller scorpion charged straight at it, grabbing one of its pincers. The two fought a tug of war, spinning in a wide circle, pincers interlocked.

Brank raised the .50 caliber, but Hansie put his hand on the barrel, stopping him. "Don't waste the ammo. I've seen this in regular scorpions; it's a mating dance that can go on for hours. If we get lucky, she'll eat him when they're done."

Hansie ran ahead, waving for them to follow. The trio dashed past the whirling scorpions. Emily slowed down, snapping photos as she went.

Brank yelled, "You doing scorpion porn now?"

She kept running alongside him. "Don't you want something to remember this by?"

"Yeah, old age!"

Brank saw the brightly lit, yellow crane in the distance. It was only a few hundred feet away, but that was all through twisting alleyways of gas processing equipment. Every scorpion they saw forced them to make another turn and loop around. It was like running through the maze on a children's placemat.

Hansie took a left then skidded to a halt. A pair of scorpions was crawling down the network of pipes. They dropped to the ground and turned in their direction.

Brank said, "They look more hungry than horny."

The trio turned and ran down another, wider laneway. Brank knew Goon's team should have reached the rig tower by now—this was taking too long.

"There!" Brank shouted, pointing to a thousand-gallon water tanker parked ahead. They ran towards it, the scorpions in hot pursuit.

Hansie shouted, "I'll ride on the back," climbing onto the rear platform.

Brank jumped into the driver's seat and pulled down the visor. No keys.

Emily hopped into the passenger side, dangling a set of keys. "They were under the gas cap."

Brank grabbed them and turned the ignition. "Let me guess, you wrote, 'Top Ten Places to Hide Things.'"

"Something like that."

The engine sputtered twice then rumbled to life. Brank slammed it into drive and floored it. The truck shimmied forward, reaching an unimpressive ten miles an hour.

"Not exactly a Ferrari."

Emily said, "Beats walking."

When he saw the scorpions gaining on them, Hansie grabbed the thick rubber hose spooled on the back of the truck. Anchoring himself behind the ladder, he unleashed a high pressure stream of water at the pursuing scorpions. The force of the fire hose threw the lead scorpion off balance. The second was moving too fast to stop and the two wound up in an entangled mass.

Brank saw a ten-foot scorpion drop down from the pipes, directly in their path, poised to attack. He floored the truck, getting it up to a whopping fifteen miles an hour. It slammed into the beast, crushing it under the tires.

Emily slammed the dashboard, shouting, "Squashed it like a bug!"

"Yeah, a thousand gallons of water makes for a pretty hefty boot."

The jolt almost threw Hansie off, but he clung to the rear ladder, cursing in Afrikaans.

Brank hung a left, putting them on a straight-line course to the crane.

"Almost there!"

Something heavy slammed down onto the roof, and the truck swerved wildly.

Brank wrenched the wheel, barely recovering. "That ain't good!"

Hansie hooked one arm around the rear ladder while using the other to operate the hose. He heard something rattling above and looked up. A scorpion peered down at him from atop the water tank. It lashed out with its pincer, tearing away the top of the steel ladder. Hansie directed the hose up. The high-pressure blast of water forced the creature back. It pivoted, shifting its attention forward.

Brank kept the tanker floored. Emily heard a sharp thud on the roof and looked up just as a pincer sliced through the roof. She dropped to the floor, barely avoiding the claw. The pincer withdrew. A second later, the scorpion's stinger jabbed down, shredding the seat. It rose then slammed down again like a jackhammer, coming closer each time.

Brank cut the wheel sharply to the right. The truck swerved under a low-hanging network of steam pipes. The pipes scraped along the roof, shattering the windshield in a shower of glass.

The pipe clotheslined the rooftop scorpion, throwing it over the side of the truck. It hit the ground hard, lashing out. Its left pincer sliced through the rear tire, reducing it to ribbons. The truck slewed, smashing into a network of pipes. The contents of the half empty water tank shifted, throwing four thousand pounds of water to the driver's side. The passenger side tires left the ground.

"Hang on!" Brank yelled as the truck rolled.

Hansie felt the truck shifting, shouted, "*Fok!*"and slipped under the ladder, using it as a roll cage.

The truck slammed down onto the driver's side, careening forward in a shower of sparks. It crashed into a wire storage cage full of steel cylinders at the base of the crane.

Hansie crawled out from behind the ladder and dropped to the ground. A half-dozen five-foot steel cylinders rolled past him. Two had their stems sheared off and were hissing angrily.

Shouting, "*Fok me!*" he dove for cover, but the expected explosion never came.

To his relief, both damaged tanks were green, meaning they were full of oxygen as opposed to acetylene. Hansie got up onto his feet, amazed that nothing was broken. Even his rifle was intact. The truck lay on its side, water gushing from its ruptured tank.

Hansie slammed his rifle butt on the hood, shouting, "Hey! You two alive in there?"

Emily crawled out of the shattered passenger side window,

momentarily unsure which way was up or down. Seconds later, Brank kicked the door open and crawled out. Hansie was relieved to see the .50 caliber rifle was intact.

Brank looked up at the crane and said, "Hey guys, we're here. Emily, are you good?"

She nodded. "Yeah, I think so. You?"

Brank patted himself down and said, "I think one of my nuts climbed up inside me, but otherwise I'm okay." His face was peppered with cuts from the glass.

Hansie pointed back the way they came, declaring, "If you want to stay that way we better get moving. Those two bastards I gave a shower are still coming, with friends."

The central part of the crane, known as the mast, was a hollow square of 12mm forged steel lattice. An enclosed ladder ran straight up its center, all the way to the control cabin at its peak.

Brank hustled Emily to the access ladder and said, "Start climbing." Then he waved Hansie over. "You're right behind her. I'll pull up the rear to give cover fire." He looked up at the yellow crane bathed in blindingly bright halogen lights. "I just hope they're not waiting up there."

Hansie said, "Those bright lights might save our ass. They like it dark."

Emily scurried up the ladder, Hansie following two steps behind her, fireman style, to ensure the person above couldn't fall.

Brank looked up at the bright lights, muttering, "Except now they can see us better." He climbed a few steps, the thirty-pound rifle hanging like a boat anchor. The crane's control cabin was a good sixty feet up. He watched the pace that Emily and Hansie were moving at and remembered how fast the scorpions could climb. A quick mental calculation told him one thing.

They were screwed.

Goon finally reached Rig Tower-1. Taking his first up-close look, he muttered, "Jesus, Mary and Gretzky, that's high."

A flight of steel stairs ran from the ground to the second level, known as the drill floor platform. From there it would be a hundred-foot vertical climb.

Flynn ran up behind him, looking winded, and said, "You gotta be kidding! We're climbing that thing?"

"Only if you want to live."

Ruby trotted past Goon, shouting, "What're you waiting for, Sasquatch? Afraid of heights?" and bounded up the stairs.

"Damn it, wait for us!" Goon stomped up the steel steps, Tigger and

Flynn right behind.

The second level was known as the drill floor—a labyrinth of grey steel girders clustered around the central drill. From there, the access ladder ran straight up. Ruby was already climbing.

Goon turned to Tigger and Flynn. "I'm going up to cover Ruby; you two stay down here. Tigger, you play spotter so Flynn can fry anything that gets up to this level. Once you see us hit the halfway point, ditch the flamethrower and start climbing."

Flynn asked, "Why ditch it?"

"'Cause fire rises, numb-nuts, so you can't shoot down." Goon popped the twenty-round dual magazine from his Mossberg. Fishing through his pockets, he pulled out a smaller ten-round mag marked with red tape, proclaiming, "Time to break out the Dragon's Breath," and started up the ladder.

Ruby was already fifteen feet above him, moving like a gymnast. She stopped, shouting, "I got two bogies above me at three o'clock."

Goon saw them and leaned back, hooking his leg around the ladder's rung, freeing his hands. He shouted, "Shut your eyes!" and fired a specialty shotgun shell known as "Dragon's Breath." The blindingly bright magnesium buckshot hit the first scorpion like a wave of fire. The searing heat and sledgehammer force blasted the creature off the rigging and sent it plummeting to Earth. His second shell was just as effective. Goon yelled, "You're clear, Ruby, keep moving!"

Down below, Tigger positioned himself directly behind Flynn, calling out targets. "One coming up at six o'clock."

Without aiming, Flynn pivoted to his six o'clock, unleashing a jet of flame, scorching the monster.

"Another climbing over the lip at two o'clock."

Flynn shifted to his two o'clock. The inferno engulfed a five-footer, proving the effectiveness of a two-man fire team.

Despite their success, Flynn couldn't shake the voice in his head repeating, *You ain't going to make it.* His mind reeled back to the humiliating day when his fear of heights had washed him out of airborne training. Desperate, he looked around for some alternative. He found it. The main drill assembly was encased in a ten-by-ten-foot safety cage constructed of thick steel grid. It was solid and the machinery inside was loud enough to confuse the scorpions. The sliding entry gate was secured by a foot-long deadbolt and the padlock was open. The place was made to order.

He was too lost in thought to hear Tigger shouting, "Yo, yo, two of them, eight o'clock, eight o'clock!"

Flynn snapped out of his daze, but it was too late—the scorpions were on them. The closest was barely six feet away when he torched it. The flaming beast rolled onto its side, hissing.

The second was already on Tigger, its pincer clamping down, snapping the bones in his forearm. His rifle clattered to the floor as the scorpion dragged him backwards. Using his free arm, he drew his machete, aiming for the only vulnerable target—the scorpion's row of lateral black eyes. Tigger drove the machete straight down into one, rupturing it in a geyser of grey fluid. The scorpion jerked back, releasing his arm. It backed up a few feet, contemplating its next attack.

Tigger lay on the deck, his arm shattered, screaming, "Shoot it!"

Flynn was frozen in terror. The scorpion was too close to Tigger, rendering the flamethrower useless. Helping Tigger meant forgoing it to unsling his rifle. But more scorpions were already climbing the deck. Instead of helping Tigger, he backed up toward the steel cage, releasing jets of flame as he went. He slid open the safety cage door, ducked inside and slammed it shut—leaving Tigger to fend for himself.

Brank climbed the access ladder, legs pumping, never looking back, certain he'd be grabbed from behind any second. He saw Emily and Hansie safely crawling into the control room—a steel and Plexiglas cabin protruding from the crane's mast.

Emily looked down, shouting, "Come on up, you're okay!"

That's when Brank glanced over his shoulder and saw ... nothing. Despite their being easy meat, the scorpions weren't climbing up after them. He kept powering upward until Hansie grabbed his shoulder, yanking him into the cabin.

Brank took a deep breath and glanced at Hansie. "You okay?"

The old soldier looked pale, his breath coming in short rasps. He said, "*Fok* you, I'm fifty-eight years old and climbing around like an *aap*." Then he went back to fishing through the maze of exposed wires under the control console.

Brank leaned out the control room window, rifle ready. The ladder was clear, as were the girders around it. He asked, "Why didn't they come up after us? Not that I'm complaining, mind you."

Emily leaned out, peering down at the base of the crane. The scorpions were clustered around the damaged green cylinders strewn across the ground. "Brank, I think I just figured it out. What's in those green cylinders we crashed into?"

"The green ones are universally oxygen, mostly for welding."

"Well, the scorpions are huddled around the ruptured ones like frat boys doing whippets."

Brank looked down. "Yeah, they're really sucking it up."

"I think I get it. Back in the Viséan Age, the atmosphere was really oxygen rich. That's why insects and other stuff grew to be so huge. At least that's the theory."

"So, you think these things are struggling to breathe?"

"That's why they're huffing that oxygen. It's like we're fighting an army of asthmatics."

"I'm gonna have to find that monster article of yours and like it on Facebook, or whatever normal people do."

Satisfied that they weren't in immediate danger, Brank took in their new surroundings. The cramped control cabin was mounted to the side of the crane's mast assembly, roughly sixty feet off the ground. The hundred-foot crane arm jutted out from the assembly. Its telescoping arm would double that length, making it long enough to reach Rig Tower-1. One problem—it was facing in the wrong direction.

"Hansie, can you get this rig running?"

Without looking up, Hansie said, "The key isn't here."

"Can you hot-wire it?"

"What the *fok's* it look like I'm doing?"

Brank raised the .50 caliber, studying the distant tower through its scope. Ruby was well on her way up. Then he shifted his attention to the base. "Oh shit!"

Emily asked, "What?"

Brank said, "Cover your ears!" then fired.

The scorpion advanced on Tigger, stinger poised to strike. But instead of running, Tigger went on the attack, lashing out at its raised tail with his machete. The razor-sharp blade slashed across the base of the stinger, slicing open a patch of muscle tissue. The apex predator backed away, sizing up this shockingly aggressive prey. Two more scorpions loomed behind, watching the battle—eager to dine on the loser.

Tigger swung the machete again, his broken arm dangling uselessly at his side. He egged the beast on with a Honduran street fighter's cry. "*Te voy a dar una galleta!*"

The creature lurched forward to deliver the killing strike—then its head exploded.

The shower of viscera threw Tigger back onto the steel flooring. He instantly recognized the .50 caliber's distinctive thunder and waved his machete in the air, yelling, "*Yupi* Brank!"

The other two scorpions lurched forward, only to be blasted apart.

From up above, Goon yelled, "Quit screwing around and get up here! Now!"

Tigger stood, scraping entrails off his shirt, and yelled, "Chill out

Hermano." Then he peered over the edge of the platform and saw why Goon was freaking out. The ground below them had been transformed into a blanket of squirming black scorpions. Yelling, "*Hijo de puta!*" he raced for the ladder—broken arm or not, he wasn't spending an extra second down there.

CHAPTER NINE

Nhamo watched the mercenary approaching the plane, his heart pounding. It wasn't that he was afraid of a standup fight. As a child soldier he'd cut down men twice his size with guns, knives and even his fists. But he knew that a single shot or even a loud noise would alert the rest of the mercenaries. For the children that would be a death sentence.

He whispered, "Prince, get over here."

The young boy scurried over.

"Prince, I need your help. Can you do that?"

The boy nodded, eyes wide with fear.

"And you must be very brave. As a Ndbele warrior you must protect your family."

The boy nodded again, this time with a new determination.

The mercenary circled around the plane once, seeing nothing suspicious. He knelt down, panning his flashlight under the aircraft.

Four glowing eyes stared back at him. Scrambling backwards, he fumbled with his machine gun, trying to fire. The pair of startled jackals yipped once and raced out from under the plane and into the night.

He lowered his weapon, laughing at his own panic, muttering, "You scavenging bastards." Securing this village had been easy, but the monsters he'd fought earlier had him on edge. He pondered just walking away from the airplane despite there possibly being stuff to loot inside. But greed won out over caution, so he pressed on. Eyeing the battered plane, he muttered, "What a piece of shit."

The thing looked like it was held together with tape. In fact, there were patches of peeling speed tape plastered all over the wings. Closer scrutiny revealed a faded Angolan Air Force emblem stenciled on the fuselage, right next to some rusty bullet holes.

Shaking his head, he muttered, "Kruger probably shot this junk heap down."

He shined his flashlight into the strange Plexiglas observation cone beneath the cockpit. It appeared to be empty. Satisfied, he decided it was safe to venture inside.

The moment he walked away, Nhamo stuck his head up, peering out from the nose cone, thinking, *So far, so good.*

The mercenary had to wrestle with the aging door just to get it open. He flicked on his flashlight and stepped into the dark interior. Sniffing the air, he muttered, "This thing reeks of goat piss."

He panned his flashlight around with one hand while the other held the grip of his machine gun. The fuselage was crammed with wooden crates and loose cargo netting.

Kicking an empty crate, he said, "Nothing but junk."

Then something rattled to his left. He turned, gun at the ready. The sound was coming from one of the crates. Using the barrel of his machine gun he shoved the lid aside and shined his flashlight down.

A small boy crouched inside, hands folded over his head, pleading, "Please don't shoot me."

The mercenary grabbed him by the arm, yanking him out. The kid fell to the floor, knocking over some more empty crates, making a hell of a racket.

With tears in his eyes, Prince begged, "Don't shoot, I was just hiding."

The mercenary snapped, "I should, you little *umthondo!*"

With all Prince's clamor and wailing, the mercenary never heard Nhamo climbing up from the lower cockpit. He crept up silently, coming within three paces, then slammed the ball peen hammer into the back of the mercenary's neck—an instant killing blow. It was a technique Nhamo had been taught as a child, when he was too short to hit someone on the head.

As instructed, Prince pushed himself against the dying man, breaking his fall. That meant no noise and less chance of his weapon accidentally discharging.

Prince asked, "Did I do okay?"

"Like a true warrior."

The boy toyed with the mercenary's machine gun and asked, "What's an *umthondo?*"

Nhamo snatched the gun away and said, "It's what you piss with. Now, help me get his clothes off, we don't have much time."

Using his rifle scope, Brank could see a carpet of scorpions swarming around the rig tower's base. The eager creatures were fighting each other to be the first to climb. Goon, Tigger and Ruby were midway up the tower with no scorpions around them. They were as close to safe as it got in this place.

Brank pulled the rifle's empty magazine and tossed it to Emily, along with the .50 caliber belt she'd found. "Load that up for me, ten rounds." He slapped his last full magazine into the rifle, adding, "The back rim slides under the—"

"Got it," Emily said, already on her third bullet, "pointy end in front."

Without looking up from his efforts, Hansie asked, "How many rounds left?"

"Not enough. Ten in this magazine and about twenty loose. It won't even make a dent in what's crawling around the tower."

Hansie twisted two wires together and, after a short spark, the control console lit up. "Don't get excited, that's just the DC power coming on. I'm still working on the crane engine."

Brank said, "If I can't lure those things away from the tower it won't matter."

Emily tossed Brank the loaded magazine and rushed over to the control console. "Can scorpions hear?"

Hansie said, "Yeah, sort of. Why?"

Emily keyed a microphone mounted on the console and started throwing switches. "This is a PA system, right?"

"Uh huh, it's to warn workers when the crane's moving."

She pressed the switch on the microphone and turned the volume up till it rang with feedback. Her voice boomed out from speaker horns on the control room's roof. "Hey, you eight-legged shit heads! You hungry? Come on over here!"

Brank watched the scorpions shift their attention in the crane's direction. "It's working!" He fired twice, killing a pair of scorpions that had made it up to the drilling platform. He lowered the rifle and began rooting through his pockets.

Emily said, "I knew that time in AV Club would eventually pay off," and continued shouting pep rally nonsense into the microphone.

Brank found his MP3 player and tossed it to Emily. "Plug that in and hit play!"

Emily disconnected a cable from the PA and jammed it into the headphone jack. There was a shrill ring of feedback; then the opening cords of Metallica's "Master of Puppets" blared through the PA.

Brank looked through his rifle scope and said, "It's working! They're turning and coming this way."

Emily said, "I guess they like Metallica."

"Everybody likes Metallica. Nice save on the PA system; I bet you were the hot nerdy girl on the AV Squad."

"I'll take that as a compliment."

Brank shifted his rifle scope away from the rig tower to the opposite side of the compound. His enthusiasm vanished. "Uh, Hansie, you need to see this!"

Hansie fished a set of binoculars from under the console, took a look and shouted, "*Fok me!*"

Emily strained to see what they were looking at.

Hansie handed her the binoculars, saying, "Have a look, but you ain't gonna like it."

He was right. The fracking zone looked like it had been carpet bombed. A steel drilling tower had collapsed, huge machinery had been demolished and pumping trucks were strewn around like Tonka toys.

Brank shouted over the blaring music, "Hansie, is that the rift that opened in the earthquake?"

"Yeah."

Emily saw what he was talking about—a huge gash in the shale rock at the far end of the compound. Dozens of scorpions were clustered around it. Even worse, a steady stream of the creatures was crawling up from the depths. "It must be some colony that was trapped for millions of years."

Brank said, "There must be a hundred of them. And that's just what we can see."

"But aren't scorpions solitary creatures, like tarantulas?"

"It's been four hundred million years. People change, I guess they do too. Hansie, how deep do you think that rift goes?"

"If they were sleeping in that gas pocket, it's thousands of meters, plus however far the fracking went horizontally."

Brank lowered his rifle. "Well, that means my plan B's officially shot to shit."

Emily asked, "Why, what were you thinking?"

"There's a natural gas storage tank over there, maybe thousands of gallons." He fished two red-striped .50 caliber rounds from his pocket. "As a last resort I was going to shoot it with these incendiary rounds, blow it, and fry 'em all."

Hansie shook his head. "They burnt off all the gas last night, but even if they hadn't, your idea still wouldn't finish the job."

Emily asked, "Why?"

Brank shook his head. "Hansie's right. That sinkhole's like a bunker. The gas would burn for a while on the surface, but it wouldn't get down into the pit. We might kill half of 'em, but the rest would just crawl out and get fat on the remains."

Hansie added, "Plus we'd all be dead from the blast. So, unless you have some more depressing news, I've got work to do." And he went back to fidgeting with the wires.

Brank moved his scope slightly to the right. Something caught his eye. "So, maybe we don't burn them." He was looking at a pair of three-story white cylindrical tanks standing near the chasm.

"Are those white tanks full of liquid nitrogen?"

"*Ja*," Hansie said, "they use cryogenic separation for the natural gas. Then they started injecting it into the fracking core just to *fok* things up worse."

"Well, liquid nitrogen would flow straight down into the pit and freeze-dry those fuckers."

"If you're thinking of shooting the nitrogen tanks, it won't do shit."

"Why not?"

Hansie sighed in exasperation then explained, "It's a safety feature to keep terrorists from doing exactly what you're thinking. If the bullet only punches a hole through the cast-iron outer shell, it won't do anything. And even if the bullet hits the inner shell, the extreme cold just re-seals the puncture. To get what you want, you'd have to tear the whole tank wide open at the base."

"What would do that?"

"Maybe a few RPG rounds, which we don't have."

Emily said, "If Ruby gets through, maybe the Zimbabwean Air Force could drop napalm down the pit."

Hansie snickered and said, "They couldn't hit the ground with their own piss."

Brank studied the chasm for a moment and saw something he'd missed. "Hansie, you know how we thought all those drilling guys were dead?"

"Uh huh."

"They're not. It's something worse."

Six members of the drilling crew had been dragged to the pit alive and were herded into a circle of scorpions. The largest scorpions were using their pincers to drop immature ones into the circle. The infant scorpions were charging at the terrified men, jabbing at them with their stingers.

Emily watched through the binoculars in horror. "Are they—"

"Practicing? Yeah," Brank said. "The adults are teaching them to hunt. I don't think they're injecting venom with those stingers. They're just learning how to attack." He studied the mass of scorpions and said, "Look at the size of that one!"

The scorpion in the center was twice the size of the others, at least seventeen feet. The infant scorpions clustered around her, while the older ones maintained a respectful distance.

"I think that's the momma bear of the bunch."

After enduring six more vicious stings, a worker finally collapsed. His body was dragged off and shredded by the mature scorpions while their children moved on to the next victim. That man charged at an adult, slamming it with his fists.

Emily realized that he wasn't trying to escape; he was trying to provoke the scorpions into killing him quickly. It didn't work. The adult just dragged him back into the circle so his unimaginable suffering could continue.

Emily tore her eyes away, and her voice, barely above a whisper, said, "Brank, please don't let them drag me over there."

Brank slid his arm around her. "I'm not letting that happen. I promise." He wanted to say more, to somehow ease her pain, but they didn't have that kind of time. He turned his scope down onto the crane mast and didn't like what he saw. "Um, Hansie, how's that hot-wiring going?"

"As fast as it can. I never said I was an expert."

"Well, in about five minutes that crane's gonna come in real handy."

Emily saw what he meant. At least a dozen scorpions were closing in on the crane and the ones already at the base were moving away from the oxygen cylinders. Now they were climbing.

Brank said, "I think those oxygen bottles are empty."

Emily added, "So are their stomachs."

Ruby was midway up the drilling tower, with Goon right behind.

He shouted, "You got a signal yet?"

She looked down at the satellite phone hanging from her shoulder. "Nothing. This place is like a void." Glancing down, she added, "Hey, Tigger ain't looking so good."

Goon saw that she was right. Tigger was climbing using one arm and his progress was painfully slow.

Goon shouted, "Look out below!" then shifted his legs outside the ladder rungs and slid down, navy style. Tightening his grip brought him to a hard stop a few feet above Tigger. The Honduran was deathly pale and drenched in sweat.

Tigger looked up and, gritting his teeth, said, "My arm's fucked."

Goon said, "Climb up behind me and wrap your legs around my waist.

"I can make it."

"Quit bitchin' and do it."

Tigger climbed up and over Goon into a piggyback position and said, "I'm on, now giddyap."

Goon started climbing and said, "Smart ass. You're lucky I'm strong as a horse."

"More like a burro."

Goon laughed and kept climbing. "What happened to Flynn?"

"That *culo* left me and took off."

"Where?"

"I don't know, I was kinda busy."

Goon climbed a few more rungs and asked, "Is that your machete poking me or are you just glad to see me?"

"You ain't my type." Tigger heard something in the distance, like a swarm of angry bees, growing louder. "What the—"

A dark shape whipped past, almost knocking Goon off the ladder. Twenty feet to his right, a black gyrocopter was moving into a hover; a few seconds later, it started to ascend.

"It's a drone." Goon pushed himself even harder, taking the rungs two at a time. "We need to get up top and warn Ruby."

Kruger sat next to the drone operator, studying the video feed, amazed to discover that some of the Americans were still alive. Hertzog hovered over his shoulder trying to see the monitor.

Kruger said, "There are two of them."

Hertzog asked, "What are they doing?"

"Trying not to get eaten I suppose." He tapped the operator on the shoulder. "Take it up higher, let's see if there's anybody else up there."

The drone slowly ascended. Through the haze, Kruger made out a figure climbing the steel rigging just below the crown block.

Kruger snapped his fingers. "There's another one! Move in closer." The shaky image was difficult to make out. "Can you hold it still?"

The operator said, "No, the heat draught from that flare stack's throwing it off. I barely have a signal."

Kruger leaned closer. "It's that American *hoer* from the State Department."

Hovering over his shoulder, Hertzog asked, "What's she doing?"

"She's climbing up to the highest point." He had a sudden realization. "I think she's trying to get a clear satellite signal." Kruger cracked his knuckles. "That means they haven't managed to call for help yet."

"If she makes that call, we're screwed. Can't you knock her off the tower with the drone?"

The operator shook his head. "Too much interference. I can barely keep it aloft, never mind hitting anyone."

Kruger couldn't resist adding, "I requested an armed drone, but your bean counters said it cost too much."

"Don't you have snipers?"

"Yeah, until they got eaten."

Hertzog grew more petulant. "Well, you have to do something!"

Kruger nodded silently, sucking his teeth, and then turned to Hertzog. "May I borrow that elephant gun of yours?"

Ruby finally reached the crown block platform—the highest point on the rig tower. She leaned forward, palms pressed to her knees, coughing up phlegm. She prided herself on being in peak condition, but the past few hours had pushed her to the limit, and the soot-filled air wasn't helping. Her skin bristled from the heat of the burning flare stack only ten feet above. The flaming stack roared like a jet engine, belching fire into the sky.

She looked down at the satellite phone, pumped her fist and shouted, "Yes!"

Without wasting any time, she pulled up the prewritten message and the zip file of photos then waited impatiently for it to cue up.

Between the roar of the flare stack and her preoccupation with the phone, Ruby failed to notice the black gyrocopter hovering over her.

Kruger climbed onto the roof of the Mamba armored car and lay down in prone position. The elevation offered him an unobstructed view of the rig tower.

One of his most reliable men crouched beside him, his eyes pressed to a pair of binoculars. "I've got her, one o'clock." Holding up a digital anemometer, he added, "The wind's fifteen kilometers from the west."

Kruger adjusted his grip, savoring the rifle's feel. The handmade bolt-action rifle was the pinnacle of the gunsmith's art, costing more than he earned in six months; just as importantly, its .404 bullets were powerful enough to stop a charging rhino yet still deadly accurate at extreme range. Truly a rifle of kings.

He pressed his eye to the scope, lining her up in his crosshairs. The shot was long, and he'd only get one crack at it before she dove for cover. But Kruger was an expert marksman who'd killed men at greater distances. He exhaled slowly, finger tightening around the trigger.

Goon climbed, his leg muscles burning, until he made it to the crown block.

Ruby saw him and waved the phone, shouting, "We've got a signal."

He screamed, "Ruby, take cover!"

A .404 round struck her squarely in the shoulder, severing her left arm and slamming her back against the steel rigging. Goon ran towards her.

She choked out, "Stay down!" The phone clattered onto the steel deck. "Make the call!"

The second bullet struck her squarely in the chest, catapulting her off the platform. Her body tumbled, bouncing off the steel girders until it slammed onto the drill floor platform.

Screaming in rage, Goon raised the shotgun. The drone operator saw him and tried an evasive maneuver. The big Canadian was faster, snapping off two shots. The drone exploded like a clay pigeon. Instinctively, Goon dropped down low, just as a sonic blast of wind roared past his ear. The sniper's third bullet had barely missed him, slamming into a steel girder with a shower of sparks, the impact digging a one-inch crater into the hardened steel.

Diving for cover behind the block and tackle, Goon yelled, "Tigger, you good?"

Tigger had found cover behind a steel cable spool. "I'm good. I saw a big muzzle flash below at six o'clock."

Goon crouched down, unsure of his next move. The phone was lying on the deck, barely twenty feet away, but the sniper would make mincemeat of him before he reached it. The crane was to his right—far away but in direct line of sight. Up till now, his walkie talkie had been useless, but with direct line of sight it might get reception.

Tigger shouted, "Whatever he's shooting ain't military, 'cause there's no suppressor. But it's *muy grande!*"

Goon said, "Yeah, well, I know somebody with a bigger one." He keyed the walkie. "Stumpy, it's Goon, you copy?"

Brank responded, his voice choked in static. "Go ahead."

Goon sighed in relief. "We've got trouble. Ruby's dead."

Brank was silent for a few seconds then asked, "How? I don't see any scorpions."

"A sniper. He must be out by the gate with those other assholes. I need some cover fire to get to the sat-phone."

Using his scope, Brank located Goon's hiding place. Further out, beyond the fence line, he could see the mercenaries' camp. But his view was distorted by the rippling heat coming off the flare stack. Through the haze, he could barely make out two figures crouched atop an armored car—exactly the firing position he would have chosen.

Brank keyed his walkie. "When you hear my first shot, go. I'll give you three rounds total."

"Copy."

Brank zeroed in on the blurry armored car and fired.

Kruger maintained his position, waiting for one of the men to reemerge.

His spotter said, "I've got eyes on one of them. He's hunkered down behind—"

Brank's .50 caliber round literally blew the spotter in half, drenching Kruger in gore.

Kruger rolled left just as a second round tore into the roof an inch from his hand, leaving a grapefruit-sized hole. He dove off the roof, landing hard in the sand, and scuttled under the armored car. Hertzog hunkered down next to him.

Kruger said, "Looks like the one with the big gun's still alive," and he handed Hertzog what was left of the Heym Express rifle, amounting to the barrel and forestock. Brank's second bullet had reduced the rest to splinters of hand-carved walnut and etched blue steel. "Thanks for loaning me that. A truly fine weapon."

Hertzog stared at the remnants of his treasured rifle. Kruger thought he was going to cry.

The vehicle rocked as a third .50 caliber round reduced the bulletproof windshield to shards. Then everything went silent.

Kruger's men returned fire, blindly aiming for the distant rig tower.

Kruger jumped to his feet, shouting, "Cease fire! You'll blow the damn thing up!"

Reluctantly, the men followed his orders.

Kruger stood, brushing flecks of meat off his shirt. He looked over at the fence line. The scorpion still sat there, motionless, like some monstrous Buddha, its black eyes boring into him.

Kruger tore his eyes away and shouted, "Someone bring me those fucking nuns!"

Goon scooped up the fallen satellite phone and ducked down into his hiding place as Brank fired his third shot. Sometime during the melee, Tigger managed to crawl over to join him. A barrage of automatic weapons fire clattered in the distance. Goon ducked lower as rounds pinged off the steel rigging around them.

A searing pain shot through his side, and he screamed, "Goddamn it!"

Tigger said, "Sit still," and probed his buddy's side. His hand came back bloody. "You caught a ricochet." He pulled disinfectant and a pressure bandage from his belt pouch. "Grit your teeth, 'cause this is gonna hurt."

Goon winced in pain and said, "Lucky bugger nailed me just below the vest."

"It's not in too deep. You're lucky it was going slow and you're made out of beef jerky."

After doing what he could to control the bleeding, Tigger scanned the fence area through his M4's Trijicon scope. "They ain't shooting at us no more."

Goon nodded. "Stumpy must have messed 'em up good."

Brank's voice crackled through the walkie. "What's your situation?"

Goon replied, "Mission accomplished."

"Good. I've got a situation on my end, so you're flying solo for a while."

"Copy that," Goon replied, not wanting to burden Brank any further.

Tigger said, "Hey *hermano*, those fucks have the villagers lined up outside the fence."

Goon leaned over and peered through the scope. "Son of a bitch. What're they doing?"

Tigger took his rifle back and studied the scene. He saw the bald, one-eared guy surveying the group. He gestured to his men, who dragged a woman wearing a white robe forward.

"Those *cabrons* brought the nuns over too."

He watched as the one-eared man slapped the nun to the ground then kicked her in the side.

Tigger's grip tightened around his rifle. "I should pop that fucker right now!"

Goon calmed him down, saying, "Don't! The range is too far and the wind's too high, you'll wind up hitting the good guys. But don't sweat it, 'cause I'm calling in the cavalry right now."

Tigger watched Sister Estelle being beaten, his fury rising. His mind reeled back to that horrible day. It was back to Honduras where he led an elite team of *Policia Tigres*—a paramilitary force dedicated to fighting the gangs and cartels. Tigger and his men had been assigned to take down a murderous Barrio 18 group terrorizing the region. After a bloody fight, his men had prevailed, killing over a dozen cartel members, ending their reign of extortion and murder. Justice was served, and the locals were grateful. But Barrio 18 demanded revenge. Too cowardly to fight the *Policia Tigres*, they settled on another target—a local convent. They came in the evening and left at dawn, leaving behind a scene of unparalleled barbarity. When Tigger, a devout Catholic, saw the women's mutilated bodies, something inside him died. He and his men went rogue, avenging the fourteen nuns while breaking all the laws of God and man. It was along that bloody path that Tigger earned his Honduran nickname, *el cuchilla*— the blade. But no matter how much blood his machete drew, it couldn't wash away his shame over failing those fourteen women. Since then, he'd barely been able to look a nun in the eye without sinking into despair. Now these bastards were about to do the same thing, and he was powerless to stop them.

Goon shouted, "Shit!" snapping Tigger out of his despair. The big Canadian almost threw the phone off the well tower, shouting, "I knew she was fucking CIA!"

Tigger took the phone from him and looked at the screen. The onscreen message was short and simple. "Press thumb to screen to verify identity."

The cavalry wasn't coming.

CHAPTER TEN

The mercenary named Langa leaned back against the Mamba, eyeing the distant airplane, muttering, "What the hell is taking so long?"

It had been forever since Langa's buddy, Bafana, had gone to check the aircraft. Langa wasn't concerned for his friend's welfare; he just wanted to make sure he got his cut of anything Bafana looted.

Van Shoor wandered over, asking, "Where's the other one?"

Langa pointed to the plane.

Taking a swig of Klipdrift, Van Shoor asked, "Are you bored?"

Knowing his commanding officer was drunk, Langa said, "No sir, I'm fine."

"Relax." Van Shoor cocked his head towards the villagers squatting on the ground. "I'm just thinking about how we can, you know, pass the time."

"Like what?"

Van Shoor smiled and said, "Like that one with the nice tits over there." He pointed to a pretty young girl. "I mean they're all going to die anyway, so why not have some fun?"

Langa shrugged. "You're the boss."

Van Shoor staggered off, saying, "White men first, then you can take your pick."

Langa felt relieved to see the asshole go.

Van Shoor hovered over the bound villagers, silently appraising the young woman. The terrified girl kept her eyes fixed on the ground.

Van Shoor grabbed her, wrenching her onto her feet. "Come on, honey, it's your lucky night."

She whimpered but didn't cry out. The villagers around her just watched in silence as he dragged her behind the nearest homestead.

Langa shook his head, muttering, "You sure are the quietest bunch

I've ever seen." He heard the airplane's door slam shut in the distance. A flashlight flicked on, and someone started climbing down the gangway. He tensed for a moment then recognized Bafana's red beret and belt-fed machine gun. He shouted, "About goddamn time!"

Bafana started walking over, practically dragging a small boy behind him, always keeping the flashlight trained in Langa's direction. Slowly he came closer.

Langa yelled, "All that time and that's the only thing you found—" A burst of 7.63mm rounds catapulted Langa backward. He landed in a cloud of dust, chest torn open, his organs spilling out onto the sand.

Nhamo ran to the bound villagers, shouting, "The other, where is he?"

One of the tied-up men shouted, "Behind the hut!"

Nhamo sprinted around the hut, rounding the corner as Van Shoor raised his rifle. Nhamo dove to the ground as bullets shattered the rain barrels behind him.

Van Shoor was firing one handed while struggling to pull his pants up with the other. He backed away, firing wildly, and tripped over the girl lying on the ground. He'd just managed to get back up when the girl slammed her foot into his groin. Van Shoor crumpled to his knees, whimpering, then felt Nhamo's gun barrel pressed to his head.

Nhamo grabbed Van Shoor's rifle then turned to the girl, asking, "Did he hurt you?"

She shook her head. "But he wanted to—"

Nhamo held up a calming hand. "I know, but you're safe now."

Prince raced around the corner, embracing the girl, shouting, "Dakalo!"

He turned to Nhamo and said, "Dakalo's my sister."

"And you saved her, boy." He yanked a knife from Van Shoor's belt and tossed it to Prince. "Now cut her loose, then everyone else. Quickly now!"

The boy cut the flex cuffs off his sister while jabbering out his heroic tale then ran off to free the rest of the villagers. Dakalo looked over at Nhamo and was about to thank him.

He shouted, "Go with your brother. This isn't for you to see."

The frightened girl ran away.

Nhamo kicked Van Shoor, shouting, "Keep undressing, you piece of shit!"

Visibly shaking, Van Shoor stripped down to his shorts, the sweat gleaming off his pale skin in the moonlight.

"Keep going!"

Seconds later, the mercenary was on his knees, naked, hands locked behind his head.

"Why did you take those people?"

Van Shoor stammered out, "It wasn't me, I was just following orders."

Nhamo kicked him in the stomach. "Tell me the truth or I'll slice your tendons and leave you in the desert for the hyenas. Have you ever seen what they do to crippled men? Well, I have." He leaned closer, putting his lips to Van Shoor's ear. "It was how we entertained ourselves in ZIPRA, back during *Gukurahundi*."

Van Shoor stiffened. He considered himself a hardened killer, but compared to the Zimbabwe People's Revolutionary Army, or ZIPRA, he was a choirboy. He'd heard all the stories about how *Gukurahundi* hadn't been so much a civil war as a five-year massacre.

Nhamo kicked him again, shouting, "Tell me the truth!"

And Van Shoor did, from discovering the scorpions right up to dragging the villagers off as food.

Nhamo listened in disbelief, the beast inside him raging more with each word—the beast he'd struggled his whole life to keep chained.

In measured tones, Nhamo said, "I should feed you to those things."

Looking up at him with bloodshot eyes, Van Shoor said, "You won't get away. Those things will get out and eat every one of you kaffir—"

And in that moment, the beast broke its chains.

Prince raced among the villagers, cutting their bonds like a conquering hero. The freed villagers embraced, alternately laughing and weeping.

A single gunshot rang out from behind the hut. The crowd fell silent. Moments later, Nhamo emerged carrying Van Shoor's rifle and uniform.

Prince ran up to him, but one look into Nhamo's eyes stopped him short. An hour ago, they'd shined bright with mischief—now they were shrouded in darkness and cruelty.

Nhamo addressed the villagers. "Which of you men have fought?"

Nine men stepped forward.

"Who's the most experienced?"

A lean man in his mid-forties stepped forward and stated, "It was a long ago, but I fought for eight years."

"Your name?"

"Fhatu."

Nhamo asked, "You fought with ZANU?"

He referred to the Zimbabwe African National Union, an organization he'd once called the enemy.

The man nodded.

Nhamo tossed him the uniform and rifle. "Then you'll be my second in command. Put that on and select three other men to join your squad, the others will go with me. Are there any more weapons?"

"Just one rifle I keep for killing jackals."

"Well, these jackals can shoot back. Someone run and fetch the AK-47 from my plane."

Fhatu began barking orders to the men. Other villagers slipped into their huts, emerging with shovels and rakes—anything that could serve as a weapon.

Nhamo contemplated the odds. They were bleak. They had only five rifles against at least a dozen seasoned men holding thirty hostages. As he studied the villagers, his gaze fell on the young girl, Dakalo. For a brief moment she smiled at him then shyly looked away. But in that brief flash, Nhamo felt a warm ray of humanity shining through the darkness. Slowly, the nexus of a plan began to form in his mind.

He asked, "Do any of you men have mechanical experience?"

Two men stepped forward.

"Then meet me over by the plane, and get the children off it. I want every rain barrel emptied and brought to the plane. And grab those cases of soap and bring them along too."

One of the women ran over shouting in Venda.

Prince translated, "She says a vehicle is coming. It looks like the bus that took the others away."

Fhatu asked, "What should we do?"

Nhamo adjusted his newly acquired red beret and flatly said, "We're going to get on the bus."

Flynn slunk back into the shadows of the steel cage, banging the side of the dying flamethrower, muttering, "Come on you piece of shit, work!"

The flamethrower sputtered and died. He unstrapped the backpack, careful not to make any noise. He still had his M4 and two full magazines, so he wasn't completely defenseless. The scorpions had abandoned the deck, drawn away by some distant music. He was certain he could hide here, behind the loud drilling equipment, undetected by any strays. All he had to do was wait things out until somebody, anybody, arrived. All things considered, his situation was pretty good.

He heard shots in the distance but couldn't see what was going on.

Something slammed onto the platform, right outside the cage, echoing like a timpani drum against the steel flooring. He crept forward for a look. It was a body, so badly mangled that it took him a few seconds to even make out that it was a woman.

He muttered, "Oh shit, it's Ruby."

The twisted body was missing an arm. Worse than that, the falling corpse had burst like a water balloon on impact, spewing gore in every direction. To the scorpions, the smell of her blood would be like waving bacon in front of a dog. A stream of blood was already flowing from the twisted body—directly into the steel cage.

Looking down, Brank counted six scorpions already climbing the crane's central mast. Leaning out, he fired a round, hitting the lead scorpion. It fell away, knocking off another one right behind it.

He muttered, "Two for one," then turned to Hansie. "How's it going, buddy?"

Hansie twisted a pair of wires and gruffly said, "Please keep asking the same question over and over. That makes it go much faster."

The cabin trembled, followed by the roar of an engine starting. A yellow, rotating beacon light atop the operator's cab lit up. The hundred-foot jib arm rose a foot.

Emily embraced him. "You did it!"

Hansie proclaimed, "You're lucky I'm such a genius."

"Never doubted you for a second."

Hansie grabbed the controls. "Let's see if I can swivel this over." The jib arm sank a good five feet. "Oops." Hansie re-engaged the locking mechanism.

Emily said, "I think that button was up and down."

Hansie pointed to a gage. "No, I was doing it right. See, that's the hydraulic pressure readout. I need to let it build up or the jib arm will just sink."

Brank asked, "How long?"

"*Fak* if I know … probably not too long."

Brank fired another round, knocking a scorpion off the mast. "I think any time is too long."

Hansie said, "This cabin's too small; if one gets in, we're all screwed. I suggest you two climb out onto the arm. That way, you can keep picking them off while I shift it over to your pals."

Brank asked Emily, "Are you afraid of heights?"

"At this point, I'm afraid of everything, but let's do it."

Tigger held the rifle scope to his eye, watching helplessly as Kruger beat the nuns. The other mercenaries gathered around, egging him on, enjoying the spectacle.

He said, "Those bastards are going to murder them."

Goon asked, "I don't get it. Why'd they bring the villagers here?"

Giving it some thought, Tigger said, "Maybe to feed those things. They probably figure they're worth something, like for a *zoologico*."

"I hope to hell it ain't a petting zoo." Goon glanced below them and said, "Shit, looks like we missed a couple." He pointed one level down.

Tigger panned his scope over and saw a pair of five-foot scorpions perched on the girders below.

Goon asked, "Why aren't they coming after us?"

The two scorpions were balanced among the steel girders, snapping their pincers at each other.

Tigger said, "Looks like they're fighting over something."

The two scorpions were focused on something each wanted, but Tigger couldn't see what it was.

Goon raised his shotgun. "Say goodnight, assholes."

"Wait!"

Goon lowered the shotgun. "What's up?"

"I can see what they're playing with."

"What is it?"

Tigger turned to him, eyes wide. "It's Ruby's arm!"

Looking through Tigger's scope, Goon saw he was right. Ruby's arm had been blown clean off by the first shot, but the severed limb had landed on the steel girders below. Now the scorpions were sparring for the prize.

Tigger said, "If we grab it, we can make the call."

"I'll go get it." Goon tried to stand but winced and sank back down, groaning. "Or maybe I can just shoot them from here."

"If you do that, the arm might fall, and we'd never find it."

"Okay, then down I go." With gritted teeth, Goon managed to stand but had to lean on the pump housing to steady himself.

Tigger saw fresh blood soaking through Goon's bandage and shook his head. "They're way out on those girders, so your gorilla ass would never be able to get to them. I have to go."

"Except your arm's busted."

Tigger held up his machete. "Yeah, but this is my blade arm. Don't argue 'cause you know I'm right." He set the machete down. "Now take off your belt so I can tie off my bad arm."

Goon wrapped his belt around Tigger's chest, securing the broken arm against his side. The tough Honduran didn't so much as groan, but Goon saw the tears welling in his eyes.

Tigger picked up a rag soaked in Goon's blood. "I got to split those two up, so I'll need some bait." He wiped the bloody rag across his face.

Goon said, "If you can draw one far enough away, I'll pop it from here."

"That'll just freak the other one out and it'll take off with the arm. Don't shoot unless I tell you to."

After a deep breath, Goon said, "Okay, but no screwing around. Just toss the arm up to me and get out of Dodge. Be careful, brother."

Tigger nodded and started climbing down. "Easy stuff *compañero*."

Flynn hid behind the central drill housing, watching with a mix of awe and revulsion as a ten-foot scorpion picked through Ruby's remains. Its back was covered in a squirming mass of pale infants. Flynn counted roughly twenty of the foot-long hitchhikers and remembered just how fast and deadly they were. The scorpion was only a few feet from the cage entrance, allowing Flynn a front row seat to its feeding process. The razor-sharp pincers crushed Ruby's bones and ripped her torso apart before dragging the pieces to its mouth. That mouth was a vertical slit, lined with sharp curved teeth—like some Freudian vaginal nightmare. Short arm-like appendages at each side of the mouth held the meat. Once in place, the scorpion vomited up acidic yellow mucus, reducing the tissue to a gelatinous state.

Bile rose in Flynn's throat, yet he couldn't tear his eyes away from the spectacle.

A five-foot scorpion crept up behind the mother, grabbing at scraps. The mother whirled around, lashing out with its pincers, defending its meal. The intruder slunk back submissively, allowing the dominant one to dine in peace. It hovered there, greedily eyeing the human feast.

Emboldened by hunger, the smaller scorpion dashed forward, plucking one of the squirming youngsters off its mother's back and stuffing it into its maw. The enraged mother turned, striking out at the attacker. The two locked pincers grappling ferociously. Flynn jumped back as the mother's tail slammed against the steel cage's gate. Then the mother's body quivered, shaking the youngsters off its back. The scorplings instinctively retreated behind her for protection.

They were heading straight for the gate.

Flynn's heart raced as the foot-long monsters squirmed under the steel gate. Gripped by panic he backed up, stumbling over the discarded flamethrower. The clattering fuel tank alerted the young ones to his presence. Without their mother to protect them, the infant creatures' only defense was staging a group attack. With stingers raised, they swarmed at him. Flynn fired his M4 blindly, hitting a few whilst sending a hail of bullets ricocheting off the steel drill housing. One round pinged off his ballistic helmet. It was like being hit with a baseball bat. He staggered for a moment before a rush of adrenaline snapped him back to clarity. The lead scorpling latched on to his boot, jabbing its stinger at the thick rubber sole. Flynn slammed his foot against the drill housing, crushing the scorpion. In desperation he pulled himself up onto the central drill housing and climbed. Halfway up, his boots slipped in a layer of protective axle grease. He tumbled off, landing face down, clutching his rifle. Thankfully he'd only landed a few feet from the gate, leaving the cluster of newborns behind him.

The infant horde did an about face and went back on the attack. Flynn knew if he stayed inside the cage, he'd wind up dying like Easy. He fumbled for the bolt, slid open the gate and scrambled outside. The infant scorpions charged forward, stopping just inside the open gate, defending their newfound shelter.

Flynn looked back at them and muttered, "You can keep it."

To his right the adults were still locked in combat, providing him a clear path to the stairway. He took five steps and saw a stray scorpling in front of him, defiantly waving its pincers.

Muttering, "Eat this," he slammed down his rifle butt. The half dead scorpling lay there, quivering in a puddle of indigo blood.

It might have been some cry beyond the range of human hearing or a sudden discharge of pheromones—but somehow the mother knew her child had been attacked. The beast pivoted and in one lightning-fast motion slung the smaller scorpion off the platform and charged. Flynn barely got off a shot before its pincers locked around his waist, hoisting him into the air. The vice-grip pressure cracked his ribs, squeezing the air from his lungs. Suffocation blurred his vision until the scorpion's grip slackened just enough for him to breathe. When Flynn's vision rolled back into focus, he saw the scorpion's stinger hovering over him, venom oozing from its tip.

Drawing what was surely his last breath, he screamed, "Just do it!"

But the creature didn't strike, nor did it crush him. Instead it held him, suspended in the air, waiting patiently as her young crawled onto the safety of her back. With its family reunited, the scorpion made its way down the steel steps, clutching Flynn in its pincer. His screams were lost in the din of drilling equipment.

The mother scorpion was dragging Flynn to the pit.

Brank popped open the access hatch on the control cabin's ceiling and climbed out. He cautiously stepped off the cabin's roof onto the main jib arm then stopped to get his bearings.

The horizontal jib arm was constructed of steel lattice, with a three-foot-wide top deck that was never intended for walking on. Despite that, it was still wide enough for him to stand securely. Housed within the jib arm's steel lattice was a second, narrower telescoping section. Brank estimated the main jib arm at a hundred feet—a length that would double once the telescoping arm was extended. The crane trolley sat parked at the far end of the jib, its massive hook block swaying like a pendulum below it.

To his rear was the shorter counter jib, housing the winch motors and hydraulics along with the crane's twenty-ton counterweight.

Above him was the tower peak—a fifteen-foot span of vertical lattice connected to the main jib by a steel cable.

Currently the jib arm was facing in exactly the wrong direction. It was up to Hansie to pivot it one hundred and eighty degrees to reach Goon and Tigger. And it was up to Brank to keep them from being eaten in the process.

With a few tentative steps, Brank discovered just how challenging it was to walk on the jib arm. The jib was designed to move with the air currents as opposed to fighting them. As a result, it constantly swayed a good six inches from side to side. It was like walking in a canoe—on the ocean—in a storm.

"Glad I didn't eat anything."

He reached down into the control cabin and hoisted Emily up. Hansie handed up his .50 caliber along with the Vektor rifle Emily had acquired. Taking her hand, Brank led Emily out onto the jib arm.

Emily shouted, "Wow, that music's way louder out here!"

Realizing which song his Metallica mix was playing, Brank said, "Oh great, it's 'For Whom the Bell Tolls'."

"Irony's a bitch."

The music cut out mid-chord. The only noise was wind and the steady drone of the crane's engine.

Hansie shouted, "We don't need the music anymore, they'll find us just fine."

Emily took three solo steps then dropped to all fours, gripping the lattice for support. "It's falling!"

Holding up a calming hand, Brank said, "No it's not. They're designed to sway with the wind like that."

"Oh good, 'cause otherwise this wouldn't be terrifying enough!"

"I know it sounds crazy, but try standing, you'll get your sea legs pretty quick."

She slowly got up, muttering, "Or just fall to my death … got ya."

To Brank's surprise she took a few wobbly steps then found her balance. He caught himself wondering if she was seeing anyone then realized the absurdity of pondering any kind of future.

Pointing to the top of the control cabin, Brank said, "If you see that yellow beacon light come on, grab a hold of something, that's the signal it's going to move." Then he walked along the jib arm in search of a clear firing position.

Emily tried to keep up, asking, "Any more advice?"

He pointed to the distant, rhythmically swaying, hook block and said, "Don't stare at that, the movement will hypnotize you, which is bad."

"Good safety tip. You sure know a lot about these things."

"Before I joined the army, I spent six months working on drilling rigs."

"Why'd you quit?"

"I saw a guy fall off one of these cranes."

"Thanks for sharing." Emily took a few more steps while singing the Temptations' "My Girl."

Brank asked, "What're you doing?"

Emily's steps grew more confident, and in a sing-song voice she said, "Try it. The song's tempo matches the swaying."

Brank smiled and found a spot that offered a decent visual on the crane's mast. He crouched down, rifle to his shoulder. The jib's constant swaying may have been good engineering, but it was making his job a lot harder. He tried putting the scope's crosshairs on a scorpion that was nearing the top of the crane's mast.

He muttered, "Come on, relax, feel it," And Then began singing the Temptations song. "I got bullets for you today… Keep climbing and I'll blow your ass away." It worked, allowing him to mentally compensate for the sway. With a long, steadying exhale, he fired.

The round severed the scorpion's tail, knocking it off the mast.

"Yeah, talkin' bout my gun… My gun."

He fired two more rounds, successfully blasting three more of the scorpions off the mast. The yellow rotating beacon came on, and Emily dropped down, clutching the steel lattice. The crane shook, and the jib arm began to pivot.

Brank glanced over at Emily, who smiled. Brank caught himself smiling back and muttered, "Maybe we get to have a future after all."

Using his rifle scope, he looked down at the lower half of the mast. His smile vanished. When they'd started climbing, the steel mast had been bright yellow; now it was black with climbing scorpions. He was down to ten rounds—not even enough to make a dent.

CHAPTER ELEVEN

Tigger slowly climbed down the ladder, placing both feet on each rung, eyes fixed on the scorpions. He was only going down ten feet, but with a broken arm he was completely vulnerable every step.

The two scorpions were perched on girders twenty feet away, the severed arm lying between them. The creatures snapped their pincers at each other, neither one willing to give up their claim to the prize.

Tigger said a silent prayer for guidance, tactfully reminding Saint Miguel that a hundred lives depended on him recovering the arm. Right now, one dead arm was worth more than his life.

Goon lay on the platform above, cradling the Mossberg even though he didn't dare use it. Just one shotgun blast would drive the scorpions into a frenzy and likely send the arm plummeting over the edge.

Tigger stepped down onto the steel girder and paused. The scorpions didn't react, too engrossed in their sparring to notice. Rising onto the balls of his feet, Tigger took a few heel-to-toe steps back and forth then did a three-hundred-sixty-degree turn, testing his balance. It helped that he'd been a gymnast in his youth, but the foot-wide girder still made for a terrible fighting platform. He looked around for a better option. To his rear, a small working platform, known as a monkey board, jutted out from the derrick. The six-by-six platform held a vertical stand of twenty-foot drilling pipes all secured in place by a chain—a definite improvement.

He studied his opponents, remembering everything he'd learned about scorpions back in the Honduran jungles. Modern ones only had rudimentary vision and no sense of smell, relying on their sensory hairs to detect prey. Brank had proven they still had poor vision, but these monsters had a keen sense of smell, especially when it came to blood. The biggest ones had shown cunning, but he was hoping these smaller ones were younger and reckless.

In fact, he was counting on it.

Through trial and many errors, Hansie mastered the rudiments of crane operation. The slewing unit was working at full speed, pivoting the jib arm towards the rig tower. He'd learned that the jib wouldn't telescope while the slewing unit was in operation. It was a good safety feature, unless you had man-eating scorpions climbing up the mast.

He heard another .50 caliber round and glanced down to see if Brank was hitting anything. The crane's yellow mast was now black with crawling scorpions.

"*Fok* me!"

Putting his faith in Brank, he went back to pivoting the arm until it was lined up on the rig tower. He locked the slewing unit and engaged the telescoping arm. It began to extend, clicking like a giant metronome. Its speed was agonizingly slow.

Hansie dug the last cigarette from the pack and lit it. There was nothing to do but wait.

Brank fired a round at the highest scorpion, knocking it off the mast. By his count he was down to eight rounds. But the next wave was so densely packed that his weapon wouldn't do much good.

Emily shouted, "I think we're lined up!"

Hansie must have shared that opinion because the jib lurched to a stop. A few seconds later, the telescoping arm slowly began to extend.

To Brank, everything seemed to be moving at a glacial pace—except the scorpions. He said, "I should go out to the end of the jib to help 'em across."

"What if we need the big gun to cover Hansie?"

Brank didn't have an answer.

Emily said, "I'll go. It's not like I'm useful here."

"It's too dangerous."

"As opposed to this?" She handed Brank the Vektor rifle. "Here, it's not like I can hit anything further than three feet away."

All Brank could think to say was, "Please be careful."

"Okay, but only 'cause you said please." Emily started walking along the weaving jib arm, humming the Temptations song, arms outstretched for balance. Once she reached the telescoping portion she turned back to Brank, smiled and mimed an extended arm surfing pose as she rode it outward.

Brank held up his hand, giving the surfer's "hang ten" sign and muttered, "Crazy." Then he used the rifle scope to survey the drilling platform—something was wrong. He saw Goon, still hunkered down behind the block and tackle, but there was no sign of Tigger. He panned the scope down and shouted, "What the hell!"

Tigger was one level below, about to face off with a pair of scorpions. Brank considered taking a shot, but the swaying jib arm and Tigger's close proximity to the creatures made it impossible.

Tigger tapped the machete blade against the girder, catching the scorpions' attention. The closest pivoted around, rocking up and down on its eight legs, pincers outstretched. Tigger kept tapping, helping it zero in on the target.

The second scorpion snapped the severed arm up in its pincers but made no attempt to eat it. Instead, it went perfectly still, ready to defend its prize.

The first scorpion took a few steps forward. As soon as it did, Tigger slammed the blade against the derrick harder and faster. The scorpion paused, confused by the conflicting vibrations. Tigger hoped uncertainty would make it overly cautious—nervous adversaries made more mistakes.

Rattling the blade, Tigger shouted, "Come on, *cabrón*! Don't be shy, here I am!"

Another tenuous step brought it close enough to smell the blood on Tigger's face. Enticed by the scent, the scorpion continued inching forward.

Tigger heel-toed back four steps, bouncing on the balls of his feet.

Goon yelled, "You can't beat that thing with a machete!"

"Chill, *hermano*, I got this. Now, when I turn around, you start banging on the steel up there, real hard."

The scorpion took five huge strides and attacked. Its left pincer shot out at Tigger's head. In one fluid motion he ducked while swinging his blade upward, glancing the pincer's tip. The scorpion's other pincer lashed out but missed, sweeping just over his head. The tail jabbed down, but Tigger was already moving back, narrowly avoiding the stinger.

The scorpion took a step back, wary of this aggressive prey.

Seizing the moment, Tigger turned, heel-toeing it toward the distant monkey board.

Taking his cue, Goon banged on the metal above, momentarily confusing the creature.

As soon as Tigger made it to the monkey board, he shouted, "Now stop!"

Goon quit hammering.

Tigger knelt down low, reviewing what he'd just learned. Most of the scorpions had made running, lightning-fast attacks. But this one had advanced, stopped, and made a stationary attack. Clearly it wasn't comfortable fighting on this narrow girder. Slapping the machete blade against the steel, he yelled, "Hey *hijo de la puta*, come for me!" Once he had its attention, he slid the machete into its sheath and prepared.

The scorpion took two measured strides then bolted forward.

With his good arm, Tigger grabbed the nearest vertical pipe, hoisting himself up.

The scorpion charged onto the monkey board. Zeroing in on Tigger's position, it reared up, striking out with its pincers.

Tigger sprang upward, using the safety chain; the scorpion lashed out, aiming for Tigger's foot but instead clamping down on the chain. Tigger swung onto the monkey board's railing just as the pincer's crushing force snapped through the links—freeing a dozen twenty-foot pipes. Using both feet, Tigger kicked the wobbling tubes, sending them crashing onto the scorpion. The rolling pipes swept it over the edge and tumbling into space, along with an avalanche of steel pipes.

Tigger hopped down, drawing the machete, shouting, "One down!"

Goon yelled, "Nice job, but don't get sloppy."

The other scorpion remained glued to its spot, the severed arm still clutched in its pincer.

Slamming the machete against the girder, Tigger yelled, "Come on!"

It didn't move.

Goon said, "He ain't going for it."

"This one's smarter, making me come to it."

Tigger unhooked the chain from the monkey board, smacking its grab hook against the girder as he walked forward. The thirty feet of chain was too unwieldy to be a weapon, but he had another idea. "I'm throwing this end of the chain up to you. Wrap it around the girder." He tossed the grab hook end up.

Goon secured it around the girder, leaving twenty feet hanging straight down.

Tigger said, "Now make a loop."

"Seriously?"

"Yeah, we're making a snare. When it comes at me, you'll know what to do."

Goon did it, creating a chain loop suspended just above Tigger's head. He rolled onto his back, feeling a fresh rush of blood trickling down his side. Once in place he gripped the chain, knees bent, feet braced against the edge of the platform. "Okay, I'm good to pull."

With his machete sheathed, Tigger advanced on the scorpion, stomping his foot on the girder to provoke it, shouting, "Come on, *pendejo*!"

The scorpion just stood, motionless, until it caught a whiff of the blood on his face. After a few seconds, hunger overcame common sense and it took a measured step forward.

Knowing what was coming, Tigger turned, quickly heel-toeing just past the hanging loop of chain.

Still clutching its prize, the scorpion scrambled forward, its pincers raised to attack.

Tigger shouted, "Get ready!"

The scorpion came straight at Tigger, its upraised right pincer going straight into the looped chain. The grab hook slid down, tightening the chain just below the pincer. Goon yanked with all his might, hauling the scorpion's right arm upward, forcing it to cling to the girder with its four left limbs. Its stinger lashed out, stabbing at the chain to no effect.

Tigger raced for the other pincer, grabbing Ruby's dead fingers in a handshake. Fighting to defend its prize, the scorpion clamped down, slicing through Ruby's arm just below the wrist.

Tigger pulled away, clutching the severed hand. He lobbed it upward. It landed on the platform a few feet from Goon.

The scorpion's short mouth pincers snapped, slashing Tigger's left calf, drenching the wound in acidic mucus. Tigger's leg buckled, forcing him to clutch the girder with his good arm. The right pincer clamped down on his wounded leg, lifting him into the air. Now dangling upside down, Tigger pulled the machete, slashing at the scorpion's row of lateral eyes.

Goon grimaced in pain, desperately hanging on to the chain, fresh blood gushing from his gunshot wound.

Tigger's machete blow slashed open the scorpion's eyes, bathing him in gray ocular fluid. The agonized creature's pincer clamped down harder, sawing through flesh and bone, severing Tigger's leg.

The brave Honduran plummeted, screaming, into the darkness, the machete still clenched in his hand.

With an agonized howl, Goon released the chain and collapsed.

The untethered scorpion dropped, rolling into space until its pincer caught the edge of the girder. It hung there by one claw, flailing, unable to pull itself up.

Goon looked down at the dangling scorpion and screamed, "You still hungry? Eat this, you murdering piece of shit!" and pumped three rounds of buckshot into its face.

The wounded beast finally released the girder, tumbling into the night.

Goon stood there, screaming Tigger's name, knowing he'd never answer. Eventually the pain in his side forced him down onto his knees. He slammed his fists against the girder, weeping for the first time since childhood. He shouted, "Stop!" and took a few long breaths, telling himself, "Got to pull it together, got to finish the job." He crawled to the severed hand and pressed Ruby's cold thumb to the satellite phone's touchpad.

The screen message switched over to, "Sending message," then "Sending attachments." After what felt like an eternity, the screen lit up with, "Message sent."

Goon set down the phone, looked into the night sky and screamed, "You did it, brother!"

Brank screamed, "No! No!" as he watched Tigger plummeting to his death. Watching his friend die was like an emotional punch in the guts. Looking across at the tower, he saw Goon slamming his fists against the steel derrick, howling like a wounded animal. It was heartbreaking. So many deaths. First Easy, then Ruby, and now Tigger—all people he'd failed to save. In that moment he wished he'd been the one to fall off that crane so many years ago.

Hansie's voice boomed over the PA system. "Hey! A moment of your time!"

Snapping back into reality, Brank climbed onto the control cabin's roof and looked down. "Aw shit!"

Four scorpions were clustered at the mast's peak, bullying each other to reach the top first. He popped out the rifle's magazine and slipped an incendiary round into the chamber.

He shouted, "Hansie, get down on the floor!" and lined up his target, muttering, "You bastards aren't taking anybody else," then fired into the cluster.

The round ripped into the largest scorpion before detonating in a ball of fire. Flaming shrapnel of steel and exoskeleton struck the others, sending them tumbling into the darkness.

The close-range blast concussion knocked Brank over and shattered the control cabin's Plexiglas windows. He got up and leaned his head down into the cabin shouting, "You okay, Hansie?"

After a coughing fit, Hansie yelled, "Oh sure, I'm great!"

"I can do that trick one more time; after that, we're in deep shit."

"If you do that again we'll be dead anyway!" Dusting off the shards of Plexiglas, Hansie went back to the controls. He said, "The jib's reached the drilling tower. Once your people are aboard, I'll start pivoting it toward the fence. Then I'm coming out. We'll have to climb down while it's still moving, but it's pretty slow. I can't take it any lower than thirty feet, otherwise the electric fence will arc up and fry us."

"How do we get down?"

"There's a maintenance switch on the hook block, so we can lower it manually and shimmy down."

"Sounds good!"

Hansie went back to the controls, muttering, "No, it sounds *foking* insane! But what else is new?"

Kruger eyed the moving crane, piecing together what the Americans were up to.

Hertzog said, "I can't believe they're still alive."

"It is impressive. I'm not sure whether to kill them or hire them." Lowering his binoculars, he shouted, "Steyn!"

The lieutenant ran over. "Yes sir."

"The Americans are using the crane to get over the fence. Send two men over to the east side and have them wait. As soon as they're close enough, kill them."

"Yes sir." Steyn turned to leave.

Kruger stopped him. "And don't send any idiots. That man with the fifty-caliber is a damned skilled soldier."

"Yes sir. Anything else?"

After a moment's thought, Kruger asked, "How soon till all those villagers are in position?"

"The bus should have grabbed the final load by now. They'll drop them at the midway point and we'll be ready."

"Good, let's finish this."

Emily hung on tight, shocked by the telescoping jib's wild rocking. She muttered, "We went from "My Girl" to Motörhead."

The jib was positioned directly over the drilling tower and she could see Goon down below. She stood, waving in Hansie's direction and giving him a thumbs up.

He must have seen her because the telescoping jib lurched to a halt then began to descend.

Emily hung on, repeating her new mantra, "This is working, we're going to be fine," until she almost believed herself.

The passing arm dipped dangerously close to the flare stack, forcing her to crawl back a good fifteen feet until it came safely to rest on the drilling platform.

She jumped down, shouting, "Come on guys, your Uber's arrived."

Goon slowly got to his feet and hobbled towards the jib. Emily ran over, reaching him just as he crumpled to his knees.

Putting his arm over her shoulder she hauled him upright. "What happened?"

In a weak voice, Goon said, "I'm shot."

"Where's Tigger?"

Goon just shook his head.

"Alright, hang on to me. We're getting out of here."

Goon's usual booming voice was barely a whisper. "I saw him die, but there was nothing I could do. If I don't make it, you need to tell Brank something."

Nearly buckling under his weight, Emily said, "He knows you did all you could."

"Not that. It's the villagers; those bastards are going to feed them to the scorpions."

"That's insane!"

Wincing in pain, Goon said, "But true."

Emily half dragged the two-hundred-and-fifty-pound Canadian to the jib. After laying him out flat, she gestured in Hansie's direction.

A Mamba armored car idled alongside the eastern side of the fence line. Two of Kruger's men sat inside, monitoring the crane's progress.

The driver asked, "Can that thing move any fucking slower?" He strained to make out something in the distance. "Wait, I can see people on it."

The gunner popped open the roof hatch for a better view. "I bet I can nail them from here."

"Steyn said to wait till they were real close before we shoot 'em."

"And then what? Leave the crane arm hanging there so those things can use it as a drawbridge?"

"I hadn't thought of that."

"I say we hit them now and get it over with. Maybe we've still got time to break in one of those village girls before feeding time."

The driver slapped the bolt on his Vektor rifle. "I'm always up for that." He climbed out, taking a firing position behind the hood of the Mamba.

The gunner asked, "Why're you down there?"

"'Cause I want an engine block between me and that fifty-caliber. Remember what happened to Kruger's spotter? It blew his ass in half."

"Suit yourself." The gunner took aim. "I got 'em lined up."

"Me too, fire on three. One, two…"

Hansie raised the jib arm until it was safely above the burning flare stack. Satisfied it was clear, he engaged the slewing unit. The two-hundred-foot arm began pivoting towards the fence.

Brank knelt down on the control cabin's roof, alternating his gaze between the rescue operation and the cluster of scorpions climbing the crane's mast.

He shouted down, "It's getting ugly out here!"

Hansie replied, "Just a few more seconds."

Brank yelled, "I need to shoot again," and raised his rifle.

Before he could pull the trigger, the mass of scorpions ceased climbing and slipped inside the crane mast's steel lattice, leaving Brank without a shot.

"The bastards are learning."

Hansie shouted, "Brank, the arm will be over the fence in about two minutes!" He dug an empty shell casing from his pocket, tossed it on the floor and stomped on the open end. Once it was flattened, he wedged it into the slew motor control, effectively putting it on auto pilot.

He shouted, "I'm done; let's get the *fok* out of here!"

Brank heard gunfire in the distance and saw Emily dive flat onto the jib. Another burst of automatic weapons fire followed. Bullets pinged off the steel jib, creating a cascade of sparks.

"They're firing at the jib!"

Hansie yelled, "Then go deal with it!"

Emily dropped down onto the jib arm as bullets ricocheted off the steel lattice around her.

She crawled toward Goon, repeating, "This is working, we're going to be fine," but the crane was still pivoting, drawing them ever closer to the gunmen. "Christ, in another minute even I'd be able to hit us."

Goon rolled over onto his side, struggling to aim the shotgun. There was another burst of gunfire, and rounds clattered against the steel.

Emily finally reached him. His shirt was soaked with blood, but she couldn't tell if it was new. She asked, "Are you hit?"

"No more than I was before." He fumbled with the shotgun. "Help me sit up."

Emily got behind him, pushing him into a seated position. He fired twice, knowing the shotgun would have little to no effect at this range and angle—but at least they were returning fire.

Brank quick stepped for fifty feet along the jib then knelt to return fire. Although he had the advantage of high ground, the angle was too steep. Plus, the shooters were masked by prison-quality hardened steel fencing. He fired six rounds from Emily's Vektor rifle. Half were deflected by the fencing while the others ricocheted off the armored car.

He went another twenty feet until he was halfway to Goon and Emily and shouted, "Can you crawl over here?"

Emily yelled, "Goon's hit, but we'll try."

Brank fired another six rounds for cover, but their progress was slow. He only had seven bullets left in the magazine and no spares.

He considered using the .50 caliber but knew the rounds could detonate on contact with the fence, breaking the electrical circuit. That fence was the only thing keeping the scorpions inside.

With every second, the jib pivoted closer to the fence line. Emily and Goon were about to be sitting ducks.

Hansie tapped the bullet shell one last time, feeling confident it would hold.

The control room shook, as if struck by a bomb, slamming him to the floor. A ten-foot scorpion clung to the outside, shredding the metal walls with its pincers.

Hansie ducked just in time to avoid it. He scooped up his rifle, shouting, "Come on, you *vokken gedierte!*"

Ten rounds struck point-blank into the creature's face, shearing off its mouth appendages. The scorpion slunk back, vomiting a jet of yellow bile. The acidic mucus splashed across Hansie's leg, searing his skin. Despite the pain, he managed to pull himself up and out of the ceiling hatch and onto the roof.

The injured scorpion was already climbing after him. Hansie loosed another burst into its face. The ballistic force knocked it back, and, with no footing, it tumbled off the crane.

Knowing he had less than a minute to escape, Hansie turned then froze, yelling, "*Seen van 'n teef!*"

A pair of scorpions was on the jib, blocking his path. One charged forward, pincers snapping. Hansie tried to stand, but the searing pain in his leg forced him back to his knees. With no other option, he crawled backward, over the cabin and onto the counter jib.

The scorpion slowed its advance, seemingly wary of the rumbling machinery. That hesitation bought Hansie a few extra seconds, allowing him to drop down between the winch motors and reload.

The scorpion launched another attack, groping down with its left pincer. It missed Hansie, wrapping around a thick bundle of hydraulic hoses. The pincer sliced through, releasing high-pressure jets of red-hot hydraulic fluid. The spraying fluid seared the creature's eyes. It reared back then dropped down, driving its pincer into Hansie's chest.

Hansie screamed, "*Vokken kont!*" pumping twenty rounds into the creature's underbelly at point-blank range.

The scorpion squealed, entrails spilling out. Its death throes sent it tumbling off the crane with Hansie still impaled on its pincer.

Hansie's scream of, "*O Fok!*" echoed through the night until they both crashed to the ground.

The last jet of fluid sputtered from the severed hoses, leaving the crane with zero hydraulic pressure.

With a shudder, the two-hundred-foot jib began to sink.

Brank watched Emily and Goon struggling to reach him. He was powerless to help until the hypnotically swaying hook block at the end of the jib caught his eye. The jib's tip had just cleared the fence line and was about to pass directly over the shooter's vehicle. Brank hooked his leg around the steel lattice, leaning over the side of the jib, the .50 caliber in hand. But instead of aiming for the attackers, he focused on the end of the jib arm. He placed his crosshairs on the swaying steel hook block and fired.

The explosive round struck the steel assembly holding the block, reducing it to shrapnel.

Brank yelled, "Bombs away!"

The .50 caliber's distinctive roar sent the driver scrambling under for cover beneath the Mamba.

The gunner shouted, "Get back out here, you chicken shit!" and continued firing. He heard a sharp metallic snap just as the jib arm's shadow passed over him. Looking up, he stammered, "Mother fuc—"

Eighteen tons of hook block tore through the roof like paper. The bulletproof windows exploded outward. The coil spring suspension buckled, hammering the chassis down onto the shale ground.

A mixture of diesel fuel and blood flowed out from beneath.

Brank watched as the hook block pancaked the armored vehicle, ending the enemy fire. He raced toward Emily and Goon, knowing they had less than a minute to get off this merry-go-round.

The sight of Brank inspired Goon back onto his feet.

Brank asked, "How bad is it?"

"It's nothing; I've had worse in hockey games."

But Brank saw that the big man's knees were buckling. Emily stepped over to support him.

She said, "That's just macho bullshit, he's still bleeding and—" She went silent and pointed.

A pair of scorpions was creeping along the jib arm, straight for them.

Brank said, "Glad we're not going that way. Let's move."

The jib shuddered and instantly dropped a foot. Goon nearly went over the side, but Brank managed to grab him. They knelt, gripping the steel lattice as the jib dropped another foot.

Emily asked, "What's happening?"

"We're sinking, fast."

"Good, it'll be easier to jump off, right?"

"Sure, except we're on a steel jib that's dropping onto an electrified fence."

Brank looked back towards the control room. The two scorpions were closing in, moving like racehorses. But they weren't alone. It looked like a Thanksgiving Day parade of horrors was following behind them.

Brank heard a high-pitched squeal, followed by an ear-splitting whip snap. The support cable running between the jib arm and the tower peak snapped. The flying cable sent one scorpion flying into the air. Without that support, the arm lurched, dropping another two feet. Now the sinking became steady, accelerating every second. There was no way they'd make it to the end before it made contact.

Brank looked at the ground below then turned to Emily and Goon. "Do you trust me?" They nodded. "Good, then don't look, just jump... Now!"

Amazingly, they did. A split second later, Brank leapt off, barely escaping the lead scorpion.

In that same instant the jib arm made contact with the electric fence, sending eight hundred amps surging through the steel arm. Arcing lightning bolts surged down the arm, turning it into a two-hundred-foot Tesla coil. The scorpions crawling on it were launched into the air like Roman candles.

Brank landed hard, knocking every bit of air out of his lungs. He rolled to his left, gasping for breath—coming face-to-face with a ten-foot scorpion.

Then everything went black.

CHAPTER TWELVE

Kruger shouted, "What's taking the bus so long? They've been in that village forever!"

Struggling to hide the quiver in his voice, Steyn said, "I don't know, sir. They're out of radio range, so we can't reach them."

"In ten minutes I'm opening up that gate whether they're here or not."

Steyn sounded relieved. "I understand, sir; a perfectly logical decision given our situation."

"Glad you agree because I'm leaving you here with them, so you better get out there and un-fuck this situation!"

Steyn raced off, inadvertently kicking dust into the faces of the two nuns kneeling on the ground. One coughed, catching Kruger's attention.

Kruger bent down, eye level with the women. Both were seated, hips resting on their feet, knees pressed against the hard shale.

He said, "Not very comfortable, is it? It's called stress position, a marvelous tool for interrogation. Can you guess where I learned it?"

Sister Estelle sat in stoic silence.

"At the orphanage. Those nuns left me in that position for hours as punishment. Just for the sin of saying I was hungry."

Sister Estelle said, "I'm sorry you suffered that way, and I will pray for your soul."

"Pray for my soul? No, you're really praying that God will come and strike me down."

The entire complex suddenly lit up in a brilliant white flash. The men around him hit the dirt, certain the natural gas tanks had exploded. Kruger stood his ground, squinting against the blinding light. He saw the crane jib engulfed in flashes of arcing electricity and his nostrils filled with burning ozone. The generator sputtered and the scorpion sentry rose up onto its eight legs. Its tail rose then slammed down against the hard ground repeatedly, the sound echoing like a drum.

Kruger muttered, "It knows," and ran to the generator. "What happened?"

The operator was frantically throwing switches. "It overloaded, shorted out. I'm trying to get it back on line."

"Well, do it because those bastards are coming for us!" Turning to his men, he shouted, "On your feet! Form a firing line, now!"

Two scorpions were already charging at the fence. One man opened fire, but Kruger smacked him to the ground.

"Don't damage the fence! Wait until they clear it and then focus your fire. Alpha Squad left, Baker right!"

Within seconds the first scorpion cleared the fence and hit the ground running.

Alpha Squad opened fire, unleashing a hundred 5.56 rounds into the charging beast. The fusillade hammered at its exoskeleton, shearing off two of its eight legs. Despite the damage, it staggered forward until it was barely ten yards from the firing line and raised its stinger.

Then it did something that amazed Kruger.

Just before dying, the beast squirted a stream of venom into the air. Most of the firing line managed to jump aside, but one slower man was soaked in the viscous yellow fluid. He sank to his knees, screaming until his gelatinous melting skin filled his mouth, choking him.

The second scorpion clambered up and over the fence. It landed then paused, pivoting back and forth in place, searching for its prey. Then the beast charged straight at Kruger.

Maintaining discipline, Baker Squad fired in unison, but the creature's angular attack minimized their effectiveness.

Kruger shouted, "The legs! Shoot its legs!"

The barrage tore at the creature's flank, shearing off three of its right legs. Kruger watched it hobble on, hell-bent on reaching him. He yanked Sister Estelle onto her feet, shoving her in front of him. The dying creature raised its tail and sprayed, showering the nun in venom. With its venom sac emptied, the beast collapsed onto its side, thrashing as another wave of bullets tore its underbelly open.

Kruger shoved the screaming nun to the ground and heard a beautiful noise—the generator roaring back to life.

A third scorpion leapt onto the fence and hung there, its body wracked with spasms. Seconds later, it dropped to the ground, lifeless, smoke drifting off it.

The men cheered wildly.

Kruger knelt down over the nun, watching in fascination as her skin putrefied before his eyes. He said, "Thanks, Sister, I guess you saved my soul after all."

With her last breath, she proclaimed, "God as my witness, you'll burn in hell."

"I already have a first-class seat reserved." Then he stood tall, arms held high, shouting congratulations to his men, until that confidence was shattered by something he saw—or rather didn't see.

The area inside the fence line was empty. The huge sentry scorpion had vanished.

Steyn raced over. "Sir, I haven't been able to reach the men in the village. Are you still planning to open the gate?"

Kruger shook his head. "Let's wait a bit longer, give those bastards some time to settle down."

"Yes sir." Steyn ran off.

Kruger stood staring at the fence line, unsure if the sentry scorpion had gotten over during the melee or had just slipped back into the drilling site. But he was certain of one thing; those eight-legged bastards knew exactly who he was—and they were targeting him.

Brank snapped back into consciousness, his mouth and nose clogged with sand. He looked to his left and his blood froze. A massive scorpion was inches away, its hideous mouth close enough to kiss. It took one skipped heartbeat for him to register the smoke wafting off its scorched exoskeleton. It was dead.

He stood, taking a moment to ascertain that, although everything hurt, nothing was broken. He saw the sand beside him rippling.

Emily clawed her way to the surface, as if rising from the grave. After blowing out a mouthful of sand, she asked, "Be honest. Did you really know there was a sand pile down here?"

"Yeah, but it still could have been hard as cement." He kicked the scorpion's smoldering remains and said, "That's what would have happened if we'd stayed on the crane."

"I hated that crane."

Brank looked around, whispering Goon's name.

A muffled voice said, "Over here."

Brank and Emily rushed to help the half-buried Canadian.

"You okay, pal?"

Goon shot them his toothless grin. "I'm good. Playing hockey teaches you how to take hits." He looked around. "Is this like a sandbox or something?"

"Drilling sites use tons of concrete, so there's always a sand heap. We're lucky it was this close."

Goon shook the sand out of his beard. "Don't kid yourself; we ain't been lucky since the plane landed."

Emily asked, "What about Hansie?"

Brank just shook his head.

Goon said, "Damn, I really liked that old warhorse."

"Me too, but we need to get moving." Brank dug the site diagram from his pocket and studied it. "Here, this might be our best bet." He pointed a finger at a building marked *"Verbode."* "I think that means forbidden, so it might be something secure or just where the bosses locked up their booze."

Goon said, "I'm good either way."

Brank and Emily each slung one of Goon's arms over their shoulder and started walking.

"If we take a left it should be about fifty yar—" Brank froze.

A writhing mass of scorpions was clustered around the base of the crane mast.

Goon whispered, "Looks like they're having an orgy."

Emily said, "More like a barbecue."

The swarm was clustered around the smoldering carcasses of other scorpions, ripping them apart with their pincers, feasting on the steaming meat within.

Brank whispered, "Those dead ones got electrocuted. If we're quiet, I think we can get by them."

They crept on, slipping past the horde, all too engrossed in their cannibal cookout to notice.

Emily gasped and pointed to a ten-foot scorpion huddled at the fringe, viciously protecting its meal from the others.

Brank saw it too. The scorpion was tearing apart a human body. The head and arms had already been shredded, but Brank recognized Hansie's distinctive khaki shorts. He whispered, "Don't look; just keep moving."

After another white-knuckle minute, they'd cleared the horde and slipped down an alleyway lined with gas separators and heat exchangers.

Brank whispered, "Get back," and steered them in front of an exhaust fan.

Clusters of scorpions passed by them, all bound for the crane. The group huddled in front of the fan, hoping the benzene fumes would mask the smell of Goon's blood.

Emily said, "They're like seniors rushing to an all you can eat buffet."

Watching the parade pass, Goon asked, "How many of those bastards are there?"

"A shit load," Brank whispered, "like think of a stupidly high number then multiply it by ten."

Emily felt Goon's blood soaking into her shirt. "We need to get him someplace safe."

Once the coast was clear, Brank steered them right, down another alleyway. "Hang on, buddy, we're getting close. It's just up there."

After passing a row of Quonset huts they came to a low-slung, concrete-faced building covered in a layer of sandbags. The small windows were sealed with iron shutters. A yellow triangular warning sign was screwed to the steel door secured by a heavy-duty combination lock.

Brank whispered, "I'm going to have to shoot the lock, which is a really stupid thing to do."

Emily asked, "Why?"

Pointing to the triangular sign, he said, "'Cause it's full of explosives."

"Oh… Wait." Emily knelt down, twisting the individual cylinders one turn in each direction then back until the padlock popped open.

Brank asked, "Are you a burglar in your spare time?"

"It's from an online list I wrote, 'Top Ten Ways to Avoid Being Robbed.' Most people only twist one cylinder to lock up, so all you need to do is—"

Goon cut her off. "Company's coming." He pointed to a pair of scorpions rounding the intersection only thirty feet away—they saw him too.

Brank pulled the door open. "Inside now!"

They pushed through the doorway and scrambled down a short set of stairs. Brank slammed the steel door shut, throwing the bolt just as the two predators hurled themselves against it.

Emily set Goon down on a folding chair and listened anxiously to the scorpions clawing at the door.

Brank said, "I don't think they're getting through. The door's solid steel and this is a below-ground storage bunker, meaning they had to jackhammer out the shale to build it."

Emily said, "So they can't dig under it?"

"Exactly, and the roof is steel, covered in sandbags. We're safe in here."

"How'd you know all that?"

"It's pretty standard for an explosives storage bunker."

Brank dug around inside a small refrigerator and handed Goon a liter of *Twizza Cola*. "Drink some, you need the sugar." Then he examined the gunshot wound.

Emily pulled open a wooden case and held up a baseball-sized chrome device. "What's this?"

"A shaped explosive charge. Possibly depleted uranium."

She delicately placed it back in the box.

Brank said, "Relax, it won't go off in your hand. It needs a detonator." He went back to probing Goon's wound. "It isn't in too deep, but you lost a lot of blood."

Emily knelt down next to Goon, taking his hand. "You're going to be okay." She watched Brank rooting through his small first aid pouch. "Is that a tampon?"

"Yeah, junior sized, perfect for bullet wounds. Goon, this'll hurt like hell."

Brank slid the tampon into the wound, where it expanded, partially sealing the hole. He topped it with a pressure bandage then dug a tiny silver bottle out of his pouch. "Take this and chew it up."

Goon did, asking, "Is it morphine, please, please?"

"It's Zofran to keep you from puking. In ten minutes I'll give you these. One's a fentanyl lozenge for pain and the other's a dextroamphetamine to keep you alert."

With a raised eyebrow, Emily said, "You must be popular at parties."

Brank held up the silver bottle and explained, "It's an old Special Forces medic cocktail, non-regulation and totally illegal but effective."

Emily looked at the bottle and yelped, "Jesus Brank, your finger's missing!"

Brank held up his right hand, wiggling its partial index finger. "Oh, that was gone when we got here. I must have lost my rubber finger cap along the way."

Goon said, "Why do you think I call him Stumpy?" and chuckled then groaned.

Brank finished applying the bandage and said, "Sorry buddy, your fluids are bad, but I don't have an IV."

Goon groaned, took a swig of cola, and said, "It's all good."

"Did Ruby get the message out?"

"No, but Tigger managed. It was the last thing he did."

"He was a good man. I know you were tight, I'm sorry."

"He was like my bad-ass little brother." Goon went quiet for a moment.

Brank said, "It's my fault, I should have planned things out better. Maybe if I'd known about this place sooner everybody'd still be alive."

Goon snapped, "That's bullshit! Ruby, may she rest in peace, ordered us here, throwing you into a bad situation. Then we got sealed up with Godzilla monsters inside and Nazi storm troopers outside. If it wasn't for you, we'd all be dead. If Tigger was here, he'd tell you the same damn thing."

Brank sighed and said, "Thanks buddy."

"So what's the plan, Stumpy?"

"It'll be hours before the cavalry arrives and you're in no condition to move, so I'm thinking we wait it out here. These walls should keep the scorpions out, and the scorpions will keep the bad guys off our back. Sound like a plan?"

Emily said, "You want to tell him, Goon?"

Goon nodded. "There's just one problem, boss."

Brank listened, stunned by Goon's account of the kidnapped villagers being held outside the gate. One thing was clear—if they sat tight in the bunker waiting to be rescued, a hundred men, women and children would be slaughtered.

Goon added, "Tigger thought they wanted to keep these things for a zoo or something."

Brank shook his head. "No, that's not it. I think they want to shut the fence off and open the gate. Once those things smell food, they'll all come running out to chow down on the villagers."

Emily asked, "But why? What do they gain by butchering innocent people?"

"Because once the scorpions are out munching on villagers the mercenaries can slip inside, turn the fence back on and take legal possession of their precious new gas."

"They'd murder all those people just for the gas?"

"Think about it, a suspended animation gas is worth more than gold, diamonds, hell anything. The medical applications, space travel, law enforcement ... it's the golden goose. If someone owned the only known pocket, they'd be richer than Gates and Bezos combined. Plus, if they killed us and the villagers, nobody'd ever know what really happened."

"Except we got the word out."

"And when help arrives, they'll already be locked up inside. Possession's nine tenths of the law."

"But once they're inside won't they have to deal with the scorpions coming out of the pit?"

Brank laughed out loud.

Emily asked, "Uh, sorry, but did I make a joke?"

Brank said, "I'm laughing because our storm trooper friends don't know about the pit, which makes their plan sadistic and stupid at the same time."

"And what about the scorpions that get out?"

"They'll eat the villagers and move on. Beitbridge is only about forty kilometers away."

Emily gasped and said, "There must be forty thousand people in Beitbridge!"

"Not for long." Brank walked over to the row of wooden boxes, pulling out one of the shaped charges. Bouncing it in his hand, he said, "Okay guys, new plan."

Goon said, "Boss, whatever you want to do, I'm in. Tigger died trying to save those people, and I ain't letting him down. Hey, can I have my cookies now?"

"Knock yourself out."

Goon wolfed down the two pills.

Brank rooted through the cases of explosives. "Thanks for the pep talk, Goon, but you're staying here." He handed Emily some spools of red plastic cable.

She asked, "Do I even want to know?"

"It's Prima-cord ... detonating cable."

"Are you going to throw bombs at those things?"

"I wish I could, but it ain't that easy. Shaped charges are hard to detonate, that's why most explosive engineers still have all their fingers."

"So what's the plan?"

"Remember when Hansie said I couldn't shoot those liquid nitrogen tanks and blow them up?"

"Yeah."

"But I could use these shaped charges to blast them wide open. The liquid nitrogen would flow down into the pit and kill them."

"Cool, but what about the ones above ground?"

"You already solved that problem."

Confused, Emily asked, "Okay, can you remind me how I did that?"

"Once the liquid nitrogen is released, it'll turn to nitrogen gas and hang close to the ground, like dry ice fog at a rock concert. The nitrogen displaces oxygen—"

"And chokes them to death!"

"Yup, a couple bong hits of that fog and those wheezy bastards'll curl up and die ... I hope. Any scorpions that try to escape will run right into the electric fence and get fried."

"That's kind of brilliant."

"Only if it works." He pried open a long wooden case and held up a section of perforated steel tubing. "Goon, if you're up for it, I need you to slip the shaped charges into these perforating guns and wire them with detonator cord. Keep all the charges facing in one aligned direction like a giant claymore mine."

"No problem boss, the fentanyl's working and the speed's already kicking in."

"That's comforting to hear from someone handling explosives."

Emily carried an assortment of steel tubes and shaped charges over to

Goon who got right to work.

Brank popped open a plastic pelican case lined with electronics. "Hey Goon, I found a hardwired detonator. But it's a direct trip-switch with no delaying timer."

"That's perfect, if you're planning a kamikaze attack."

"That doesn't appeal to me."

Emily asked, "Can't you shoot the explosives with your big gun to set them off?"

"Shooting explosives only works in *Die Hard* movies. What I really need is a timed detonator. Usually I could make one out of a cell phone."

"Handy trick."

"I learned it from our Taliban friends, but there aren't any cell phone signals here, so that plan's for shit."

Emily dug through her cargo pants until she found her camera. "What about this?"

"You want to take my picture now?"

"It has a timed exposure setting for the flash and shutter. That means there's a timer and some kind of electrical signal, right?"

Goon said, "The little lady's correct … as usual. Give it here; I'll rig 'er up."

Brank asked, "You know how?"

"I trained for Improvised Explosive Disposal."

"I thought you were infantry?"

"I'm Canadian Forces, Stumpy; we're small but versatile."

Emily popped the flash card out. "Hope you don't mind if I keep my pictures." She handed the camera body to Goon.

Goon fiddled a bit then said, "I don't want to rain on your parade, but unless you anchor the perforating gun's back blast, these shaped charges are just going to fly off like bottle rockets and won't do shit."

Brank took a deep breath. "Goon, try to focus on the ocean of positives, not the puddle of negatives."

"You've been reading Tony Robbins again, eh?"

"Yup, and now I'm unleashing the giant monster killer within."

But Brank knew Goon was right, and he began poring over the site diagram for a solution.

The perforating gun was a steel alloy tube designed to house multiple shaped charges. During fracking operations it would be lowered down into a completed drilling hole. The gun would be snugly encased in a steel pipe, secured on all sides by solid rock. Once in place the shaped charges were detonated simultaneously, fracturing the rock layer around it, releasing the oil or natural gas deposits that were otherwise impossible to reach— essentially the perforating gun put the fracture in fracking. Brank's problem was that the perforating gun had to remain locked in place during detonation to direct its blast energy of about 30,000 feet per second. He had to improvise a way to keep the gun stationary, despite the impact pressure of around fifteen million PSI. It was a conundrum with a hundred lives depending on him finding a solution.

Emily leaned close to him. "Can I ask you something personal?"

"Go ahead," Brank replied, privately enjoying their closeness.

"You're good at this, I mean really good."

"Thanks, but what's the question?"

"Why aren't you still in the army? I mean why would they let someone like you go?"

He waved his maimed right hand. "Missing digit. They drummed me out with a partial medical discharge. Very partial, like twenty-five cents a month."

"Bullshit. That's a minor wound; I've interviewed people that were allowed to stay in with worse."

"Are you just going to badger me until I tell you?"

She nodded.

"Okay, fine. Back in Iraq, my platoon was doing recon of a village. Except when we got there all fifty residents were dead. Shot, burned, all kinds of awful stuff."

"Was it the Taliban or ISIS?"

"That's what I thought, until some drunken grunt from another platoon started bragging about how they wasted a whole village. I did some digging and found out their platoon leader, who was some green second lieutenant, ordered them to kill everyone and cover it up."

"Why?"

"Some bullshit about a roadside bomb that wounded two of his guys. It was an excuse. He was just a piss poor officer who cracked and pulled his own Mai Lai massacre. I took my evidence to command and they elected to court-martial him."

"And?"

"He got off. Hell, I think he even got promoted."

"That's nuts!"

"Well, when your daddy's a senator on the Armed Services Commission, nutty stuff happens. A couple months later, in Syria, I lost my fingertip to a chunk of shrapnel. Needless to say, Daddy Warbucks made sure I got run out, with the smallest medical pension possible."

"I'm sorry Brank, that sucks."

"Like the old saying goes, no good deed goes unpunished. Fortunately, Talos Corporation didn't mind my missing digit and hired me on. Next thing you know I was assigned to protect Ruby, who dragged us to every hot spot she could find. That lady loved trouble."

"Can I ask one more question?"

"I probably couldn't stop you anyway."

"What's your first name? And don't say Stumpy."

Brank chuckled and said, "It's Dave."

She smiled. "Well, Dave, I think you deserved better."

"Thanks, but given the last few hours, I'd say we all deserve better." Then something on the diagram caught his eye. "Hey Goon, I think I found a way to secure the back blast."

Goon asked, "Is it half assed and reckless?"

"Abso-fucking-lutely."

CHAPTER THIRTEEN

Brank focused on the site diagram, plotting the most direct route to his new destination.

Goon asked, "Hey Stumpy, how many inputs are on that manual detonator?"

"It looks like four."

"Great, hard-wire me up three long-ass runs of detonator cord with blasting caps on the end. Once you're out of here I'll set them off, one at a time, and make a racket. That ought to keep the critters off your back."

"What about the fourth input?"

"I'm wiring up a short length of perforating gun that we can toss outside. I figure six shaped charges should soften up the beach before you make your run."

"Sounds good." Brank set to work wiring the detonator. "How's the big gun going?"

Goon held up a pair of five-foot steel tubes packed with wiring and blasting caps. "Your perforating gun's ready. Just connect these two pipes, Bangalore Torpedo style, and you'll have forty shaped charges detonating at once. It ought to split that tank wide open, and if those really are depleted uranium charges ... well, who knows. I'm giving you a twenty-foot run of cord out of the tube to plug into super girl's camera. What do you want to set the timer for?"

"Two minutes."

Goon gave him a look. "That ain't much 'oh-shit' time in case something happens."

"I'm only going to be about a hundred feet from that pit full of scorpions, so if I'm stuck on the ground any longer, I'm dead anyway."

"Okay, it'll be preset. All you do is power up the camera, say cheese, and haul ass out of there."

Brank said, "There's a gas separation unit about twenty yards away. It's high enough to get me above the nitrogen cloud. Once you hear it go bang, climb up on top of those crates and, I don't know… Try not to breathe too much. This whole place'll be covered in more dry ice fog than a seventies disco, except this fog is about minus three hundred degrees."

Goon shrugged. "Hell, that's a summer day back in Alberta."

It took them another two minutes to lay out all the equipment.

Emily looked at the array of pipes, cable and Brank's weapons and said, "I'm going with you."

"No way."

"There's too much junk for you to carry alone, and even if you could haul it, you'd be going so slow they'd catch you."

Goon said, "The lady's right again. Even I could catch you lugging all that crap."

Brank knew he didn't have a choice. "Fine, but I want you glued to my ass the whole way, got it?"

Emily said, "I'll be like Velcro."

"Alright, let's get this clown car rolling."

Goon said, "Hey super girl, can you help me up? I need to be next to that window over there."

Emily hauled him over while Brank got ready to roll. After jamming whatever tools he could find into his pockets, he slung Goon's shotgun under one arm and looped the coil of detonator cord over the other. That still left him hauling the .50 caliber rifle, which was down to five rounds. Emily grabbed the two lengths of perforating gun, along with anything else they might need.

Brank declared, "We're ready."

Goon prepared to throw the third perforating gun. The four-foot tube was tethered to a length of detonator cord that was in turn hard-wired to the detonator.

Emily slid the steel window shutter up just long enough for Goon to hurl the pipe like a javelin. The moment he did, a scorpion lunged for the window. Emily slammed the shutter down and bolted it just as the creature slammed into the building.

Goon shouted, "Fire in the hole!" and triggered the detonator.

The explosion was muffled, like a low thud, but the shockwave shook the building. Emily felt her stomach lurch.

Goon shouted, "The puck's dropped, so go, go, go!"

Brank flung open the steel reinforced door and charged up the steps. Emily was three feet behind him. Neither bothered looking before they leaped.

The air hung thick with smoke and an acrid smell burnt Brank's nostrils. To his right he saw the scorpion that had lunged for the window. The creature had taken the brunt of the blast, sending chunks of it flying in every direction. A second scorpion lay writhing on the ground, skewered by the other's dismembered pincer. A third five-footer was rolling around on its back, either injured or just disoriented. They didn't wait to find out which.

Brank shouted, "Ahead fifty paces then right." He raced forward, making sure Emily was behind him.

They kept moving. A distant, smaller blast echoed through the machinery.

"That's Goon setting off blasting caps." Brank jogged another twenty feet and barked, "Hanging a right!"

He cut right, looking back to make sure Emily was still there. He dashed another thirty feet and suddenly skidded to a halt. Emily crashed into him, almost falling. Brank backed them up to one of the fans, pointed ahead, and whispered, "Something ain't right."

The entire drilling complex was lit by a network of intense work lights positioned at regular intervals. But the area ahead of them was a suspiciously dark section.

Emily whispered, "What is it?"

"There's a black hole up ahead, like somebody disconnected the work lights."

"Should we go around?"

"We don't have that kind of time." Brank thought for a moment and said, "Give me your jacket."

Without questioning him, Emily stripped it off and handed it to him.

Brank pried a leveling brick out from under the track mat and wrapped the jacket around it. He stepped out and hurled it with all his might. It landed just short of the dark spot. A second later, two medium-sized scorpions dashed out, tearing into the coat.

Brank raised the .50 caliber, taking careful aim, whispering, "Scorpions are ambush predators, so they set a trap. But your jacket was soaked in Goon's blood."

"So, too delicious to resist."

Brank said, "Exactly," and fired.

The bullet ripped through one scorpion, exited and bored into the second. The first died instantly, while the second rolled onto its back, writhing in pain.

Emily said, "Wow, two for one."

"Got to conserve ammo. Now let's move."

They dashed past the wounded scorpion. Glancing up, Brank saw that a row of work lights had been methodically smashed.

"They're learning."

Kruger turned to his men, his frustration reaching its boiling point. "Bring me the other nun!"

Before they could comply, Steyn pointed to the road, shouting, "The bus is coming!"

"About goddamn time!"

The men watched the Mamba armored vehicle bouncing down the dirt road, the Rhino-Runner bus trailing behind it. As it approached the fence line, the Mamba veered off, heading for the generator. The Rhino-Runner pulled to the left, creating a barrier between the mercenaries and the bound villagers.

Kruger shouted, "Steyn, find out what those idiots are doing."

Steyn jogged over to the bus and pounded on the door. It opened, and a burst of gunfire tore into him, launching him backward onto the ground. Another rifleman opened fire from one of the bus windows, stitching the ground near Kruger.

Kruger hit the ground, yelling, "What the hell?"

The mercenaries ran for cover. Six huddled behind the other Mamba, while the remainder jumped behind some low rocks. A hail of bullets from the bus slapped at the ground in front of them.

Fhatu jumped out of the bus, waving to the bound villagers. "On your feet and into the bus! Now!"

Three more villagers piled out of the bus to assist.

The mercenaries opened fire, their bullets pinging harmlessly off the Rhino-Runner's armor plating.

Inside the bus, one of the villagers crouched, rifle held over his head, firing blindly through the open window.

The Mamba screeched to a halt a few feet from the generator. A villager popped up in the roof turret, opening fire on the generator operator. The frightened man scrambled away, amazed that the shooter had missed him at nearly point-blank range.

Fhatu shoved the panicked villagers into the bus, shouting, "On the floor and stay down!" Only half the hostages had gotten aboard, but the mercenaries were already regrouping.

Kruger was back on his feet, erratic gunfire peppering the ground in front of him. He shouted, 'They can't shoot for shit! Concentrate your fire on the wheels!"

His men complied, loosing at least fifty rounds into the front tires. Although the wheels were hardened, run flat tires, they couldn't withstand that much trauma. Chunks of rubber flew off until there were only bare wheel rims.

Kruger shouted, "The rear tires, shred 'em!" He hated losing the bus, but there was no way he was letting these bastards get away. He looked over at the hijacked Mamba now shielding the generator and saw two of his men returning fire. "Don't waste bullets, that generator's not going anywhere! Besides, we need that vehicle intact!" Then he muttered, "Clever little shits, keeping the fence powered up while you escape."

Hertzog raced towards him, panic in his eyes. A burst of gunfire from the bus tore into him; he kept staggering towards Kruger until he toppled at his feet in a cloud of dust.

Kruger shrugged. "At least the little bastards hit something."

The last of the villagers made it aboard the bus. Fhatu slid into the driver's seat and threw it into reverse. It heaved backward a few feet before its bare steel rims became hopelessly buried in the sand.

Seeing this, Kruger shouted to his men, "I want one man to keep that bastard by the generator pinned down. Pull the last Mamba over here and form up behind it. We'll move forward, nice and slow. Measured fire, no need to waste precious rounds on these *munts*."

One of the mercenaries focused his fire on the Mamba near the generator, effectively rendering that shooter useless. Kruger's remaining men formed up behind the Mamba.

Fhatu looked out from the bus and realized what Kruger was planning. He was already low on ammunition, with men who hadn't held a weapon in years. If Kruger got up close, they were dead.

Kruger joined his men, slapping one on the back. "Don't worry; this'll be like fish in a barrel."

After narrowly escaping an ambush, Brank and Emily settled on a new defensive tactic—running like hell. They sprinted the final leg without encountering any scorpions.

Brank said, "It should be right up here."

Breathing hard, Emily asked, "So are we walking right up to the pit full of scorpions?"

"Nope, we're driving."

Rounding the corner, they came to a gated yard packed with heavy construction equipment. Among the vehicles, Emily saw dump trucks, backhoes—and a ten-foot scorpion. She froze.

Brank dropped to one knee, raising the .50 caliber. But the creature didn't attack. In fact, it didn't even move.

Emily asked, "Is it sleeping?"

"Must be a heavy sleeper, 'cause we made a hell of a racket. Stay here, I'll check it out."

"Uh uh, the deal was glued to your ass, and that's where I'm sticking."

Brank crept forward, rifle to his shoulder, ready to fire at the first sign of movement. At the halfway point he kicked a stone at the creature. Nothing.

Emily whispered, "Could it be another trick?"

Brank scooped up a rock and hurled it. The stone bounced off the scorpion's head, but it didn't move. He took a few more steps, shining his flashlight where the creature's mouth should have been. There was just a black void. Brank knelt down for a better look.

"It's hollow."

Emily asked, "Don't scorpions shed their skin, like tarantulas?"

"Yeah, I think I saw that on *Animal Planet* or someplace." He kicked the hollow shell, amazed by how light it was. "But where's the previous tenant?"

"I'll keep an eye out."

They heard gunfire in the distance.

Emily asked, "Rescue mission?"

Brank listened to the next burst and said, "No, it's too soon, plus I'm only hearing R4s and SS77s, all South African hardware." Taking a deep breath, he said, "Screw being cautious, we're out of time," and charged deeper into the construction yard, pivoting his rifle left and right. There was no sign of scorpions.

Brank said, "That's our ride," and pointed to a Cat-D6, medium-weight bulldozer. He ran to the dozer and did a quick walk-around. "Perfect, it even has a deep bucket blade like a back hoe."

"Can it get past those things?"

He patted the bulldozer, pitching like a used car salesman. "Miss, you're looking at twenty thousand pounds of steel tracked vehicle, packing two hundred horse power, guaranteed to plow through anything. Wanna know the best part?"

"What's that?"

"These babies go faster in reverse than forward, so getting out's even quicker."

"Um, can you drive it?"

"Yup, a combat engineer in Iraq taught me to drive an M9 earthmover. We used it to clear minefields. This is almost the same, without the bulletproof glass and armor."

"I kinda wish it had those things."

"The only downside is that this rig's older than I am, but once I get it started it should be the same."

Brank trotted over to a row of sheds and steel equipment cages. The first steel cage held acetylene and oxygen tanks. Next to it was a rack jammed with shovels and rakes.

"Emily, grab one of those shovels."

He walked along a row of covered pallets, tearing off the tarps until he found stacks of five-gallon drums labeled, "Rubberized Fiber Coat."

Brank muttered, "That'll work," and lugged a can over to the bulldozer. "Hand me that screwdriver."

Emily dug it out of her pocket and watched curiously as Brank pried open the can. "What're you making?"

"It's kind of a sticky bomb."

"I heard that in a movie once."

"It's a real thing. Shovel please."

Brank dug out a generous helping of the thick black goop and shoveled it into the well of the bulldozer's blade.

He said, "Once we're close, we'll jam the perforating gun into this slop, with the bang-bang side facing out. This stuff bonds to anything, so it'll hold the gun in place long enough for me to get in position."

Emily didn't look convinced.

"Trust me, it'll work. When we set off the charges, this twenty-thousand-pound backstop will direct the blast right where we want it. In theory anyway. Do me a favor and toss those perforating guns in the cab."

Brank added two more shovelfuls of goop until the rear of the deep blade was lined in black sludge.

Emily opened the cab door and heard a beeping sound. "Goddamn it."

The door alarm wasn't loud, but in the stillness it seemed ear-splitting. She set the pipes and cables inside and slammed the door shut. The beeping ceased.

She hopped down and said, "Sorry."

"My fault, I should have known about that." He stared at the dozer's engine, mentally running through a checklist he hadn't performed in years and never on such an ancient machine. "Okay, compression release down, fuel switch on, decompressor pointing out towards me, throttle halfway on the puck."

Emily leaned back against a dump truck, scanning the yard for scorpions. Something lightly brushed her ear.

She swatted at it, muttering, "Well, at least the mosquitos aren't giants."

It happened again, only when she swatted this time, her hand came back speckled with sand. More sand drifted down from above. Emily looked up and saw a ten-foot scorpion perched atop the dump truck's body. "Up top!"

Brank saw the creature and raised Goon's shotgun.

While the other scorpions had moved with almost blinding speed, this one was slow—its movements awkward, almost clumsy. The creature's body was jet white, almost translucent, and coated with amniotic fluid.

Emily said, "It looks like an albino."

"I think it's the one that just shed its skin." Brank knew that, despite its clumsiness, it was still a ten-foot, venom-packed scorpion. "I hate firing a weapon here, but no choice."

The scorpion slipped, nearly falling until it latched onto the truck's cab and took a few more tenuous steps down.

Brank fired. The buckshot tore through the scorpion's unformed exoskeleton like a hot knife through butter. The impact blew the beast in half, shredding the dump truck's door.

A deafeningly shrill truck alarm pierced the night air.

Brank said, "Shit, I didn't know it was made out of Jell-O!"

"They're gonna hear that."

Brank handed her the shotgun and went back to prepping the engine. "Okay, choke straight out." He turned to Emily and pointed to a knob, shouting over the wailing siren. "This thing's old, so once I turn it over, I need you to push in the choke."

Emily nodded then saw something and pointed to the yard's entryway. "There's one over there!"

Brank grabbed the .50 caliber, saying, "There's never just one," and fired.

The round tore into the creature, killing it. But he could already see shadows hovering in the distance. He jumped into the cab, knowing the bulldozer was their best defense.

He jammed the control levers, muttering, "Clutch out, fuel on." Satisfied, he pressed the starter motor. The machine belched then began to run. "Push the choke in slowly, till it sounds … happy."

Emily pushed the knob until the rough running engine smoothed out. She looked up at Brank and saw a five-foot scorpion crawling across the cab's roof.

She shouted, "Up top!"

The beast's pincer's swiped down at her, barely missing. She hit the ground, crawling away from the dozer. The scorpion leapt off the roof, scuttling towards her.

Brank grabbed the .50 caliber, hoping for a clear shot, when a second scorpion jumped onto the back of the dozer. It slammed against the Plexiglas, momentarily confused, then climbed up top. It tore at the roof, puncturing the metal. Brank raised the .50 caliber straight up and fired. The armor-piercing round went straight through the roof, catapulting the scorpion into the air. The acoustic pressure in the closed cab roared through Brank's skull, turning all sound into a distorted feedback loop. His head reeled and blood trickled from his nose.

Emily staggered onto her feet and turned, raising the shotgun. The blast hit the scorpion squarely in the face, knocking it back, but the recoil nearly threw Emily to the ground. She pulled the trigger again, but nothing happened. She turned and ran, silently cursing her liberal parents' "no guns" policy.

Twenty yards ahead, she saw another scorpion blocking the yard's entryway, poised to attack. It charged forward. Now surrounded, she scrambled for the only available shelter.

His senses still reeling, Brank slammed the bulldozer into gear. The twenty-ton machine lurched forward.

Then it stalled.

Emily dove for the ground and crawled inside the scorpion's shed exoskeleton. The interior was slick with thick amniotic fluid, but she kept moving.

The pursuing scorpion's pincers tore at the discarded exoskeleton. When that failed, it jabbed down with its stinger. But, like a suit of armor, the hard shell proved impenetrable.

Emily curled into a ball, her hands too slick with amniotic fluid to operate the shotgun. The scorpion pounded at the shell then lifted it into the air and hurled it to the ground.

Brank pumped the starter again, the checklist racing through his head. Nothing. Then he looked at the dozer's hood, instantly saw the problem and shouted, "You goddamn idiot!"

He'd done everything right but still made a rookie mistake. The dozer's vertical exhaust pipe stack still had the dust cover on it. Without a clear exhaust, the machine would just keep stalling. He popped open the door, scanning the yard for Emily. He saw two scorpions huddled around the shed exoskeleton and realized she was hiding inside—a clear shot was impossible.

Brank leaned out further, groping for the exhaust stack, cursing himself. His fingers were only inches away when he caught something moving in the corner of his eye. He jerked back as another scorpion sprang up in front, gripping the dozer's blade. It lunged forward, but its legs became momentarily caught on the blade, saving Brank's life. He slid back inside, slamming the cab door. Once free, the scorpion climbed onto the bulldozer's hood, smashing at the cab with its pincer. Then, in one glorious moment, it swung its pincer back, slamming into the exhaust stack, severing it from the chassis.

"Thanks, asshole!" Brank jammed the starter, praying it would turn over with the choke closed. The engine sputtered twice then roared to life.

Brank shouted, "Yeah!" just as the scorpion smashed its pincer against the cab, cracking the Plexiglas.

Jamming the steering control left, Brank spun the dozer in place, smashing the blade against the nearby dump truck. The dozer shook, throwing the scorpion off balance. Brank slewed the dozer right again, sending the creature tumbling off.

Brank shouted, "Want some more?" and threw the bulldozer into forward.

The twenty-ton machine rolled over the scorpion, crushing it with nary a bump. Brank kept rolling. Now only one scorpion was hovering around the exoskeleton. It turned its attention to Brank.

Brank raised the blade high, waiting for the creature to attack. As soon as it lunged forward, he lowered the blade, pinning the scorpion to the ground. He raised the blade slightly while turning in place. The steel tracks spun for a second then caught, grinding the scorpion into the hard shale.

Brank locked the brakes and raced over to the exoskeleton, shouting, "Emily!"

The scorpions had torn it to bits. He rooted through the pieces, yelling her name. But all he found was Goon's shotgun lying in a puddle of clear fluid.

Emily was gone.

Then, despite the incessant ringing in his ears, he heard a faint voice, far in the distance, screaming his name. It was Emily. The scorpion hadn't killed her—it was taking her to the pit.

CHAPTER FOURTEEN

Goon leaned back against the row of wooden crates, feeling weak from blood loss and fighting off the fentanyl-induced fog in his head.

He could hear scorpions outside, greedily feasting on their dead comrades, with more arriving every minute. Once the carrion supply ran out, they began pounding at the door.

Goon shined his flashlight onto the door and breathed a sigh of relief. Brank had been right; the reinforced steel was holding up just fine. Then the hammering ceased.

A few seconds later, Goon heard a new sound, like nails scratching on a chalkboard. He listened intently, muttering, "What the hell are you up to?"

After a minute, the scratching grew deeper, reminding Goon of skates being sharpened. Then he realized what was happening, visualizing it in his mind—it wasn't a pretty picture.

Goon muttered, "When a hammer doesn't work, you try a saw."

When bludgeoning had failed, the scorpions devised a new tactic. One of them was using the tip of its razor-sharp pincer to etch into the steel door, deeper and deeper until it eventually cut through. The sound continued, never wavering in speed or intensity.

"You bastards don't give up, do you?" Goon pulled himself up onto his feet, still feeling lightheaded and dizzy. He poured his canteen over his head, muttering, "Stay focused."

Rooting through the crates, he assembled a pile of shaped charges and detonator cord along with the one remaining perforating gun. These were smaller charges than the ones he'd given Brank, but in this confined space the explosion would be devastating.

Fighting back the fatigue, he began wiring the perforating gun, muttering, "You bastards come through that door and I'm making poutine out of us all."

Emily screamed, praying Brank would hear her. Initially the scorpion's pincer squeezed so tightly that she'd almost lost consciousness. Then it relaxed the pressure, instinctively keeping its prey alive. She shut her eyes, trying to blot out the memory of what she'd seen at the pit.

The scorpion avoided the alleyways by traveling as the crow flies, scaling obstacles like gas separating towers then leaping down with impossible grace. To Emily it felt like some sadistic carnival ride, offering utter terror followed by a lingering death.

She reached out, trying to claw at the scorpion's row of lateral eyes, hoping the sudden pain would force it to release her. On some deeper level, she hoped the attack would inspire it to kill her right there. Hard as she tried, its five eyes remained just out of reach—unblinking, glaring back at her.

The scorpion clattered up the side of a two-story gas separation tower then leapt off, barely catching itself on a lower piece of machinery, then jumped again. Emily's stomach rose, and her vision clouded as it leapt into the void. The scorpion hit the ground, its eight legs acting as shock absorbers. And then it stood, motionless.

They had arrived.

Its pincer opened, dropping Emily six feet onto the hard shale. She landed on her knees, the overdose of adrenaline surging through her cancelling out the pain. Looking up she saw a dozen full-size scorpions circling around her.

The group parted, and through the gap Emily saw a writhing mass of creatures clustered around the pit. There were dozens, maybe hundreds, with more emerging from the crevice every minute. Then she saw why the group had separated—they were making way for the matriarch.

Emily thought she'd reached her maximum level of terror, but glimpsing that seventeen-foot monster nearly stopped her heart. Dozens of infant scorpions huddled beneath the matriarch's legs or clung, squirming, to her back.

Without warning, one of the infants charged at her. At the last second it veered right. She turned and saw its target—a crouched figure in blood-soaked military clothing. The foot-long monster attacked, jabbing its stinger into his arm before retreating. The man clutched his arm, screaming.

Emily wouldn't have recognized him if it hadn't been for his distinctive cargo pants and knee pads. His face had been reduced to a bloody mass of stinger wounds and bone-deep lacerations.

"Flynn?"

Flynn looked over at Emily, barely registering her presence. His left eye was now an empty black socket while the other was nearly swollen shut.

Emily said, "Oh God Flynn, I'm so sorry."

Flynn stared at her with his remaining eye and, in a barely audible voice, choked out, "Welcome to nursery school. The babies don't use venom, but they sure do love stabbing and cutting."

"Hang on. Brank's coming, I know it."

Coughing up a gob of blood, he said, "I'm glad you came."

"Hang on; we'll get out of this."

He shook his head. "No we won't. I'm just glad the kids have you to play with. Now maybe Mommy will kill me." He collapsed, barely breathing.

Emily caught a flash of movement—an infant raced forward, targeting her. She swatted at the little monster, and globs of amniotic fluid sprayed off her arm. The infant froze in its attack posture. It dabbed a pincer into the glob of fluid and brought it up to its mouth. Emily sensed its confusion then remembered she was soaked in the goop. The infant took a few tenuous steps back, as if waiting for guidance, then shifted its attack to Flynn.

Emily shouted, "Watch out!"

It pounced, stabbing Flynn twice in the arm before withdrawing. He just lay there, moaning.

Two more scorplings charged at Emily. Thinking fast, she scraped some of the amniotic fluid from her arm and threw it at them. Both stopped, poking at the globs, uncertain what to do.

"That's right," she said, raising the pitch of her voice, as if talking to a puppy, "I'm one of you guys."

The infants withdrew beneath the matriarch's legs. Emily stood her ground, knowing this surreal truce could fall apart any second.

The matriarch charged forward, batting Emily with its pincer. She fell to the ground, rolled over and got right back on her feet.

The matriarch pivoted, lashing out at Flynn. Its stinger jackhammered down, impaling him.

Emily watched in horror as the scorpion hauled Flynn into the air, suspended from its tail, then slapped him to the ground. Half a dozen infants charged forward, pincers tearing at Flynn who writhed and screamed before going limp.

The matriarch turned its attention to Emily, advancing slowly. A group of emboldened infants hovered around it. Emily scanned the area, searching for any kind of weapon. There was nothing.

Tears welling in her eyes, she said, "I guess the fun begins."

The matriarch took a few more steps then froze.

Emily heard a low rumbling sound in the distance and muttered, "Great, another earthquake."

The blast of an air horn cut through the silence. It blew again, and the rumbling grew louder.

The scorpion moved back a few steps, clearing Emily's field of vision, revealing the most beautiful sight imaginable—a bulldozer, gleaming yellow beneath the halogen lights. It was barreling straight for the pit.

Brank had arrived.

From the bulldozer's cab, Brank could see the nightmarish swarm of scorpions clustered around the pit. He blew the horn again, ensuring he had their attention. The bulldozer's blade was raised to its highest position, meaning he couldn't use it as a weapon. Right now, it was a container for the offerings he'd brought the scorpions.

He saw Emily, trapped in the center of the swarm, and blew the horn three times fast, hoping she'd get the message. Now he just had to lure the scorpions far enough away to rescue her—and he'd brought the bait to do it.

To his left were more gas separation towers, which would make his attack more treacherous, so that was out. To the right was an open space, strewn with demolished equipment. Perfect.

The first attack came. Three large scorpions charged forward, one coming head on, the others breaking left and right.

"Trying an end run?" Brank drove forward, hitting his top speed of fifteen miles per hour. The dozer hit the center scorpion head-on. The creature grabbed at the base of the dozer's blade but slipped, tumbling beneath the tracks.

The left scorpion hit the side of the dozer, grabbing at the hood. Like the first, it couldn't maintain its grip and tumbled off.

Brank pivoted the dozer in place, grinding it beneath the tracks.

"What's wrong, fuck face? Things a little too slippery?"

Brank had spent an extra two minutes in the construction yard dousing the entire dozer in Super Lube Diesel Engine Oil. It was time well spent.

He spun the dozer right, knowing the third attacker was inbound. His timing was perfect. The third scorpion had just reared up, trying to latch on to the cab. The swinging dozer blade hit it like a roundhouse punch, knocking it under the steel tracks. All Brank felt was a small bump as it was ground into pulp.

Brank spun the dozer one hundred and eighty degrees, assuming at least one scorpion was making a rear attack. It was two. The moving dozer easily batted one aside. The second managed to latch on to the blade's lift cylinder. It held fast, scrambling for a grip with its front legs.

Keeping one hand on the forward controls, Brank leaned out of the cab, aiming Goon's 12-gauge one-handed and fired. The blast hit the creature's lightly armored underbelly, knocking it loose. It tumbled to the side, but its tail swung inward, directly under the steel tracks.

Brank spun the dozer in place, grinding its tail into pulp. He smiled, having almost forgotten how maneuverable tracked vehicles like the bulldozer were. The tailless scorpion lay on its back, writhing in agony. Brank rolled the bulldozer across its head and powered forward.

The scorpion he'd batted aside didn't pursue him. Likewise, the massed group in front hung back, displaying a previously unseen emotion—fear. Brank had officially climbed the food chain from easy meat to apex predator. But he knew it wouldn't last. If he attacked the pit the scorpions would come at him en masse, protecting their home. The trick was not to directly threaten their breeding ground.

Emily watched the bulldozer tear through the attacking scorpions, fighting back the impulse to cheer Brank on.

The matriarch remained fixed in place, its attention focused on the new threat. The scorplings clustered around her legs for safety. Emily took a few baby steps to her right, cautiously putting some distance between them, but every time she did, the matriarch sidestepped, always keeping the same distance between them.

"Holy shit," Emily muttered, "the bitch is using me as a hostage."

Kruger stood behind his men, shouting encouragement as the Mamba advanced on the bus. They were within thirty yards, gaining ground at a slow, but steady pace.

One of the villagers grabbed Steyn's fallen rifle, joining Fhatu at the bus window. Disciplined fire clattered against the window frames, so all they could do was hold up their rifles and fire blindly.

Fhatu turned to another villager and shouted, "Do it now!"

The man climbed out of the bus holding two aerial flares. He held one up high and pulled the cord. The flare rocketed up five hundred feet and popped open, casting a brilliant light over the area. A second followed.

Kruger saw the flares go up but dismissed it as either desperation or stupidity. He slapped the nearest mercenary on the back, shouting, "Don't worry, they're such lousy shots that if you get hit, your number was probably up anyway." Glancing back, he swore he saw something in the aerial flare's flickering light. It was the massive sentry scorpion, crouched among the rocks behind them. An instant later, it was gone. Shaking his head, he muttered, "Just a trick of the light."

Fhatu felt a searing pain in his shoulder and dropped to the bus floor. One of the villagers crawled forward, pressing a rag against his bleeding arm.

Looking up at the woman, Fhatu could see the terror in her eyes. He said, "Don't give up. Soon, soon."

Kruger shouted, "Alright, let's get ready. On my order, hit the gas and ram that goddamn bus broadside. Don't stop till it's on its side."

The men ceased firing for a moment. Kruger heard something in the distance, a low rumble barely audible but growing louder. He saw nothing to his left or right. Then he looked up, gulped and shouted, "You got to be kidding!"

A large twin engine plane was coming at them from the west, low and almost impossibly slow.

He yelled, "Incoming aircraft!" suddenly realizing why the villagers had fired the aerial flares—they were lighting up the area for the aircraft.

At the same instant he saw muzzle flashes coming from just below the cockpit. The ground around him exploded.

Nhamo brought *The Mayor Urimbo* in low, taking advantage of the Russian plane's insanely low cruising speed.

A pair of villagers was lying prone in the lower cockpit, aiming a pair of SS77 belt-fed machine guns they'd liberated from the bus crew. Neither was a competent marksman, but with Nhamo in the cockpit, all they had to do was fire straight and the plane would do the rest.

He bellowed, "Fire! Fire!"

Both men opened up, raining a continuous stream of bullets onto the Mamba below. A truly glorious sight.

Hitting the intercom, Nhamo said, "Drop as soon as you have them in sight."

Two men squatted on the plane's open rear cargo hatch, ready to release a pair of open topped, fifty-gallon drums. Each contained a mixture of aviation fuel and powdered soap. The jellied fuel served as a crude but effective homemade napalm. Two other men stood behind them, safety ropes lashed around their waists, Molotov cocktails in their hands. A relay line of men stood behind them clutching more flaming bottles.

One shouted, "Now!" and they pushed out the open drums. The other men hurled their Molotov cocktails.

One of the barrels went wide, but the other crashed down onto the roof of the Mamba, followed by a flaming cocktail. The thickened aviation fuel burst into flames, painting the Mamba in a coat of fire.

Nhamo swung around for another pass. Their attack hadn't been precise but had done serious damage. From personal experience he knew just how terrifying an aerial assault was. Even if it didn't kill the enemy, it would break their will.

Kruger ducked as machine gun fire tore into the Mamba. The man in front of him toppled backward, knocking him to the ground. He pushed the dying man aside just in time to see two more drop.

Something crashed down onto the Mamba and, a moment later, its roof burst into flames. A stream of burning aviation fuel flowed down into the open gun port, immolating everyone inside. The driverless vehicle careened left, running down a wounded man while leaving the rest unprotected.

The plane banked around, setting up for another strafing run. This time, its gunners opened fire at longer range. Initially their volley went high, but they quickly found their targets. Two lines of gunfire stitched the ground, killing another man.

The aircraft roared over at treetop level, releasing a second wave of Molotov cocktails. The burning jars missed their targets, but their bonfires, combined with the drifting aerial flares, bathed the scene in a flickering, hellish light.

That's when Kruger saw the true sign of a lost battle—blind panic.

One of his men ran headlong into the electrified fence; his spasming muscles catapulted his smoldering body backward like a Roman candle.

The scorpions, excited by the spectacle, charged the fence. One tried to climb over, only to be roasted in place. The others backed off to a safe distance and waited, their eight legs rocking in anticipation.

The villagers piled out of the bus, firing their weapons and shouting curses in Venda.

Kruger rallied his three surviving men, ordering, "Form a line and return fire!"

The men did as ordered. Kruger knew it was pointless, but he needed to offer the villagers a viable target other than him. It worked, the villagers focused their weapons on the three men, allowing Kruger to slip away unnoticed.

He scrambled toward the Mamba parked near the generator. But that gunner saw him and opened fire. He dove to the ground and crawled into the shadows, grateful that the bastard couldn't hit the side of a barn. Kruger couldn't get a clear shot at the gunner, so he chose another target, firing a long burst at the generator. A billowing cloud of steam told him he'd hit the target—the radiator. He smiled and crawled for cover, knowing that in a few minutes the generator would overheat and seize. The scorpions would get their meal after all.

The plane made another strafing run, concentrating its fire on his three remaining men. Its twin guns tore up the ground, killing two. The survivor threw down his rifle, raising his hands in surrender.

Peering out from the shadows, Kruger watched the villagers advancing on the surrendering man and muttered, "You were better off with the bullets."

That final strafing run had kicked up a huge cloud of dust. Moments later, the sputtering aerial flares drifted to the ground, plunging the area into darkness. Kruger knew this was his last chance to escape, but all his vehicles had been captured or destroyed. Then he spied the old Range Rover parked near the fence line and ran for it. It was an ancient piece of junk, but he only needed it to run for a few hours.

He climbed inside, shouting, "Come on keys."

He found them over the visor, and, after three tries, the engine rumbled to life. Without turning on the headlights, he jammed it into gear, peeling out in a cloud of dust. Once he reached the edge of the fence he cut right, racing along the east side of the perimeter fence, an escape plan already forming in his mind.

The Mwenezi River was roughly eight kilometers away. The water would be high from the previous night's rainfall, so all he'd need was a boat, or even a raft, and the current would carry him across the border to Mozambique. The false passport and wad of American dollars sewn into his shirt would get him home from there. Things were looking good.

Something bolted out of the darkness, charging straight at the Range Rover. Kruger tried to swerve, but it was coming too fast. The head-on impact stopped the Range Rover dead in its tracks, hurling Kruger against the windshield. His chest slammed against the steering wheel with an audible crack. He flopped back against the seat, tasting blood, and then clung to the door handle as the vehicle rolled onto its passenger side. It crashed down, jolting him again. Then everything was still. His first deep breath told him he'd broken a rib.

A pincer slammed against the cracked windshield, showering him in glass. But then the attack stopped. He fished through his pockets, found his flashlight and flicked it on. Its beam revealed a scorpion draped across the hood, barely alive, flailing at the shattered windshield.

The damned sentry scorpion had found him.

CHAPTER FIFTEEN

Brank drove forward, angling the dozer away from the pit.

Two bold scorpions launched a frontal assault. The first grabbed the bottom lip of the raised blade with its pincers, its legs scrambling desperately to find purchase. The second, being more innovative, used the first as a ladder, crawling over it. The first lost its grip, falling beneath the tracks, while the second scrambled onto the hood.

Brank threw the dozer into a spin, trying to dislodge the beast. It clung on, inching forward, until it could use its pincers as a battering ram, jabbing at the cab. The second strike shattered the Plexiglas.

Brank raised the .50 caliber, knowing he couldn't survive a third strike. The round slammed into the creature's face and punched straight on through, exploding out the back in a shower of viscera. The carcass tumbled sideways, only to be sucked beneath the steel tracks.

"Anybody else feeling froggy?" Brank was glad he'd taken a few extra seconds to jam his ears full of toilet paper.

The scorpions hung back, keeping a protective perimeter around the pit—and Emily.

Brank had intentionally skirted the horde, driving about thirty yards to their right. Upon reaching a suitable spot, he stopped and spun the dozer in three-hundred-and-sixty-degree turns.

"Come on, I need some of you to get stupid." He stopped the bulldozer, its upturned blade facing the wall of scorpions.

Seeing this as a challenge, two scorpions cautiously advanced, waiting to see this new monster's next move.

"Keep coming, keep coming." Brank waited until they were ten yards away. "Here you go!"

The deep blade lowered to ground level, releasing what Brank had been hiding. Fifteen hissing green cylinders clattered to the ground.

Brank backed away, allowing them a chance to sample his offering.

Within seconds the scorpions figured out the hissing canisters were full of delicious oxygen. The pair clustered around them, inhaling greedily; then, whether by sound or pheromones, those scorpions sent an invitation to their oxygen-starved brethren.

At least twenty-five of the beasts charged forward, clustering around the oxygen bottles. A few eyed the bulldozer, so Brank backed up further, ensuring they didn't feel threatened. The group went into a gaseous feeding frenzy, fighting each other to reach the bottles.

Brank muttered, "Suck it up, boys, it'll be your last," and took a circuitous route around the pack.

The mass of scorpions around the pit made no move to attack. Most were too busy helping new arrivals climb out of the crevice, while those newbies tried to acclimate to this brave new world.

Emily was up ahead, standing alone save for one scorpion—but it was the biggest Brank had seen, easily seventeen feet long. He rolled forward, lowering the blade.

Emily watched the bulldozer slowly rumbling closer. The matriarch scorpion was also eyeing it but hadn't moved a muscle.

She said, "Come on, Big Momma, just take your babies and run for cover."

It just stood like a statue.

Emily tried shuffling away, but the creature just sidestepped towards her until it was only ten feet away.

"Staying close but leaving yourself some maneuvering room. Smart."

Brank kept coming, slowly, trying to be as inconspicuous as a twenty-ton machine could be. He came within twelve feet and stopped.

Emily's only hope was to make a dive into the lowered blade, but the moment she took a tentative step, the matriarch dashed forward, positioning itself between her and the dozer. The beast stood its ground, rocking up and down on its eight legs, sending a clear signal that it could kill Emily with one pincer swipe or attack the dozer. Probably both.

Brank stood up in the cab, clutching the .50 caliber rifle. As he raised the weapon the mother scorpion's pincer shifted, hovering directly over Emily. Shocked that the creature had learned to recognize a rifle, he muttered, "So much for you critters being half blind and stupid." Using this to their advantage, Brank only lowered the weapon halfway, forcing the scorpion to split its attention between him and Emily.

"Okay," Emily muttered, "Dave did his part, now it's my turn." She wiped the sweat off her brow and remembered she was still soaked in amniotic fluid. Running her hand across her shirt, she collected a glob and threw it on the ground at her feet then repeated the action.

Attracted by the fluid, an infant scorpion ventured out from beneath its mother.

Emily whispered, "Come on, baby, come to Surrogate Momma," and wrung another glob from her shirt.

The scorpling ventured out further, nearly within reach. It took two more steps. Then Emily did the craziest thing she'd ever done. Her hand shot out, grabbing the end of the scorpling's tail, just below the stinger.

"Gotcha!"

The mother scorpion whirled around, eyes locked on her. Emily held the baby out at arm's length, using a grip she'd seen on the old *Croc Hunter* show. The infant flailed wildly, unable to get its pincers high enough to grab her.

Emily screamed, "Back off, or I'll kill this little brat!" and signaled that she was willing to smash the baby to the ground.

Emily knew the matriarch scorpion couldn't understand her, but it instantly got the drift. It took two measured steps back, lowering one pincer to protect the young huddled around it.

"You better back up, Momma, 'cause I'm a goddamn baby killin' machine!" With her free hand she gestured for Brank to pull up.

Brank eased the dozer forward until it was only two feet from Emily. She gestured again, this time to raise the blade. It moved up slowly, until it was at knee level. Emily gestured for Brank to stop.

She shouted, "Can you hear me, Brank?"

"Yeah."

"I'm going to sit down on the scoop thing, then you back up real slow and casual."

"Got it. I put some things inside the bucket to help you."

Emily sat down on the lip of the dozer's blade, still clutching the infant in her outstretched arm. "Move back, nice and easy."

The dozer drifted back, slowly building speed. The mother eyed it, sensing its baby was about to be kidnapped. Emily leaned forward till her outstretched arm was only inches from the ground and tossed the infant away.

She yelled, "Go, go, fast!"

The infant scrambled toward its mother as the dozer lurched into high speed. In the same moment, Brank turned the blade control, twisting the lip upward. Emily tumbled back against the rear of the bucket.

Brank bellowed, "I told you reverse was faster than forward!"

The matriarch scorpion shook violently, throwing off the infant hitchhikers. Now unencumbered, it bolted forward, its eight legs easily matching the bulldozer's top speed.

Emily bounced around, trying to gain her footing while swimming in the black gunk lining the bucket. Her hand settled on something wedged in the gunk—a CO_2 extinguisher.

The scorpion's pincer reached below the dozer's blade, grabbing on to the lift idler. It pulled itself up, gripping the blade's lower lip, and climbed.

Emily looked up and saw the creature peering down at her. She squeezed the CO_2 extinguisher, enveloping the scorpion in a cloud of ice-cold vapor. It lurched back but attacked again.

Brank was between a rock and a hard place. He could lower the blade, potentially crushing the scorpion, but that would spill Emily onto the ground, leaving her vulnerable. He saw the creature on the hood, but firing at it risked putting a bullet through the engine block, leaving them marooned in scorpion central.

Emily let loose with the extinguisher. Even if the CO_2 didn't stop the thing, at least it couldn't see down into the bucket. The scorpion's pincer came down, groping blindly. Emily slunk back into the corner, hitting her head on another of Brank's leave behinds. It was a steel cylinder, about five feet long, wedged in the black gunk. For a second she thought it was oxygen but remembered that those canisters were green—this one wasn't. With two pulls she managed to pry it out of the goop and shove it at the groping pincer. Thinking it had grabbed Emily, the scorpion locked on, withdrawing its pincer.

Emily shouted, "You grabbed the wrong snack!" and stood up, her head coming just above the bucket's lip—nose-to-nose with the scorpion. She emptied the CO_2 extinguisher straight into its mouth.

With an unearthly hiss the beast recoiled, losing its footing. It tumbled over the side of the bulldozer, barely clearing the steel treads.

It rolled once then sprang back onto its legs, still clutching its prize—an acetylene tank.

Brank slammed on the brakes and spun the dozer, blade facing the scorpion.

Grabbing the 12-gauge, he screamed, "Get down!" and unleashed two loads of double-aught buckshot.

The buckshot tore into the acetylene tank, detonating it in a ball of fire. A hailstorm of shrapnel and exoskeleton chunks rattled off the dozer's blade. The blast had reduced the matriarch scorpion to a lingering bonfire.

A hundred yards away, the scorpions clustered around the oxygen bottles heard the blast but made no move to attack. Apparently the matriarch's death wasn't worth relinquishing their seats at the oxygen bar.

Brank stood up in the cab and shouted, "Emily, stay down. I've got one more trick up my sleeve." He yanked the magazine out of his .50 caliber rifle and inserted his last incendiary round. With a long exhale he trained the scope on the mass of oxygen-starved scorpions. But his target wasn't the creatures or the oxygen tanks—he was aiming for a pair of sealed acetylene tanks he'd mixed in with the oxygen cylinders. He'd even tossed in four jerry cans of diesel fuel as a chaser. As a precaution he'd wrapped the acetylene tanks in some fluorescent orange safety vests he'd found. Thanks to the roaring bonfire of matriarch scorpion, the vests presented a glittering target.

Brank yelled, "Fire in the hole!"

The .50 caliber round tore into one of the tanks, detonating it. The second tank exploded a millisecond later, along with twenty gallons of diesel fuel and twelve hundred cubic feet of pure, fire fueling oxygen. The shockwave knocked Brank back into his seat, and the ensuing fireball rose fifty feet into the air. Of the two dozen scorpions, most were blown to pieces, while the remainder lay crippled and dying.

Poking her head up, Emily saw the inferno and screamed, "Yeah bitches! That's four hundred million years of evolution shoved up your ugly asses!"

The dozer spun around, knocking her back inside the bucket.

Brank yelled, "Calm down, we ain't done yet."

Emily slammed her fist on the metal, howling, "Bring it on, Stumpy!"

The dozer rolled towards the twin liquid nitrogen towers.

Scorpions swarmed out of the pit, most ravenously descended on the smoldering remains of their fellow arachnids, while a smaller group eyed the departing dozer, plotting revenge.

Goon dragged the last of the wooden crates to the back corner of the bunker, forming a crude barrier. The scratching at the steel door grew more frantic with every passing minute.

Then it stopped.

He saw the tip of a pincer poking through the steel door. With a metallic squeal, the scorpion twisted it back and forth, widening the slit with each turn.

Knowing he had a minute, maybe two, before the scorpions breeched the doorway, Goon got to work. He placed the perforating gun lined with shaped charges near the door then fed the detonator cord out behind his improvised barrier. It only took him a few seconds to connect the cord to the yellow pelican case housing the detonator. Once that was done, he connected a second bundle of explosives lying next to him. The yellow circuit tester lit up, indicating the detonator was ready to go. After a moment's hesitation he switched it to standby, meaning he was one button away from detonation.

"All those years of fightin' terrorists and I wind up being a suicide bomber."

The charges by the door were meant for the scorpions—the second set would just guarantee Goon an instant and painless death.

Now the scorpion's entire pincer was through the gap, scissoring through the metal as though it was cardboard.

Goon grabbed the last crate and tried to drag it over to the barrier, but it refused to budge.

"Either I'm getting weaker or this goddamn thing weighs a ton." Feeling curious, he popped the crate open and peered inside. His face lit up in a toothless grin. "Jesus, Mary and Gretzky, now there's something you don't see every day!"

The scorpion used its pincer to hammer open the gap until it grew into an ironing-board-sized gash. Flattening its body, the creature squirmed through. It hit the ground running, pouncing onto a wad of blood-soaked bandages. A second scorpion wriggled through the doorway, already sniffing the air for prey. As soon as it was through, a third, larger scorpion tried to slip through the gap, becoming stuck.

Goon huddled behind the crates, listening to the creatures, his finger hovering over the detonator.

Like a bloodhound, the second scorpion alighted on his hiding place and scrambled up onto the barrier of crates.

As soon as Goon heard it coming, he shouted, "Game on!"

The charges detonated with a thunderous roar, reducing the crates to splinters. Flying steel and lumber shredded the two scorpions. The explosive back pressure rocketed the third creature backward, out of the doorway, leaving most of its legs behind.

The air hung thick with smoke and nitroglycerin vapors. Another scorpion poked its head inside, but, unable to breathe the noxious atmosphere, it backed out.

The smoky room became as silent as a tomb.

Leaning on another man, Fhatu limped towards the generator; the gunner who'd been protecting it saw him and started waving frantically.

After pushing his way through the jubilant throng of villagers, Fhatu asked, "What's wrong?"

The gunner pointed to the antifreeze-soaked sand and said, "It's been shot. The fan's dead and the radiator's ruptured."

Fhatu turned to the rejoicing villagers, shouting, "Quiet!" The crowd went silent. "We need water!" He pointed to a dead mercenary. "Pull his canteen and any others you find. Do we have any more water?"

But one look at the sea of faces answered his question.

"Then find buckets or bottles and piss in them, otherwise the fence will switch off!"

The terrified crowd dispersed.

The generator lurched sickeningly. Eying the temperature gage, the gunner announced, "It's way up in the red, I don't know how much longer it'll run!"

Fhatu looked over at the perimeter fence. The scorpions on the other side had already sensed that the power was failing. They must have communicated the good news because more were emerging from inside the site to join them. They stood there, silently waiting for their chance to strike.

Brank pulled within ten feet of the first liquid nitrogen tank, jammed on the brakes and shouted, "Get out!"

Emily climbed out of the bucket and into the cab, embracing Brank. "I knew you were coming."

Brank smiled and said, "Good to see you in one piece."

Emily looked over at the pit, only a few hundred feet away. "This is way closer than I expected."

"Yeah, but we gave them one hell of a black eye, so I'm hoping they're scared. Plus, in about a minute, this area's going to be real unappetizing."

The dozer backed up then rumbled forward, slamming into the tank. It took another two attempts before Brank tore open the steel and fiberglass outer shell. Once it was broken, he used the dozer's blade to dig out a chunk at the base. Fog billowed out, forming a low-hanging cloud around the bulldozer.

Emily asked, "Did you break it open?"

"No, I only broke the insulating shell, the fog is just condensation. Even a bulldozer couldn't rip open the inside."

The inner tank, technically known as a Dewar vacuum flask, was actually two steel containers joined at the neck, with an airless vacuum in between. Tower-sized tanks like these were nearly impossible to accidentally fracture. But what Brank was planning was no accident.

He backed up until they were clear of the spreading fog, which would cause serious frostbite.

Grabbing the two perforating guns, he climbed out, saying, "I'm hoping that fog keeps them back. Here we go." After connecting the wires joining the two guns, he jammed them into the well of the dozer's blade, the layer of black goop cementing them in place.

Emily said, "Remember, it's bang-bang side out."

"Listen to you, getting all technical." He was indeed careful to ensure the perforated side of the pipe was facing the tank. "Keep an eye out for critters."

"Got it. They're all still hanging back by the pit."

"Yeah, munching on their barbecued cousins."

After jamming the perforating guns in place, Brank ran a wire out from the dozer's blade. He knew that forty conventional-shaped charges detonated simultaneously would slice the tank wide open. But if the explosives were, as he suspected, depleted uranium charges ... well, it was going to be one hell of a show.

Spooling out the wire, Brank said, "Once I hit the timer, we beat feet for that two-story structure over to the left." He pointed away from the pit. "We should be safe up top."

"What if they start climbing?"

"I'm hoping they won't have enough breath, but if they do, I've only got one fifty-caliber round and six buckshot loads."

They heard propellers in the distance, coming in fast. Nhamo's plane roared overhead, its rear cargo door hanging wide open. The plane barely cleared the top of the liquid nitrogen tanks then slowly banked around.

Emily pointed up and asked, "Rescue mission?"

"Nope, that's the maniac that flew us out here. But what the hell is he doing?" Brank wired the detonator cables to the camera, handed his weapons to Emily and climbed into the cab. "Wait here and be ready to run!"

The bulldozer rumbled forward, slamming against the gash he'd made in the tank. He kept it in forward, pressing against the tank until the steel treads spun in place.

He muttered, "Nice and snug."

Pressing the blade to the shell meant all the explosive energy would be focused forward—right into the nitrogen tank.

Brank hit the camera's power button. A digital message came up in the viewfinder reading, "Timed exposure 2:00," then, "1:59, 1:58."

Brank climbed out of the cab and over the back of the bulldozer, trying to avoid the cloud of freezing vapor. He ran to Emily, grabbed his .50 caliber and shouted, "Let's boogie!"

Emily turned to run then froze in place. She pointed towards their destination.

Brank saw what she was pointing at and yelled, "Aw shit!"

CHAPTER SIXTEEN

Brank and Emily saw five scorpions coming in their direction, blocking their escape route.

Emily said, "They must have been wandering around the complex—"

"Till they smelled all that delicious barbecue by the pit."

"Except we're the appetizers."

Brank turned to the pit and saw a group of scorpions advancing. "That direction's screwed too."

The countdown ran through his head—they were down to ninety seconds.

Emily pointed to the second liquid nitrogen tower. "How about there?"

He grabbed her hand, shouting, "No choice."

They ran full tilt to the second nitrogen tower. Thankfully, the access ladder was on the far side, away from the blast wave. Rounding the corner, Brank stopped, nearly yanking Emily's arm out of the socket. Two large scorpions were coming at them, blocking their path.

Brank raised the .50 caliber and fired. The round tore into the first scorpion's midsection, bursting out the other side in a shower of gore. But the second one charged forward, pincers extended. Brank swung the empty rifle like a bat. The scorpion grabbed it, yanking it from his hands. Using its pincers, it bent the rifle like a pretzel.

Emily brought up the 12-gauge, firing point-blank into its face. The beast staggered back, still blocking the stairs.

She thrust the shotgun into Brank's hands. "I don't know how it works."

He said, "You done just fine," and pumped two more shells into the scorpion. It backed up enough for them to reach the ladder.

Brank pushed Emily toward it, shouting, "Up, up, and don't look back!"

Without argument, she scrambled up. Brank estimated they had twenty seconds.

The scorpion came back for another round. Brank fired twice, forcing it to retreat around the corner. But he knew that as soon as he started to climb it would come back and pluck him off the ladder. Even worse, he had only one shell left.

The scorpion returned, poised to attack, then stopped. A cloud of freezing nitrogen drifted around the corner, clinging to the ground. With a hissing sound that Brank could have sworn was a cough, it backed up then turned and ran away.

Brank scrambled up the ladder taking two rungs at a time, counting down in his head... *Ten, nine, eight.*

His count was eight seconds off.

A deafening explosion tore through the night, rocking the ground like an earthquake. Barely hanging on, Brank looked up and saw Emily dangling from the ladder by one arm. But somehow she managed to swing over, grabbing the rungs, and clambered up like a monkey.

He shouted, "That's my girl."

Feeling the rising wave of cold air, Brank kept climbing. Glancing down he saw ... nothing. The entire site was blanketed in dense white fog. In the distance he could make out a tidal wave of minus-three-hundred-and-twenty-degree liquid nitrogen washing over the pit, flowing down into its deepest recesses. The liquid nitrogen tower he'd blasted groaned, listing forward. Then it collapsed into the white void with a thundering crash.

He kept moving, rung by rung, the rising cold gnawing at his legs. After what seemed like an eternity, he reached the top. Emily was waiting at the edge to pull him up.

Brank lay back on the cold steel roof, breathing heavily.

Emily smiled down at him and said, "You did it."

Brank smiled. "We did it."

Slowly and painfully he got to his feet, fear and adrenaline numbing the pain of at least a dozen injuries. He said, "I think those were definitely depleted uranium charges 'cause that was one hell of a blast."

And then he heard the squeal of twisting metal, and the liquid nitrogen tower shifted beneath their feet. The entire structure listed right. Brank peered over the edge and saw a fresh tsunami of nitrogen gushing out of it. The now ruptured tower shifted a few degrees more.

All Brank could say was, "I think we did too good a job."

The Range Rover lay on its passenger side, tires still spinning. Kruger kicked open the driver's side door and crawled out. Catching a whiff of gasoline, he leaned inside and turned the ignition off. The vehicle teetered beneath him, so he shined his flashlight at the ground.

"Well, I'll be damned!"

The scorpion was pinned beneath the upturned vehicle. Three of its four right side legs were twisted at grotesque angles—shattered by the impact. One of its pincers had been reduced to splinters of black exoskeleton over grayish-blue meat. It tried to raise its crushed tail, but the effort was futile.

Kruger shouted, "Alright, you bastard, let's finish this!" He climbed down, his broken ribs screaming with every move. Standing just beyond the creature's reach, he bellowed, "Look at you, all busted up. Come on, you've been after me all night, so come and get me!"

The scorpion raged against the vehicle, rocking it up and down to no avail.

Kruger kicked sand into the scorpion's face and mockingly declared, "Face it, the better species won!" He started to laugh, but the sharp pain in his ribs cut it short.

Knowing the scorpion wasn't a threat, Kruger assessed his situation. Thankfully, the vehicle had come to rest just beyond the electrified fence's "zap zone." Another two feet to the right and he could have been fried like bacon. He knelt down, shining his flashlight on the undercarriage. The front axle was bent beyond recognition, steam billowed from its crushed radiator and the air reeked of gasoline.

"Fucking totaled. Looks like I need to find another way to get—"

A massive explosion rocked the night. The ground trembled, throwing Kruger to the ground. Looking up, he saw a white cloud rising from the drilling complex.

"What the hell?"

The explosive tremor jarred the upturned Range Rover. The scorpion took advantage of its shifting weight by hammering down with its intact legs and rocking the vehicle upward. Gravity did the rest.

Kruger tried to scuttle backward but wasn't fast enough. The vehicle crashed down, landing on its four wheels, crushing his foot beneath the front tire.

He screamed, struggling to free his shattered foot. But every attempt sent new waves of agony shooting through his body. After several futile attempts he just lay there on his back, a puddle of gasoline forming around him. Through the cloud of pain, he realized something—the scorpion was loose.

Kruger heard it moving then saw it slowly inching its way across the hood on shattered legs. Knowing he couldn't free himself, Kruger groped around until he found his rifle. The scorpion's face appeared, looming over him. He raised the rifle one-handed, loosing a long, full auto burst into its mouth. The beast rocked in place, bullets tearing through its already shattered exoskeleton. It struggled desperately to attack until it went limp, too weak to move.

Kruger shouted, "What's wrong? Can't finish the job?"

With its dying breath the scorpion raised its shattered tail, spraying a stream of venom behind it—directly into the electrified fence. A bolt of electricity shot out, following the venom stream. Hundreds of amps surged through the dying scorpion and the Range Rover.

Kruger watched in amazement as the scorpion's body quaked spastically, smoke pouring off it. Yet, by some miracle, Kruger wasn't being fried along with it.

In a flash, it came to him. "The tire!" His foot was wedged beneath the rubber tire, grounding him.

He laughed then shouted, "You almost did it, you stupid bastard!"

That's when he saw the cluster of sparks around the shattered gas tank. He watched, horrified, as they turned to flames, engulfing the undercarriage. Burning fuel dribbled to the ground, igniting a river of fire flowing straight at him. The puddle of gas around him burst into flames. Kruger screamed, the smell of roasting flesh filling his nostrils.

In those final moments he swore he heard the nun's voice, proclaiming, "God as my witness, you'll burn in hell!"

But it took another two minutes of searing agony for him to get there.

Fhatu watched as the last bucket was emptied into the generator. It had barely been half full and there wasn't another drop of water, urine or even spit left to pour in. The lurching generator's temperature gage hovered squarely in the red, rising with every second.

He smacked the hood of the Mamba and shouted to the gunner, "Take this to the village, pack every child inside and drive away. Don't stop until you reach Beitbridge!"

The gunner nodded and drove off.

Turning to the villagers, Fhatu ordered, "Put the women and wounded into the bus for protection. Grab every weapon and form up around it. Once they come out—"

A deafening explosion shook the ground. Fhatu stumbled back against the generator as the men around him dove for cover.

One yelled, "Did the gas tanks explode?"

Fhatu watched as a huge white cloud rose from the drilling complex into the night sky—an almost heavenly sight. The cloud was so dense that even the hundred-foot derrick was swallowed in the haze. It settled into a thick fog blanket that drifted towards them.

Fhatu addressed the crowd. "Stop gawking and get to the bus now!"

Through the encroaching haze, Fhatu could see the scorpions hurling themselves at the fence, only to be electrocuted. The fog drifted beyond the fence, and the air became ice cold.

Shivering, he muttered, "What is this?"

A man grabbed him by the shoulder and helped him back to the bus where the others were forming a firing line. But Fhatu knew the men barely had thirty bullets between them. Their only real weapon was hope.

The generator shuddered violently and stalled, and their last hope died with it.

The electrified fence was off. The scorpions were coming.

Nhamo saw two figures standing atop the remaining white nitrogen tank, gesturing frantically. Then the entire tank swayed, nearly throwing them over the edge. The three-story tank was listing to one side, right on the verge of collapse.

Nhamo keyed the intercom. "Those must be our people. Listen very closely and do exactly as I say."

After giving the instructions, he brought the plane around. One of the gunners climbed out of the lower cockpit, the loaded weapon tucked beneath his arm. The aircraft banked sharply, knocking him to the floor. The machine gun fired twice, blasting two holes in the ceiling, inches from Nhamo's head. The shocked man stared up at the holes, afraid to make eye contact with Nhamo.

Keeping his eyes glued to the windscreen, Nhamo shouted, "Put that down before you kill us! Now get in the back and help the others!"

The nervous man raced out of the cockpit.

Nhamo brought the plane around for his run, repeating to himself, "*The Mayor Urimbo* will always bring you home. *The Mayor Urimbo* will always bring you home."

The plane banked around until it was on a collision course with the crumbling tank. Brank jumped up, waving his arms.

The nitrogen tower trembled, shifting further. Its metal frame screamed, seconds from total collapse.

The plane kept coming, its altitude low enough to give them a haircut.

Brank saw the cargo nets dangling from the rear compartment and yelled, "You beautiful lunatic!" then knelt down, shouting to Emily, "Put your arms around my neck and wrap your legs around my waist, and whatever happens, don't let go!"

She did and asked, "Are we—"

"Going home? Damn right!" He turned to the oncoming plane, arms extended, and yelled, "You should probably close your eyes!"

The plane bore down on them, impossibly low, its prop wash nearly blowing them off the tower. It roared overhead, clearing them by mere feet. Brank felt the cargo net slam into him and latched on to it with all his remaining strength.

A heartbeat later, he was swinging midair like a trapeze artist, Emily clinging to him. Looking back, he watched the tower buckle and collapse into the heavenly white cloud below. The rescue had been a miracle, except for one problem—try as he might, Brank couldn't find the strength to pull himself up. Every drop of adrenaline and ounce of strength he possessed had been spent.

He muttered, "I can't—"

There was a sharp upward jerk. Brank thought they were falling until he felt another tug and looked up. A row of men were leaning out of the rear cargo hatch, straining to hoist the net into the plane.

Brank yelled, "They're pulling us up. Just hang on."

Emily shouted, "Okay," as if there was anything else to say.

Brank lost all sense of time and space, so it took either hours, minutes or seconds to pull them into the aircraft. When he landed on the floor, all he could do was lie there, exhausted beyond measure.

With a groan, he asked, "Emily?"

"I'm right here." Emily curled up with him, equally spent, content not to get up right away, or ever.

Brank grabbed the nearest man by the wrist, asking, "The village?"

The man smiled, giving him a thumbs up.

A few seconds later, the plane's PA system came on. Nhamo's voice chimed through the speakers with maniacal enthusiasm. "Hey Brank, do you remember what I told you?"

Despite his exhaustion, Brank still mouthed the words along with Nhamo.

"Remember, *The Mayor Urimbo* will always bring you home!"

Brank smiled and quietly passed out.

Scorpions stampeded through the alleyways of machinery, desperate to escape the spreading white fog. For the already oxygen-starved creatures, even a few breaths of the nitrogen gas proved fatal.

One scorpion sought shelter in the explosive bunker, but the haze of acrid smoke and nitroglycerin fumes proved as toxic as the cloud outside. The suffocating creature thrashed wildly, trying to escape, only to be forced back inside by the encroaching nitrogen cloud. Within a minute it became too weak to move and lay there, slowly dying.

The smoke-filled room was quiet again, until a hacking cough broke the silence.

Something stirred beneath the debris; then a hoarse voice bellowed, "Aw, fuck me in the arse!"

Goon wriggled out from under two hundred pounds of explosive proof blankets. After another stream of profanities, he managed to sit up, his body wracked with pain. Not only was his gunshot wound throbbing, but the explosive back pressure had hammered his kidneys and chest like Mike Tyson.

He yanked off a pair of ceramic lined ear protectors and waggled his head, trying to shake out the ringing. It didn't work. He muttered, "Christ, I'm gonna be hearing bells and shitting blood for weeks."

He glanced around the room, now plastered in scorpion entrails and splintered wood. Among the wreckage he spotted the scorched lid of the crate that had saved his life. Stenciled across it were the words, "Property Jaco Botha—Gun Engineer. Do Not Touch!"

Jaco must have been the site's demolition expert. His crate had been packed with three explosive-proof blankets designed to protect demolition crews. Each of the Kevlar-and-aramid-weaved blankets had the explosive absorbing power of a bomb disposal tech's blast suit. The blankets had saved Goon's life, while the ear protectors had just been a bonus.

Goon tossed the lid onto the dying scorpion, looked up and proclaimed, "Thanks Jaco, wherever you are!"

Wisps of white fog drifted through the shattered doorway, growing steadily into a cloud. The scorpion coughed, taking its last breaths.

Goon watched it die and said, "Now there's a sight that's truly … breathtaking," then laughed hysterically at his joke. The frigid cloud settled around him, feeling good against his bruised … everything. He looked up, raised his arms in triumph, and shouted, "Wahoo! You did it, Stumpy!"

Fhatu leaned back against the bus, straining to make out the fence, but the fog was so thick he couldn't even see the man next to him. Raising up his rifle, he shouted, "Get ready!"

He heard weapons cocked, prayers from inside the bus, and the rapid breathing of a terrified man. It took him a moment to realize it was his own. He inhaled deeply, trying to remain calm, waiting for the inevitable.

It never came.

They stood silently for five minutes, weapons at the ready, as the fog slowly dissipated. The moonlight finally pierced through the veil, revealing a sight that left Fhatu awestruck. He looked to the other men, but they all just stared at the fence, dumbfounded.

Mounds of dead or dying scorpions lay behind the fence,

wrapped in a low-hanging carpet of fog. A few struggled vainly to climb up before collapsing onto the heaps of bodies. They twitched furiously then died as if the icy vapor were some kind of insecticide.

Villagers slowly filed out of the bus to gaze at the incredible sight. At first they were silent until one old woman began to sing *Siyabonga Jesu Wa Hamba Nathi*. More voices joined hers until the entire village had raised their voices in praise.

Fhatu looked up into the night sky, his spirit buoyant, the wound in his side forgotten.

The *Mayor Urimbo* soared low overhead, its prop wash nearly drowning out the hymn.

Fhatu raised his hands up high, calling out, "Thank you, brother!"

Brank slowly opened his eyes, still feeling as if he was swaying beneath the plane. He was aware of his injuries but couldn't muster the energy to care.

A dark-skinned man wearing a lime-green beret crouched over him, adjusting an IV needle. Brank gradually pieced together that the man was a medic with the Zimbabwean National Army, he was in a tent, and the sun was up.

The medic announced, "He's awake."

Emily sat down on a stool next to him and smiled.

Brank said, "More like barely awake."

She patted his hand. "Relax, they gave you morphine, along with fourteen stitches and treatment for frostbite, taped up some cracked ribs, oh, and you were right about your testicle ascending."

"Huh?"

"Just kidding, all your junk's where you left it."

Brank smiled, even though it hurt. "So how long was I out?"

"About four hours. What do you remember?"

"Well, there was a cowardly lion and a tin man ... and you were there too."

"Well, Dorothy, you look more like that witch the house landed on."

Brank tried to sit up but changed his mind. "Are they dead?"

"One hundred percent. The liquid nitrogen killed everything in the pit, and the nitrogen fog choked out the rest. The army arrived a few hours ago to mop things up, but if it hadn't been for you, the villagers would be dead and those things would be on the loose."

"What about Goon?"

A booming voice said, "Oh, now he finally asks." Goon was laid out on a nearby cot with a pint of whole blood hanging from an IV stand along with a bag of what Brank assumed was morphine. The big Canadian looked even more disheveled and frightening than usual.

Brank said, "Glad you made it, buddy. How're you feeling?"

In a slurred voice, Goon said, "I'm ripped out of my skull. These *Zimbos* sure love doling out the morphine."

"Were you okay in the bunker?"

"Oh yeah, I had a blast. But once you knocked down those towers it got cold as the Yukon in there. I was freezing my arse off until Emily told the troops where to find me. Do you know I'm the first case of frostbite these medics have ever seen?" Goon laughed uproariously at his own joke.

Brank said, "Yeah, that's a lot of morphine," then pulled himself upright. Through the tent's mosquito netting he could see a cluster of Zimbabwean soldiers being regaled with tales of a heroic rescue. Brank recognized the braggart's voice as Nhamo.

Brank said, "Somebody drag flyboy in here."

Nhamo strode into the tent, accompanied by a pretty village girl.

Brank saw the young woman and asked, "Who's your lady friend?"

Nhamo was beaming. "This is Dakalo, my fiancée, though I haven't been formally introduced to her father yet."

"I'll put in a good word for you, like telling him how you saved our sorry butts. Thanks."

Emily threw her arms around Nhamo and said, "Thank you so much. I'm Emily by the way."

A harsh look from Dakalo inspired Emily to take a step back.

Noticing this, Nhamo politely shooed the girl out and said, "You don't want to make a Ndebele girl jealous. They can be more dangerous than scorpions."

Brank added, "I want to officially take back any disparaging remarks I ever made about your plane."

"As I told you—"

"I know, I know, *The Mayor Urimbo* will always bring you home."

Goon laughed hysterically, though Brank wasn't sure if he'd even been listening. During the round of laughter, a dour-looking man in his mid-forties quietly entered.

Brank took one look at his sports jacket and pressed slacks and instantly pegged him as an American official. He leaned over to Emily, whispering, "Here we go."

The man stepped forward, extending his hand. "Mr. Brank, my name is Jeff Foster. I'm with the US State Department."

Brank shook it and asked, "Can't any of you guys just say CIA for once? It'd be so refreshing."

Ignoring the joke, Foster said, "I wanted to thank you for your fine work. It's a terrible shame that Ruby Jenkins was lost."

"Along with most of my men. I didn't do a bang-up job protecting anyone."

Goon shouted, "Cut that whining shit or I'll body slam your ass," then fell into another morphine-induced round of laughter.

Jenkins said, "I'm sure you did the best job possible under extraordinary circumstances. I'll need a full report from you and Ms. Lennox. I must stress that, for the foreseeable future, this incident must remain classified."

Emily exhaled theatrically and said, "There goes my Pulitzer Prize."

Brank said, "I'll buy you a pizza instead."

Foster continued, "There's a chopper outside waiting to take you and Ms. Lennox back to Harare."

Brank cocked his head toward Nhamo and said, "Thanks for the offer, but I think we're catching a ride with my amigo here."

Nhamo's face lit up.

Goon shouted, "Fuck that noise, I'm getting my arse on the chopper," then laughed himself into a peaceful stupor.

CHAPTER SEVENTEEN

Isla Roca Lobos, Mexico
Eight weeks later

Dave Brank lay back in his hammock, sipping a cold bottle of Montejo Pilsner while flipping through a complimentary copy of the *London Times*. Isla Roca Lobos was the third five-star resort he and Emily had stayed at since "The Incident," despite being more or less broke. He took an admiring glance down to the beach where Emily was gathering shells or some such beachcomber thing. Being a private island, she'd deemed swimsuits an encumbrance. Watching her bounce around brought on a nagging, previously unfamiliar sensation—happiness.

After "The Incident" she'd been offered a year-long contract as a travel writer for an exclusive tourism site. They both suspected it was a CIA front, designed to lure despots and drug lords to private destinations for easy kidnapping; but as long as the lodgings were five star and the drinks and meals complimentary, neither of them cared. She still worked her tail off between gourmet meals and was also writing a novel. It was something about giant spiders.

Talos Corporation had granted Brank three months' medical leave in return for him reconsidering his resignation. Though "The Incident" was classified, Talos had gotten great press for killing Kruger and his band of murderers. Apparently his band of killers was wanted by the Hague Court for crimes against humanity, among other offenses.

But things hadn't been all fun and frolic in Margaritaville. For weeks he'd woken up screaming, soaked in sweat. Poor Emily could barely close her eyes for the first month, sometimes weeping uncontrollably for hours. Together they'd worked through it, clinging to each other and coming out stronger in the end.

After healing up, Goon had been promoted to a senior management position at Talos, where, Brank assumed, nobody called him Goon. Tigger's wife had received a massive cash settlement and American citizenship. Easy's family had also been awarded the same amount, which they used to create a chapel in his memory. Flynn's ex-wife had also been given a generous settlement, which, in true white trash fashion, she was drinking up with his best buddy from high school. Nhamo had been granted a US government contract to fly relief supplies around Zimbabwe, along with getting a newer but still antique plane, also named *The Mayor Urimbo*. These had all been the conditions for Brank remaining silent about "The Incident."

Brank took another sip and mused, "Bribery can be pretty sweet."

There had been many other developments, though none of them could be found in the *London Times* or any other newspaper. Graaff Energy had been forced to surrender the drilling site to the Zimbabwean government, ostensibly due to their illegal use of depleted uranium. Company executives had attempted to re-enter the site to remove confidential documents, only to find it cordoned off by Zimbabwean troops.

No mention was ever made of the mysterious gas, though the US State Department quietly authorized a massive humanitarian aid package to Zimbabwe in return for, "certain considerations."

Brank's afternoon beer and meditation was interrupted by a float plane circling overhead. After a few passes it set down, gently pulling right up to the dock. Being a five-star, private island, Roca Lobos came equipped with a float plane dock because you can't have drug lords getting their Cucinelli shoes wet.

Emily dashed up the beach and into the cabana to grab some clothes, giving Brank another opportunity to admire her flawless bottom.

He muttered, "Life's good."

A tall, red-haired man climbed out of the float plane and sauntered up the beach. It took Brank a few seconds to recognize him.

"Goon! This is a surprise."

Goon waved, yelling, "How's it hanging, Stumpy?"

He fished a beer out of the cooler and plopped down in a wicker chair. The burly Canadian was a man transformed. His hair was shorter, his beard neatly trimmed, and he wore pressed khakis with a *Reyn Spooner* Hawaiian shirt.

Brank said, "I like your executive meets tropical look."

Goon grinned, revealing a gleaming set of dentures, and said, "So what's new?"

"Absolutely nothing, and that's the way I like it. By the way, I'm loving those new choppers. Can you toss me that towel over there? 'Cause, as you may have noticed, I left my swim trunks inside."

Goon shrugged. "It don't bother me, brother. Hey, I thought your finger was the only thing that had been blown off."

Brank held up his beer and cheerfully said, "Fuck you very much." After a long sip, he asked, "So is this a social call?"

"It will be, right after we talk. Talos Corporation got a new contract with the State Department, who in turn asked me to come talk to you. They think you're some kind of superhero, despite your … obvious shortcomings."

"What are we talking about?"

"A big problem, the kind only you and I have dealt with."

Brank sat up, suddenly feeling very naked. "Aw shit, not scorpions."

"No, well, not exactly. I'm not authorized to give too many details until you say yes. It's a situation down south."

"Ooh, I wish I could help you, buddy, but Emily and I have been … how you say—"

Emily stepped onto the porch wrapped in a fetching sarong and said, "I think the term was 'preemptively deported' from South Africa."

Goon shook his head. "That's not the south I'm talking about, and it's bad, Stumpy … like really bad. Buddy, the world needs you."

THE END

ACKNOWLEDGEMENTS

Thanks for reading Scorpius Rex and I hope you enjoyed it. I endeavored to be technically accurate, because you, as a reader can always tell when I'm bluffing. Writing this book involved great deal of research and I wanted to thank the consultants who lightened that burden.

Huge thanks to Prince Tafadzwa Kurupati for his insights regarding Zimbabwean culture, language and geography. *Ndatenda* (or *ngiyabongo* Ndebele)* and I hope I captured some of the spirit of your wonderful country.

I'd also like to thank Drilling engineer Jose Luis Parraga Cardozo for his technical insights regarding Natural Gas drilling, fracking, perforating guns and all related topics—even if I did take a few dramatic liberties.

When it comes to Afrikaans names, products and language, including Hansie's profanity fueled vocabulary, I'm indebted to Nadine Matthysen of South Africa. *Baie Dankie* for all your assistance and I'll raise a *Klippies And Coke* in thanks.

And to Ken, better known as Mr. Proofreader who's spent years making me look functionally literate.

Many of these experts can be found on the website Fiverr.

And of course to Severed Press for their assistance and support.

On a parting note, please, under no circumstances attempt to make a flamethrower out of a fire extinguisher, diesel fuel, gasoline and acetylene! It will blow up in your face. In fact, don't attempt to make a flamethrower of any kind. Read a book instead. Severed Press offers plenty of adrenaline-charged options that won't kill you.

Scorpius Rex is William Burke's second novel, following a long career in film and television. He was the creator and director of the Destination America paranormal series Hauntings and Horrors and the OLN series Creepy Canada, as well as producing the HBO productions Forbidden Science, Lingerie and Sin City Diaries. His work has garnered high praise from network executives and insomniacs watching Cinemax at 3 a.m.

During the 1990's Burke was a staff producer for the Playboy Entertainment Group, producing eighteen feature films and multiple television series. He's acted as Line Producer and Assistant Director on dozens of feature films—some great, some bad and some truly terrible. Scorpius Rex is the glorious result of a childhood spent immersed in late night creature features, monster magazines and horror comics.

He can be found at www.williamburkeauthor.com

His YouTube Channel is http://www.youtube.com/c/BillBurke

His Facebook page is
https://www.facebook.com/pg/williamburkeauthor/

CHECK OUT OTHER GREAT HORROR NOVELS

DEATH CRAWLERS
by Gerry Griffiths

Worldwide, there are thought to be 8,000 species of centipede, of which, only 3,000 have been scientifically recorded. The venom of Scolopendra gigantea—the largest of the arthropod genus found in the Amazon rainforest—is so potent that it is fatal to small animals and toxic to humans. But when a cargo plane departs the Amazon region and crashes inside a national park in the United States, much larger and deadlier creatures escape the wreckage to roam wild, reproducing at an astounding rate. Entomologist, Frank Travis solicits small town sheriff Wanda Rafferty's help and together they investigate the crash site. But as a rash of gruesome deaths befalls the townsfolk of Prospect, Frank and Wanda will soon discover how vicious and cunning these new breed of predators can be. Meanwhile, Jake and Nora Carver, and another backpacking couple, are venturing up into the mountainous terrain of the park. If only they knew their fun-filled weekend is about to become a living nightmare.

THE PULLER
by Michael Hodges

Matt Kearns has two choices: fight or hide. The creature in the orchard took the rest. Three days ago, he arrived at his favorite place in the world, a remote shack in Michigan's Upper Peninsula. The plan was to mourn his father's death and figure out his life. Now he's fighting for it. An invisible creature has him trapped. Every time Matt tries to flee, he's dragged backwards by an unseen force. Alone and with no hope of rescue, Matt must escape the Puller's reach. But how do you free yourself from something you cannot see?

CHECK OUT OTHER GREAT HORROR NOVELS

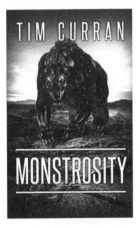

MONSTROSITY
by Tim Curran

The Food. It seeped from the ground, a living, gushing, teratogenic nightmare. It contaminated anything that ate it, causing nature to run wild with horrible mutations, creating massive monstrosities that roam the land destroying towns and cities, feeding on livestock and human beings and one another. Now Frank Bowman, an ordinary farmer with no military skills, must get his children to safety. And that will mean a trip through the contaminated zone of monsters, madmen, and The Food itself. Only a fool would attempt it. Or a man with a mission.

THE SQUIRMING
by Jack Hamlyn

You are their hosts

You are their food. .

The parasites came out of nowhere, squirming horrors that enslaved the human race.They turned the population into mindless pack animals, psychotic cannibalistic hordes whose only purpose was to feed them.

Now with the human race teetering at the edge of extinction, extermination teams are fighting back, killing off the parasites and their voracious hosts. Taking them out one by one in violent, bloody encounters.

The future of mankind is at stake.

And time is running out.

CPSIA information can be obtained
at www.ICGtesting.com
Printed in the USA
LVHW092037070621
689597LV00005B/472

9 781922 323668